To Mandy

Payback

Christine Lawrence

Lots of Love

Christine Lawrence
x

1

Published by Christine Lawrence
Copyright Christine Lawrence 2018
The moral right of the author has been asserted.

ISBN 9781787232204

This novel is entirely a work of fiction. Any resemblance to
actual persons, living or dead, is entirely coincidental.

Acknowledgements

Thanks to all of those people with whom I have had the privilege of working with during their journeys through addiction and recovery, and to all those wonderful characters that I have worked with in Mental Health services throughout my colourful career. Thank you also to those writer friends who have given so much of their time and encouragement to help me achieve this novel. Special mentions to Will Sutton, Amanda Garrie, Charlotte Comley and all at the Writers @ Lovedean, Matt Wingett, Zella Compton, Jackie Green, Diana Bretherick, Tom Harris, Tessa Ditner and all at the Portsmouth Writer's Hub. And of course, thanks to my brilliant and patient husband who always has to be the first to read anything I write.

Chapter One

1984

Karen

It was hot and she couldn't move - so hot that the air was like thick soup. She sucked it in, desperately trying to keep awake. Heat was pressing down on her, holding her in its deadly embrace. Panic started as a sudden beat, a beat of fear, and recognising it, she immediately wished that she hadn't. Just let me get back to before, before when I was asleep and drifting in complete ignorance of what was going to happen next. But she was powerless - she would never be able to go back, not in real life, anyway. You can only go back in your mind, changing your memories and re-inventing the past. Perhaps none of this ever happened after all. Maybe the whole of her life so far had been a dream, a bad dream.

The curtains were open wide and there was sunlight streaming through. Not a dream then, surely not? Then she heard the tapping, tap, tap, tapping on the door. She craned her neck to look towards the doorway but there was just a blank wall where it should have been. She wanted to call out, to cry for help but as she opened her mouth she realised it was not air she was breathing in, but water - thick, broth-like fluid rushing into her throat, choking her, flowing into her until she became at one with it and was floating, peaceful now, free of everything.

A thought suddenly shocked her to her senses: I don't want to die! I can't die - there's too much to lose! She struggled against the current and took a hold of the window latch. Forcing it open she felt herself caught in the rush as she was sucked out on a wave to the ground far below...

Suddenly awake, but wet and hot, wet with the sweat of another bad dream, she could taste the saltiness around her mouth. How much longer will I have to live with these nightmares? She waited until her breathing slowed. Each time these dreams happened it got a little better though - she could recover from them much quicker now. They were always much the same - she was trapped in some way - facing death, but had always managed to escape at the last minute. This morning was like many others and the best way to get over it was to just get on with whatever needed to be done. Let go of the past, she constantly told herself, but the past didn't always want to let go of her.

***

Karen looked at her watch. It was ten past and Gem was late again. She sighed and picked up the file from the table. I'll give her five more minutes then I'm going out. Her eyes were drawn to the ceiling where she noticed a damp patch by the light fitting in the shape of a man's head. A man with curly hair. Unwelcome memories of the past pushed their way into her mind. She started to feel the familiar panic rising inside her. How many times will all that stuff come flooding back. Like the nightmares I would rather forget. Ten years ago still seems like yesterday sometimes. She shuddered, looking down at the file in her hand.

There was a knock at the door.

'Come in,' she called brightly.

The door opened and Gem entered. A young woman, slightly built, she was dressed in black leggings and a baggy purple top, her long brown hair tied up in a pony tail. Her dark eyes flashed at Karen defiantly.

Karen stood up, relieved Gem had finally arrived and she'd been brought back to the present. 'Sit down,' she smiled, trying not to look at her watch again.

'Sorry I'm late. I got waylaid...' Gem lowered her eyes as she sat in the chair opposite Karen.

'Never mind, you're here now. That's all that matters.' Karen smiled again. 'Coffee?'

Gem shook her head. 'No thanks.'

'Have you done your pee specimen?'

'Not yet, I didn't want to keep you waiting any longer - I'll do it in a minute.' She produced an empty specimen pot from her jacket pocket and placed it on the table.

'That's ok. There's no rush.' Karen paused. 'So, how have you been getting on since our last meeting?'

'Alright, I guess.' Gem shrugged.

'You're picking up the Methadone alright? Are you managing with the dose?'

'It's OK. I can get to the chemist alright but the dose never lasts the whole day any more.'

How many times have I heard that one? Karen thought.

'It should settle down, just takes a little time,' she said.

'It's already been a month.'

'Well, I know it's not the perfect answer but it's all there is. Have you given any thought to what we talked about before? About the volunteer work, I mean.' Karen opened the file, checked the notes and looked up again.

Gem grimaced. 'I don't think it's really me, working with all those old dears. Charity shop work's not my thing.'

'Look,' Karen leaned forward in her chair and sighed before going on. 'I don't mean to be pushy, and it's not for me, you know that - but the judge did say you needed to prove you're turning your life around, didn't he?'

'I know.' Gem shifted uncomfortably in her chair.

'And doing a few hours in a charity shop would be a good way of doing that. Giving something back in a practical way.' Karen paused. 'And they're not all old people working in them anyway.'

'Old people and the dregs that can't get a proper job, like me.'

'Like you? You shouldn't think like that, Gem. Look, this is how I see it. You've had a hard time of things, made some stupid choices but now you've got the chance to turn it around. I know this isn't the ideal start but it is a start.'

'I don't know.' Gem slouched in her chair. 'I still think it's a bit of a nerve, expecting me to work for nothing.'

'Well, if you can get paid work, do that instead. Only there's not that much paid work about and you'd need some good references.'

'I can get those. I wasn't always like this.' Gem sighed. 'I did have a good job before all that shit happened to me.'

'Yes, I know - but that was before. It's almost like starting from the beginning again. You've got no choice if you want to prove yourself to others.' Karen paused. 'And the shit didn't just happen to you, Gem. You need to start taking responsibility for your own actions. Only you can change your life, you know that.'

'I suppose,' Gem said as she stood up taking the specimen pot from the table. 'I'll go and do the pee then.'

***

Ten years since her daughter Lucy was born, seven years since Karen had qualified as a psychiatric nurse, she was loving her job as a drug worker. Life was so much easier now Lucy was old enough to let herself into the house after school. Karen could relax and focus on her work. And there were no late shifts or nights so she could be home for Lucy every evening and at weekends.

The past years hadn't always been easy. When Lucy was born, Karen was staying with Evelyn and her Mother, Mrs. Chapman. They'd helped her a lot, treating her as part of the family, looking after Lucy whilst Karen completed her training. Mrs. Chapman, already ill, had spent years hiding her pain and finally succumbed to cancer, slipping away early one morning in December a few years ago. Then the Council decided to demolish the lovely old houses in Trinity Street to make way for a Juvenile Court and a car park. Evelyn was rehoused in a bungalow in Longfield Avenue and Karen found herself a terraced house to rent in Wickham, still visiting Evelyn frequently in her new home. It was hard to believe Evelyn was the same woman who had suffered so much locked away in Highclere Hospital for all those years. Now she was independent, looking after herself and enjoying the small garden behind the bungalow. She was happy to look after Lucy in the school holidays too, if Karen couldn't get time off, which was wonderful. Lucy loved her and thought of her as a grandmother figure.

Karen had also kept in touch with her foster mother and one time mother-in-law, Margaret, although she rarely saw her now Peter was out of prison. Peter, her ex-husband, was not the father of her child. How had it all gone so terribly wrong? It was still painful to remember what he'd tried to do to her all those years ago and Margaret was still his mum after all. Karen knew he wasn't living in the area but couldn't be sure as to where he was. She sometimes worried that he would just turn up one day and try to take over her life again. She knew these fears were mostly unfounded but you could never be too careful. She still had flashbacks to those terrifying times - like when she saw something that reminded her of him, even if it was only a damp stain on a ceiling. And she had the nightmares.

Sometimes Karen thought her own past troubles helped with her work - she understood how people could drift into situations, make the wrong choices and then struggle to get back on track. And every one of her large case-load of clients was different. Different people with similar problems. Some people said they didn't understand how she could work with drug users. But they are just people with problems, the same as you and me, would always be her reply. Unfortunately, not many people understood that. She had always believed it was important to have a positive view and try to find something good in everyone. Otherwise what could you work with? You might as well give up before you've even started.

Abandoned at birth, she remembered how hard she'd tried to find her own mother and had once thought maybe it could have been Evelyn. Evelyn, who had given birth to a daughter and never knew what had happened to her after she'd been locked away in the mental hospital. Evelyn who had spent twenty odd years in the institution, hardly speaking to anyone until Karen had come along. When Karen finally discovered Evelyn definitely wasn't her mother, rather than being devastated, she realised it didn't really matter that much and the relationships she had with Evelyn, Margaret and Mrs. Chapman were more important to her than finding her real mother. And of course, by then she had her own daughter, Lucy, to fill her life with love. Margaret had stood by her after Lucy's birth even though she knew her son, Peter, was not Lucy's father. Any other mother-in-law would have turned against me after what happened, Karen realised. Even though at the time she'd felt justified, Karen always felt guilty when she thought about sleeping with someone else whilst she was still married to him.

Watching Lucy grow from a baby to a little girl was the best thing ever in her life although Karen was still determined to make a career out of nursing and worked hard with her studies, finally passing her exams in 1977. She then worked on the wards as a staff nurse for a few years before moving out of the hospital to work in the Community Drug Team. Keeping busy was the best way to leave the past behind.

Chapter Two

Gem

She'd walked past the window five times already and was beginning to feel ridiculous.

'Pull yourself together woman', she snapped under her breath then spun around and marched to the door, determined this time to just get on with what she had to do.

Her hand on the door, Gem hesitated again, losing her nerve. She glanced through the steamy window half-hoping she'd not been noticed. Catching herself and recognising the unfounded fear, she swallowed it down, opened the door and stood just inside looking about her. The shop appeared to be deserted of all life apart from the musty smell of old books and other people's recycled lives. About to turn and escape through the door, she was halted by the sound of raised voices from a room at the rear of the shop.

'We're a great team Catherine.'

'Yes we are Kevin. But now you must put the labels on these garments. For the one pound rail.'

Gem wondered again whether she'd made a great mistake. I'll never fit in here. I told Karen. Dregs of the Earth, losers, old people whose lives are over with nothing better to do.

Pretending to be engrossed in the bric-a-brac, she took up a jade rabbit and peered closely at it as a young man appeared in the rear doorway, struggling under a heap of clothing, plastic hangers clattering to the floor as he moved. Somehow finding the counter he dumped the lot on the already untidy surface. It was only then he noticed Gem.

'Good morning Madam.'

She jumped at the suddenness of his attention.

He smiled across at her as he spoke. 'Are you looking for anything in particular? We have a lot more stock in the back room. Are you after jade rabbits?'

'No, no, just browsing,' Gem stuttered, dropping the rabbit back down onto the shelf as if it were burning her hand.

She blushed, unsure of how to react. The young man - Kevin, she supposed - seemed out of place - dressed as he was in black suit and tie with his altogether too-professional manner, his dark hair short and parted on the side. Perhaps he was the manager, not merely a volunteer, although Catherine had been the one giving out the orders. Maybe she should speak to the woman called Catherine? She was still was trying to pluck up the courage to ask when the shop door opened again.

An old lady struggled to wheel her shopping trolley through the door and over the threshold. The young man was by her side in a flash.

'Good morning Madam,' he gushed as he held open the door and ushered her in.

Oh, my God. Is this to be my destiny? Gem hid behind a rail of men's overcoats, the smell of damp wool wafting to her nostrils.

The old woman made a bee-line for the display of cardigans, all sorted on rails in order of size. Kevin was soon back to his task of labeling the one-pound bargains, whilst Gem wondered again whether to take the plunge today, to come back another time or not bother at all. She browsed around the shop - found herself inspecting the summer blouses, pulling out flimsy tops, size eight, equally unsuitable for both the time of the year and her size. Feeling self-conscious, Gem glanced across at the only other customer. Well, the only customer really, as Gem knew she herself was a complete fraud, there under false pretenses. The pit of her stomach was churning as she made her way to the window and watched the rain running down the glass pane.

How did it come to this?

I'm Gemma Wylde, I'm twenty six. People usually call me Gem for short. I grew up around here. Lived with my parents and sister. My mum and dad were, and still are, quite well off. Dad made his money from setting up a business as an insurance broker. We weren't really posh but Mum liked our lifestyle and used to dress up to go to events even though

Dad only went reluctantly. He said it was good for the business to "hob-nob" with all those other business people.

My sister Amy was younger than me and was always my parents' favourite. She'd be twenty three now. I worked hard at school but however hard I worked it was never good enough for Mum. Dad was OK but as he got busier at work, he was home less and less and when he was home, the rows started. I could hear Mum nagging at him late at night. Sometimes I even heard her shouting. Dad was always quiet though. Amy and I got on well - I was like a second mum to her, always looking out for her if she got in any trouble. Even though Mum spoilt her I still loved her dearly and was always there for her.

Disaster hit our family when Amy died. She was only thirteen - such a waste. The one day I didn't hang around and wait for her at the school gates and she has to go and get run over by a drunk driver whilst she was crossing the street. I used to walk from the college to her school - it was only in the next street and we finished at three so I had enough time to get to the gates and wait for her to come out at quarter past. I was sixteen and was too busy chatting to my mates to want to bother waiting for her that one time.

Dad said it wasn't my fault but I've always blamed myself and Mum has never been able to look me in the eye since then. I admit I went off the rails after that. Kids at college were all smoking weed. I tried it a few times and found it helped to relax me and forget what had happened. After a while though, I couldn't escape from the pain, nothing seemed to work any more. But I couldn't stop myself.

I was at a party when this girl got me into chasing the dragon. The feeling was amazing - like being held in a warm cocoon of love. I thought it would be OK as long as I didn't start injecting it. Surely you couldn't get hooked just on the occasional smoke? But I did.

It was Dad who took me to the clinic. He confronted me one day and I just broke down. 'I don't want to lose another daughter,' he said as he made the phone call. I went to rehab and got off. That was one of the hardest things I've ever done. I met Billy in the rehab. We weren't supposed to have relationships in there but once we were out we kept in touch and met one night in a pub. We had something a bit special and soon enough he'd moved in with me. Dad had got me the flat and was paying the rent while I went back to college. I was working on my A levels and looking at going to Uni. I fancied doing a law degree. No, don't laugh - I know it sounds far fetched now but that was where I was then.

I knew straight away when Billy started using again. He denied it at first of course but it wasn't long before he was openly using in the flat. I guess the temptation was just too much for me. Sometimes he would get angry with me - a couple of times he smacked me when I got annoyed at him. It was easier in the end to just join in and before long I was completely hooked, both on Billy and on Heroin.

It all came to a head one day when I got caught shop-lifting. I was trying to get enough money for a fix but instead ended up bailed to go to court. Billy was having trouble too. He owed his dealer money and couldn't get a supply without cash up front. He lost his temper and beat me up. I was unconscious for some time and when I woke up he'd gone out. That's when I came to my senses. I phoned my dad and got him to change the locks and took myself to the drop-in clinic where eventually I was put on Methadone. At the court appearance the judge said that I would have to keep going to the clinic if I wanted to stay out of prison. Now I've got my own key worker and probation officer. That's how come I've ended up trying to get work as a volunteer in Charlie's Choice. All part of the plan to show that I'm an upright citizen. It's not going to be easy, especially now that they're starting to reduce the amount of Methadone I'm on. Sometimes I struggle to get through the day.

Chapter Three

Catherine

She knew it would be another long day, sighing to herself for the hundredth time as she pulled another armful of clothes from the black bin liner. There was a hole in the bottom of the bag and the items were damp, the odour of someone else's washing powder mingled with the left-overs from the back of an old wardrobe.

Oh to be back in good old Woollies, she thought. But the job in Woollies was long gone, and with it any self-esteem, credibility, self-worth, and all those things people said were important. And it hadn't been her fault, how she'd lost her job. They were cutting down on managers they'd said but it was more to do with her being older because they were still taking on new younger staff. And although now in her late forties, she still looked pretty good for her age and there was nothing wrong with her mind. She coloured her hair regularly and always wore up to date clothes and kept up with all the modern music. It was so unfair.

It was the loss of the laughs she'd had with her work mates that was the worst thing. And the money, of course. Oh, don't get me wrong, she was a paid employee of the charity, but the wages are pretty poor and only part time. Still, it was better than sitting at home with the ironing, the customers were alright and the staff kept her on her toes. But she couldn't have a laugh with them, not in the same way. You have to be careful about what you said, political correctness and all that. That was the trouble with working with people with disabilities and quite a few of the people who worked in the shop had one disability or another. You're never sure exactly what it is about them, and how they would react to anything she said was purely hit and miss.

There were too many people unemployed, that was the trouble. Anyone could come in and ask for a job, and the charity was always so desperate for helpers that she couldn't turn anyone away.   Which is a disaster in the making of course. You never know who you are working alongside.

Yes, there had been some very odd people working here. Take that Geoffrey, for instance. He'd seemed alright on first impressions, although a little lacking in the personal hygiene department. She'd soon set him straight on that score though, and he turned up every Wednesday morning looking, and smelling, fresh and clean. And he was alright sorting out the new stock when it came in bagged up in all sorts of carrier bags. But it was when she let him into the front that things went wrong. They really should have told her he had issues with children. When she later discovered he'd been a patient at Highclere Hospital, then it all became obvious. They said he'd never hurt anyone before, but that didn't make it any easier for the poor little sod who came in looking for Lego and went home with a black eye. Then she found out that Geoffrey had been taking home all the children's toys in a carrier bag every week instead of pricing them up and putting them into the shop. Geoffrey's mother was most apologetic, and Catherine had to admit she felt sorry for the woman, but they should have warned her all the same.   Then any unpleasantness could have been avoided.   Still, it had all settled down once he was back in Highclere, just for a little rest, his mother had said. That, of course, was the end of his career in Charlie's Choice. Catherine had breathed a slight sigh of relief at letting him go and now she had a vacancy for three sessions a week. She was sure she'd be a bit more discerning over the next volunteer.

Kevin worked hard but he was, well, he was Kevin. By that she meant he was a little bit like hard work himself, always needing to think he was in charge of everything, always particular about how he did every little job. After all this was only a charity shop - not a proper business in the way that working in Woollies was. Of course they needed to make money out of the place and the charity was important - she knew that. But all the same, he could be a bit more relaxed, especially in how he dressed when he came to work.

Chapter Four

Gem

'Are you alright?' A woman's voice behind Gem brought her to her senses. She turned to see the smiling face of the woman called Catherine looking at her sympathetically, encouraging her to take the plunge.

'I'm looking for some voluntary work to do - do you need anyone?' she blurted before she could lose her nerve again.

Catherine looked critically at her.

'I don't know,' she hesitated and sighed. 'Well, we could do with some help - but only three half days a week. Why do you want to work here in particular?'

Gem realised she'd been holding her breath. She glanced around the shop, wondering once more what she was doing. She looked back at Catherine, trying to gather her thoughts. What to say?

'I'm out of work,' she said finally. 'I need something to do - to get me into working again. Good for my cv, you know?' She paused. 'I liked the sound of this charity. I knew someone who got caught up in taking drugs.' She trailed off, realising she'd started babbling.

'Right, well then - how about you doing Tuesday mornings and Wednesday and Friday afternoons? you can start on Tuesday morning if you like.'

'Brilliant - what time do I have to be here?'

'We open at half past nine. So you need to be here at about twenty past.'

'See you then. Next Tuesday.' Gem made to leave the shop before she could change her mind.

'Hang on - you'll need to fill in a form before you go.' Catherine moved away towards the counter, rummaged in a drawer and produced a form. 'Just fill this in and bring it in tomorrow - we need to take references but you can start straight away next week.'

Gem took the form, stuffing it into her pocket and made for the door. 'Thank you,' she smiled as she turned at the doorway.

'See you tomorrow then,' Catherine said.

What have I done, Gem wondered. She stood in the doorway of the shop next door and tried to calm herself. She hadn't realised how much courage it would take to do what she'd just done. She was still shaking inside and hadn't really expected to be taken on so quickly without even an interview. They must be desperate. Taking a few slow breaths in and out, she began to feel lighter. Walking into the street towards her home, she noticed the sun was breaking through the clouds.

Chapter Five

Kevin

My name is Kevin Franks. I still live at home with my Mum even though I'm twenty three. I'm quite short, five foot six and a half, slim, with black hair and I'm not bad looking. I don't remember much about my Dad - he left when I was five and three quarters. Mum doesn't talk about him at all but I remember sitting with him in front of the television when I was little. I remember the smell of him, warm and strong, his hands ruffling my hair and then he'd pinch my cheek. When he left I can't remember how I felt. It's all just a black hole in my memory now. Mum always said we would manage very well without him, thank you. She worked at the Doctors' surgery as a receptionist and would come home from work and scrub the house from top to bottom every evening. Our house was very clean but Mum would never let me bring any friends home to play. It still is very clean. I don't have a girlfriend at the moment. Well, I've never really had a girlfriend although there was this girl at school I used to spend time with for a while. I don't see her any more though.

The shop is quite busy at times but this morning the rain seemed to keep away the usual flurry of customers. I've always wanted to work in a shop - I should have been a manager really and could have been by now - if only things had turned out differently.

I'm a hard worker and I'd done well all through school but something had gone wrong somewhere along the way. I was half way through my A levels. I thought it was because I had tried too hard and would go over and over every piece of work I did before I could hand it in. But then it got to the point where I believed that my work would never be good enough. That was when I suffered my little "breakdown". That's what my Mum called it. To be truthful, I can't actually remember much about it and anyway, I am definitely over all that now.

I plan to get a proper job soon - I just needed to get a bit of experience under my belt. When I'd applied for jobs they'd said I had no experience, so that was why I'm here, just to get experience. Not because I'm not good enough for a real job in a real shop. So I try hard to work in such a way that people will see that this is a real shop with real customers. I know presentation is important. That's why I always wear my suit to work. Once I have my own shop I will make sure that all the staff are smartly dressed at all times. I don't like the way Catherine wears jeans and paints her toenails which peep out through the holes in her sandals. But she is the manager, so I have to keep up the pretense that she's in charge - and we do make a good team after all.

The best part of the job is helping the customers, showing them the new items that have just come in. I take great pride in my "customer service". Everyone who comes in is important - well you never know who they are do you? Take that old lady who comes in every day at the same time. She smells slightly of cats - or is it urine? I'm not sure, and if it is urine, well I don't really want to think about that. I do wash my hands after she's been in because you can't take any chances. I am always nice to her all the same. If you are nice to people they always remember you, don't they? Anyway, that old lady will die one day and may leave a lot of money to someone - and it could be me.'

Chapter Six

Gem

It was early on Tuesday morning. Gem dressed herself in a pair of black leggings and a pale blue t-shirt. She looked down at herself wondering what she was letting herself in for.

How the hell did I get into this state? she pulled her long hair back off her face, pondering her reluctance of taking on this so called job. It's not even as if I'm going to get paid! She'd done shop work before just after she'd left school - working in town in Meta Fashions. She knew what it was like to be on her feet all day - she knew customers could be a pain at times but she also remembered enjoying it in a weird kind of way.

When had it all started to go wrong?

The last thing she wanted to do was to blame anyone for how she'd ended up. There was little doubt though - if she hadn't got in with Billy she'd not be in the mess that led her to being arrested - for shop-lifting of all things! She knew what it felt like to have your stock nicked - like a body-blow - personal - even if it wasn't your own personal stuff they were nicking.

So her probation officer spent hours and hours with her taking notes and writing reports and finally got the judge to agree to putting her on probation with the proviso that she had to keep attending the drug treatment centre. Now she had to keep away from street drugs. No more wheeling and dealing - just a daily dose of Methadone with a willingess to "give something back to society".

"Charlie's Choice" - a charity shop set up by the mother of a teenager who'd died of an overdose of drugs a couple of years ago. Well - not even an overdose - just the first time she'd taken some kind of legal high at a party - probably Mexxies. Her heart had just packed up they said. Now her Mum was spending all her time going round to schools and Youth Clubs telling the kids how dangerous so called legal highs could be - using photographs of Charlie after she was dead to try and scare them into not doing it. Gem could have told her scare tactics don't really work - after all she'd seen it all but still had to try Heroin and that's not even a legal drug is it? It's just too hard to say no sometimes, and curiosity gets the better of you when you're with your mates. You just don't think it'll ever happen to you, do you? Anyway the money from the shop goes towards this drop-in charity place that kids can go to for advice. Apparantly the NHS don't have the funding for getting people off unless they're actually addicted to a hard drug. Except for alcohol of course.

***

The shop was quiet when she arrived - the door still locked. Gem peered in through the glass and smiled at Catherine who was already there tidying the rails of clothing. Soon she was inside the back room, hanging her jacket on a hook behind the door. Bags of clothing were stacked against one wall - a large high table filled the centre of the room. A row of empty hangers on a rail ready for new stock to be hung at one side, a shelf full of bric-a-brac, another with paperback books piled randomly. Catherine took up a bag and tipped its contents onto the table and began lifting up each item in turn.

'Everything has to be clean - no marks anywhere - make sure there are no rips or worn spots or bobbling. Check the labels for washing instructions and the fire regulation mark. Make sure the correct size is put on the hanger before you put it in the shop. Anything that's not perfect has to be rejected - we have a "rag-bag" for everything we don't use and the rag man comes once a week to take it all away. Just stack it all in the big bin inside the door. Any toys or bric-a-brac we don't use go in the skip outside the back door. We can't sell any electrical goods or toiletries, food, perfumes, things like that. If you get stuck - just ask.' She showed Gem the labelling machine and showed her the system for recycling stock. 'Every week has a number and after four weeks we cull what's in the shop - take out anything over four weeks old and ditch it.'

Let me die now, thought Gem. 'What about prices? How do I know what price to put on the label?'

'It's all here in this catalogue.' Catherine opened a file and showed Gem the pages for each type of garment. 'See - dresses, t-shirts, men's stuff, childrens clothing. It's all here. There's a section for Designer clothing at the front. You use your own judgement as to whether items are good quality or not.'

'What about bric-a-brac and books?'

'Just have a look in the shop at the items already priced and decide for yourself - unless you think something might be worth a lot more - then just ask. Books are all one pound fifty for paperbacks and two pounds fifty for hardbacks. But we only sell books that are in really good condition - we get too many of the things to be honest. If you want to read one of the books, you can just take it home to read as long as you bring it back when you've finished it. If you want to buy any clothes - we do a special rate for staff. It's flexible.'

The shop door opened and Kevin appeared.

'Kevin - I want you to meet our new volunteer,' Catherine said as he entered the back room. 'This is Gem - she'll be working here on Tuesday mornings and Wednesday and Friday afternoons.'

'Hello,' Gem smiled at her new colleague.

'Pleased to meet you,' Kevin held his hand out and Gem hesitated before she lifted hers. He took her hand and shook it formally. 'I'm sure we'll enjoy working together,' he said. 'We're a good team here, aren't we Catherine?'

'Great.' Gem pushed down the urge to wipe her hand on her leggings.

'Kevin likes to work on the till - so I'll help you out here today - make sure you know what you're doing,' Catherine smiled at Gem. 'Now - let's get on with the day then.'

Oh God! Gem was thinking as she fought with the sinking feeling of doom that was wrapping itself around her. Trying hard not to groan out loud, she smiled back bravely.

Chapter Seven

Kevin

There's a new member of staff started this week. Her name's Gem - I remember her hanging around in the shop last week. I thought she was interested in bric-a-brac at first, then when she dropped the jade rabbit I guessed she was just a time-waster - probably in the shop to get out of the rain. She shouldn't had dropped it like that and after she was gone I took up the rabbit and put it in my pocket. I don't know why I didn't put it back and only realised that I still had it when I got home that evening. It's just as well - I will look after it.

I was quite surprised when Gem had the gall to ask Catherine for a job. I'm not sure whether I'm going to get on with her - she looks a bit like a druggie - got that seediness about her. And she came to work in leggings and a t-shirt. She could have made more of an effort on her first day. Catherine doesn't seem to see it though and spent ages with her in the back room. I could hear them laughing together every now and again. Not very professional really.

Gem was in here yesterday morning working and she's due back in this afternoon. Catherine says I have to try and get on with her - help to show her the ropes. I'm not sure about how this will effect our little team. New people are always difficult aren't they? I think it'll be alright if she stays in the back room sorting stock - but then again - can she be trusted not to take the best things and hide them in her bag? I'll have to keep a close eye on her, won't I?

The shop's been busy today. It's always like this on market day with a lot of old ladies coming in looking for bargains. I like the old ladies, they appreciate someone like me with manners. I know how to treat customers and always try to help them find what they're looking for.

I have my favourite regulars of course. Mrs. Scott came in this morning. She's a widow now - I remember when she brought in a lot of her husband's clothes a few months ago.

You have to admire her as she keeps herself active. She was telling me today that she's just finished building a new wall in her back garden. I was most surprised and at first I thought she was making it up, but she went on to explain that her husband had been a bricklayer and she'd often helped him in his work when they were younger. She said she wasn't going to let her age stop her from doing what she wanted to do. And then her friend came up behind her and told me that it was all true. She really does build walls in her back garden! You never know do you?

Unfortunately it's not only old ladies that come in on market day. This morning we had some rather unsavoury-looking young women pushing buggies with children trailing behind them. As soon as they were in the shop, the children were into everything. There was no control at all and no respect when I gave them one of my looks. You have to have eyes everywhere with people like that. I'm sure they just bring in the children to distract me. Then when my back's turned, the mothers are stealing the stock, stuffing it into the bags hanging on the buggies. How can people steal from a charity?

I don't know how I'm going to cope with the stress of having a new member of staff in here this afternoon. It's bad enough having to watch the customers without having to worry about what the staff are up to.

33

Chapter Eight

Catherine

Catherine stood behind the counter and looked around the shop. She felt a warm satisfaction as she realised everything looked to be in its place. Things were indeed looking up - the new young woman, Gem, seemed to be very keen and as she'd had shop experience was easy to train. Catherine was confident that she could soon have Gem working on the till - if only Kevin would let her have a go at it. There was something about the girl though but she couldn't put her finger on what it was. She would keep an eye on her and reserve judgement for later on.

The door opened and soon the shop was full of customers. Catherine liked it best when it was busy although she preferred to keep the shop tidy and customers were never that. They pulled things out to look at them and then stuffed them back any old how - sometimes the clothes slipped off the hangers but did anyone else pick them up again? Hardly ever. Still it kept her busy she supposed. There were two women together - in their fifties she guessed - rummaging through the carefully colour-co-ordinated sweaters that she'd set out only a few minutes before. Catherine felt herself tense as she watched them - wondered if they would even buy anything or whether they were just wasting time as many of her so called customers seemed to do. Some people just came in to see if they could find a bargain, looking at the labels to see where they'd originally been purchased. She knew some of her customers even bought items from the shop and then went out and resold them - for a much greater profit too. But doing all that herself would have taken too much of Catherine's precious time, so she didn't really begrudge them the money they made out of it. The charity still made something out of the sale so why should she care. If only they weren't so - so messy in the manner of their shopping.

The feeling of satisfaction slipped slightly as she stood watching, trying to look busy but without much to do. She knew she was only dreaming - this charity shop would never be the ideal place to work. Second best until something better came along. And something better would come along one day, she was sure of that. You have to just believe in yourself, was her mantra. Turning she glanced into the mirror behind the counter and caught herself frowning back - she smoothed a straggled hair into place and smiled. That's better.

'Penny for them Catherine.' Kevin's voice broke the spell. She looked at him, holding the smile as she spoke.

'I was just admiring the shop. It's looking just right today.'

'Yes,' he said vaguely. 'Look, Catherine - I was wondering - have you heard from Joan? She's not been in this week, has she? She was meant to work yesterday.'

Catherine thought for a while. 'She hasn't been in touch. I thought it wasn't like her but maybe she had to go away. An emergency or something.'

'I don't remember her ever going away before. She doesn't go away - and she always comes in on her duty days. She even comes in when she's not on duty.'

'She might be poorly. She is an old lady after all.'

'I suppose. I just hope she's alright.'

Catherine sighed. 'I'm sure she'll be in soon - maybe later. Don't worry. Look, this is a charity shop. We don't pay people, so if they don't want to come in there's not a lot we can do about it. It's the nature of the business, I'm afraid.'

'Has she got any family?'

'I think she mentioned a nephew - but I don't know if he's local. Maybe she's gone to stay with him.' Catherine smiled. 'Why are you so concerned anyway?'

Kevin frowned. 'I don't know. It's only that I've just found her coat in the cupboard. She must have left it here.'

Catherine shook her head, trying to remember whether she'd seen a coat hanging there when she'd arrived this morning. 'I don't remember seeing anything.'

'I'll show you then,' Kevin insisted as he walked to the back of the shop returning almost immediately carrying a coat. 'Look - pure wool, camel coloured - just like the one she wears.'

'That coat's been there for ages, I don't think it's hers.'

'But look at what's in the pocket.' He thrust his hand into one of the pockets and pulled out a crumpled envelope. He spread it out on the counter. The address was handwritten and faded but the name was still quite clear - Mrs. Joan Clarke.

'Oh. Then it must be hers then.' Catherine was feeling slightly irritated at what she thought was Kevin making his usual fuss about things.

'I can't understand why she would just disappear and leave her coat behind and I've noticed that she seemed a bit upset, a bit short-tempered, over the last few weeks. Do you think something could have happened to her? She wouldn't just go away without her coat, would she?'

'You've got a great imagination, Kevin. I expect she'll come in soon and we'll laugh about it.'

'Maybe.' Kevin didn't sound convinced.

'Look, we'll just leave the coat in the cupboard. I'm sure she'll be in soon. O.K.?'

'Can't you telephone her? Just to make sure.'

'I already did phone her - I left a message on her answerphone yesterday.'

'So she wasn't there when you phoned? There must be something wrong.'

'Look, Kevin, just leave it for now. I'm sure there will be a simple explanation. And anyway, you have no business in going through another person's coat pockets.'

'I'm sorry,' Kevin blushed. 'I would never do something like that normally. It's just that I'm worried.' He picked up the envelope and folded it carefully before putting it back in the pocket of the coat.

Chapter Nine

Karen

The office was crowded and noisy. Several of her colleagues were sat at their desks, chatting, scribbling notes in the Kardex, or talking on the telephone. Karen started to write up her notes on Gemma Wylde. Gem seemed to have got herself on track with the new volunteering job and although she said she was struggling with the reduction in Methadone, Karen was happy with the way things were going. I must grab one of those sheets on relaxation techniques before she comes in next, she reminded herself.

Scratching her head, she could still feel the scars across her skull which sometimes ached, especially when it was cold outside. Her thoughts drifted back to her own traumas, over ten years ago now. It had taken her long months to get over the post-traumatic problems she'd faced at the time. Nights of waking up, sweating with fear, convinced Peter was in the room with her. Then she would have to get up and check on Lucy, standing over her cot, watching her for hours just to make sure she was still breathing.

There were the times when she'd be driving to work and would imagine she'd seen his car pass her. Even though she'd known it was impossible, that he was still locked up safely behind prison bars, she would still be convinced it was his car. The sick feeling in her stomach would be so overwhelming she'd have to stop on the hard shoulder until the fear passed. Then there was the time in Wickham, by the bank, when he'd been standing in front of her on the pavement, his back to her. It was only when he turned around she saw it wasn't him.

She remembered the occasion at work when a male patient had become angry and had faced up to her in the doorway of the ward office. She remained calm on the surface, telling him to move away from the door but as soon as he had, she'd slammed the door shut and crumpled to the floor in a mess of tears and had to go home before her shift was over. Even now, she jumped with fright whenever someone banged a door shut.

Gradually, and with help from a psychologist, Karen had recovered almost fully, even though she sometimes had some flash-backs to that awful night when Peter had attacked her. She guessed it would never completely be forgotten even though she had learned ways to cope with it. Now she was strong enough to work in an area where she was dealing with people who could often be volatile, to say the least. Not for the first time, she wondered to herself why she had chosen this line of work. I could be working in a nice office.

She looked at the clock on the far wall. Gem was just about due to see her. She grabbed the sheet of relaxation techniques and headed to the reception on the other side of the building.

Chapter Ten

Gem

The waiting room stank of stale alcohol and urine.

She hated this place and would rather be anywhere else than sitting amongst reminders of the world she was trying to get away from. She edged along the bench away from the other occupant and tried not to breathe through her nose.

'Wassup love?' he slurred. 'Don't worry - I'm harmless.'

She turned away, hoping he would take the hint and leave her alone.

'Please yerself then.' He stood up unsteadily and went to the window above the counter - a glass screen between the waiting room and the reception staff. He thumped on the toughened glass. 'Oi! - How much longer do I have to wait?'

Gem shrank into herself, wishing he'd just go away. The woman behind the screen was ignoring him. He knocked on the window again.

'You ignoring me?'

The woman looked up. 'Behaving like that won't get you seen any quicker.'

'But I've been here an hour already - bitch,' he added as he turned away and faced Gem. 'Think they bloody own the place.' He smiled at Gem and sat down closer to her. His unwashed body odour made her feel sick. 'What you here for, love?'

Before Gem could respond the door opened and the smiling face of Karen appeared. 'Hello Gem - can you come through,' she said.

''Ere - what about me - I've been waiting for ages. I was here long before her!' The man staggered to his feet and moved towards Karen as she held the door.

'Sorry. Do you have an appointment.' Karen glanced at him then looked at Gem whilst she spoke to the man.

'No. It says "Drop-in Centre" on the door - so that's what I'm doing - dropping in.'

'Then you'll have to wait for the Duty Officer to see you. I expect he'll be out soon.'

'Look - Miss - I've been waiting for over an hour now. I'm not hanging about in here any longer.' He pushed past Karen and was out in the street before she could protest. Gem saw him from the window staggering down the road towards the pub on the corner.

'Sorry Gem - shall we go through?' Karen ushered her into the corridor and soon they were settled into the low chairs in a tiny interview room. Gem sighed to herself.

'How much longer do I have to keep coming here?' she asked.

'Tell me about your week. How have you been filling your time?' was Karen's reply.

Gem

How have I been filling my time? Is that what it's come down to? Filling my time - what a weird expression, as though time is an empty thing I have to fill. Before I went into treatment I never thought about time or whether it was being filled or staying empty. I tell Karen that I've started working in the charity shop and she's happy about that. But am I? It's not easy changing the way you've been living. I know I only do three half days there but it's still a kind of routine and I haven't had that in my life for a while now. So what's the truth of how I feel about it all? Well, there's the people I have to work with for a start.

Let me tell you about Julie. She works there every afternoon - except Tuesdays. She won't do mornings as she says she's too busy doing her housework but I think it's really because she can't get up in the mornings. She always looks like she's half asleep. And she keeps popping out to the car park at random moments. Says she's going out for a smoke but then she comes in stinking of something else - brandy I think.

I work with Julie on Wednesday afternoons and it's always the same. I've seen it all before down at the treatment centre - those ones who drink too much - they look down their noses at us druggies but they're no better really - drink ruins just as many lives - probably more seeing as the booze makes you violent whereas heroin, well, it just eats away at you and if you're on Methadone you can still get on with your life even though you're still addicted. I wouldn't want to be her.

Kevin really gets on my nerves. If he says one more time 'Good morning madam - can I interest you in our latest raffle?' I'll scream - or lump him with that bloody jade rabbit! Actually, they must have sold that - I haven't seen it since I started there. Still, Kevin's not so bad really - can make a decent cup of tea anyway and he works hard. I can take it easy when I'm on with him as everything gets done without any effort - from me that is. Actually, I wish he'd chill out a bit. It gets boring in there if there's nothing to do. He seems to know everyone who comes into the shop, remembers every little thing that's said to him, too. He's always telling me things about the other volunteers as well. Take that old lady, Joan. She works with him on a couple of afternoons a week. I've never even met her but I know all about her from what he's told me. And what he's told me is only ever boring stuff - about her having a nephew and a cat and that she never sees her sister or any of her other relatives. As if I'm interested in all of that?

Catherine's alright but she's a bit bossy although I guess she's meant to be if she has to run the place. The first day there was a nightmare with Catherine. She started on me straight away.

'This rail needs sorting out. Someone's put the wrong hangers out.' She'd grabbed a dress off the rail and waved it in front of me as she spoke. 'Dresses should go on the black hangers.'

I found myself apologising when I knew it wasn't me who put it out. I'd glanced at the price ticket and noticed the number on it. 'It was done last week - look at the code - week seventeen. It's eighteen this week.'

Catherine had snatched back the garment. 'It can't have been - I'd have noticed. Anyway - whoever did it probably got the code wrong as well.'

'Whatever.' I'd gone to the back room and found a new hanger - black of course. 'There you go.' Catherine had glared at me at the time but soon seemed to forget the incident. I just spent the rest of the day wondering what I was doing in the place. It's not nice being the new one anywhere is it? It sticks in the throat a bit knowing I'm not even getting paid for this.

Thinking about it though, Catherine and me do get on kind of well. Even though she seemed to blame me for things, we did have a bit of a laugh. She started telling me about her days in Woollies. It sounded like a great place to work. This made me think about my own life - I'd always looked down at anyone who worked in Woolworths - thought I was above all that at one time. Look at me now - how things change. I'm doing this just to get the judge off my back. But I think I will get to like it.

Chapter Eleven

Kevin

Kevin stood alone in the back room, frowning. He hesitated a moment then, making a decision - thrust his hand in the coat pocket and took out the envelope. Before he could change his mind again he stuffed it into the pocket of his own jacket. He thought for a moment, took it out, smoothed it carefully and folded it once again before tucking it into his own pocket again.

'Put the kettle on Kevin, will you please?' Catherine's voice snapped him back to the present.

Flushing with guilt he replied 'Yes Catherine - I'm just doing it now.' He filled the kettle wondering whether he was doing the right thing, keeping the envelope. Then justifying it to himself. No-one else cares. And I'll bring the letter straight back.

The rest of the day seemed to stretch on forever but at last they were locking the shop and Kevin waved Catherine away as she walked off towards the Co-op. 'See you tomorrow then.'

He waited a moment then took the envelope from his pocket and peered at the address - 59 Station Road. Just a short walk away. Before he could change his mind yet again, still gripping the envelope in his hand, he marched towards the end of the street and turned left away from the town centre.

Station Road was long. The houses displayed neat, well-groomed gardens, lawns and flower-beds - all well-kept. The front garden of number fifty nine was no different to any of the others along this street. The hedge was a little overgrown but the gate was well-oiled and opened easily to his touch.

Feeling more than a little nervous he hesitated to go any further. She'll be there and then what will I say? he wondered. But what if she's not alright? his other self argued back. Then he found himself passing the front bay window -

curtains closely drawn against the world. Doesn't sound like Joan. Such an "open" person. He wondered if she'd just gone off on holiday and began to feel a little silly. If she's away, then she just won't answer the door. Arriving at the porch he grabbed the lion-headed knocker and swiftly dropped it to land with a thud on the door. The paintwork had seen better days - he stood there inspecting the cracks and the grime around the window panes. Peering closely through the pebbled glass in the door, he tried to see if there was any sign of life. Nothing happened. Feeling braver now, he knocked again, more firmly this time. He could hear the echo of his own heart thud in answer to the knocker and waited for what seemed like an eternity. Then, as he was about to turn away the door creaked open.

Warm, stale air gushed out - a cat dashed between his feet even before he had realised that the door opener was not Joan - was not anything or anyone like Joan. No. It was a man - tall, with shoulder length lanky hair - but no mistake - a man. Kevin's smile was fixed as he wondered what to say. Before he could utter a word, however, he was pre-empted by the low voice of its owner.

'About time - where the hell have you been?' the man began as he glared up at Kevin.

'Who the... where's Billy?'

Kevin swallowed. 'I'm Kevin. I'm from Charlie's Choice - I was worried about Mrs. Clarke. She was supposed to be at work yesterday but didn't turn up and didn't phone in sick. And she comes in every day you see and she's not been in today. It's not like her. Sorry, I don't know where Billy is.' He paused for breath. 'Is Mrs. Clarke in?'

The man scowled. Yes it was definitely a scowl. 'She's gone away.'

'Oh dear.' Kevin hesitated. 'When will she be back?'

'Not for a very long time. You won't be seeing her for a while.' The door half-closed.

'She's not unwell is she?'

'Fine and dandy. Just spending some time,' the man paused. 'With her daughter in Wales. She went a couple of days ago mate.' He pushed to door to. 'Now, if you don't mind - I'm a bit busy.'

'Oh, well, she always...' But the door had already slammed shut.

Kevin stood for a moment, puzzling over what to do next.

He must be mistaken, Kevin thought, and was about to knock on the door again when the cat, hiding in the shrubbery, started hissing. That was when he realised that there was someone else just outside the gate. Without a further thought, Kevin stepped aside and hid himself behind the same shrub the little ginger tabby was hunkering under. 'Shush,' he hissed back at the cat and waited.

The newcomer walked up the path and rapped on the door. Dressed in black jeans - low-slung, showing a pair of greying underpants - a green hoodie pulled up over his head, with an old leather jacket over the top, he looked an unlikely friend of Joan. Perhaps it's a grandchild. He was much shorter than the one who opened the door to Kevin, his spikey red hair sticking out, just visible despite the hoodie. The door opened and the newcomer looked down on the other, shorter man.

'Billy. Where the fuck have you been?'

'Hey, man, I got here as quick as I could. What's your problem?'

'Just get inside. There's been someone snooping around, looking for the old woman.' Billy was ushered in and the door slammed shut again.

Kevin was still wondering what to do when he noticed something brushing against his legs. The ginger tabby looked up at him and gave a faint mew. He stooped down to stroke the cat.

'Hey, you alright little fellow?' he whispered. 'Where's your mistress gone, eh?' The cat just sat and blinked up at Kevin who stood trying to work out what was going on. It seemed wrong somehow. Joan came into the shop nearly every day and had definitely been in on Tuesday, chatting about something. Was it about her family? If only he could remember what she'd exactly said. Kevin was sure she'd have told him if she was planning to go away - and for her to not come in to do her shift yesterday and to leave her coat behind - it was just so out of the ordinary - not what she'd normally do at all. He'd not liked the look of that man who'd opened the door and as for that Billy person, he looked decidedly shifty to say the least.

Well, there's not a lot I can do just standing here in the bushes, he told himself as he crept away back down the path and with a backward glance towards the house, slipped out of the gate. The cat followed, jumped on the wall and sat watching Kevin as he retreated down the street.

Chapter Twelve

Gem

Clutching the leaflet on relaxation techniques and slightly boosted by Karen's little "pep-talk", Gem finally left the stench of the clinic behind her and set off down the street wondering what to do with the rest of the evening. The trouble with being in treatment was that you didn't have the same purpose any more to get out and get money together. It seemed like forever that she'd had to hustle every day for a hit, and the things she'd done to get through another twenty four hours didn't bear thinking about. Working in the shop for three shifts a week was OK but didn't replace the amount of energy she'd used and the excitement she got to get enough drugs to keep her sane.

Stop thinking about all that, she told herself as she picked up her pace and headed across the road towards the park. The low sun shining in her eyes making her squint as she crossed the road nearly caused her to miss the young man in the suit as he strode straight into her path.

'Oi! Watch where you're going!' she snapped, then turning, realised it was no other than Kevin from the shop. 'You alright?' she asked, wondering what Kevin was thinking, wandering out into the road without so much as a glance about.

'Eh?' He stopped and looked up at Gem. 'Oh, it's you. Sorry.' He frowned. 'I've just been round to Joan's house. She's gone missing I think. I'm worried - it's not right you know.'

'Shall we get off the road?' Gem touched his sleeve. He flinched as though her hand was fire. 'Sorry - but we need to get off the road. The traffic.'

Kevin looked about for the first time. 'Yes - yes.'

Gem followed him to the safety of the pavement. 'Now what was all that about?'

'I was worried about Joan. She never lets us down - always likes to come in for a chat even when she's not working and yesterday she just didn't come in. She left her coat in the cupboard and in the coat pocket was an envelope with her name and address on it so I knew it was hers even though Catherine didn't believe me. I was worried about her so I went to her house, just to see if she was OK and when I got there a young man opened the door and said she'd gone away a few days ago but she couldn't have because she came in the shop on Tuesday - that's only the day before yesterday and her cat dashed out of the house between my legs and hissed. And then he thought I was someone else called Billy but I wasn't so I hid in the bushes with the cat and saw Billy when he knocked on the door.' He paused for breath. 'That's why I'm worried - they didn't look like nice people and I don't think Joan would like them.'

'Woah! Just slow down a bit.' Gem's mind was buzzing. It all sounded a bit far-fetched and she had been taking it all as one of Kevin's rants, possibly based in fantasy until Kevin had mentioned Billy. Surely not? A cold feeling crept over her. 'OK, Kevin. Let's go back and have another look, just to make sure.'

'I don't know. I didn't like the man in the house. And the other one was not very nice either. I don't want to knock on the door again and I don't think you should either.'

'We won't knock on the door - just walk past and check it out,' she reasoned. 'Maybe we could ask one of her neighbours. What's the address?'

Kevin pulled the envelope from his jacket pocket. 'Station Road. It's this way.'

'Come on then - let's do it.' Gem strode down the street. Kevin hesitated for a moment then hurried to catch her up.

Soon they were approaching the bungalow. Kevin slowed, touching Gem's elbow. 'That's the one.' He stopped walking and pointed to number fifty-nine.

'OK. Wait here,' Gem said. 'I'll walk past first. We don't want to be seen together in case they recognise you. It's better if they don't know there's more than one of you. They might be looking out in case you come back.'

'You think there's something wrong then?'

'Maybe. I don't know - better to be safe than sorry. Just wait here.' And she walked off past the gate. Glancing up the garden path she noticed the ginger tabby cat sitting under a bush to the right of the front door. Apart from the cat, the place looked deserted - the curtains were drawn tightly together. Gem didn't want to be recognised either so quickened her pace, not looking back until she'd put at least a hundred metres between herself and the house. She stopped and turned. The street was empty apart from Kevin - standing looking extremely furtive. She waved to him, beckoning him to come past the house and watched as he scurried along to meet her. Oh my God, we look so dodgy skulking about the place.

'What do you think?' Kevin asked.

'It looks deserted to me.' Gem answered. 'But it's hard to tell from the front. I wonder if there's a back alley? Let's go and look.'

They walked to the end of the road and turned left. Sure enough just a few yards behind the end house was a lane leading along the back of the properties - many of which had wooden or brick garages in the back gardens.

'We just need to work out which one's Joan's,' said Gem. 'Trouble is, there's no numbers on the back gates.'

'If we walk to the end, we could count our way along,' Kevin suggested.

Soon they were working their way back counting the gardens until they reached a rickety gate next to a weatherbeaten wooden garage. The back garden was long and overgrown with weeds and grass. Gem touched the gate which swung open with a loud creak.

'Shsh,' Gem spoke to herself as she stepped inside the gate. 'This must be it. Wait here, Kevin,' she whispered. The path was overgrown with shrubs providing adequate coverage to enable her to get close to the house without being seen. The curtains at the rear of the building were drawn together except for a small gap in one window. She made her way quickly and quietly and crouched below the sill, holding her breath. The house seemed quiet enough so she stood up and peered through the gap but the room was too gloomy to see anything much other than vague shadows. About to move away, the inner door opened and a shaft of light flooded the room. Gem gasped as the recognised the sillhouette of the man in the doorway. With a sick feeling in her stomach she stepped quickly away from the window.

Now what? She waited a moment, then hearing a door slam inside the house, she turned and ran back into the alley once again out of sight of the windows. 'Let's get out of here,' she snapped.

'What's happened? Did you see her?'

'No - but I nearly got caught. Come on, let's go!'
Gem ran before Kevin could ask any more stupid questions.

'What about asking the neighbours?' Kevin grabbed her arm when they'd reached the end of the street slowing her down.

'Ask them what?' She looked at where he held her arm.

Kevin snatched his hand away, embarrased. 'Sorry, sorry. I mean whether they've seen Mrs. Clark lately, or whether they'd seen or heard anything suspicious.'

'I think you're being a bit over-the-top, Kevin. I think we should just leave it.'

'Well I don't. We only have to ask her neighbours if she's gone away and whether they know where she may have gone. I don't see anything wrong in that.'

'But to ask if they've seen anything suspicious?'

'Alright, not that then. Just if they know where she's gone.'

'I suppose we could ask someone but I don't want to go back and be seen by ...... whoever's in the house.'

'I'll do it then.' Kevin had already begun to walk back towards the front of the street.

'I'll wait here,' Gem called. 'Be careful though.'

Kevin stopped outside number fifty-five. He marched up the garden path before he could lose his nerve and rang the bell. A dog barked followed by the sound of a woman's voice.

'Alright, that's enough Jack,' she called. Then 'Just a minute.'

Eventually the door was opened with much rattling of chains and locks and there stood a woman of short stature, her grey hair tightly curled. She looked up at Kevin enquiringly.

'So sorry to trouble you, but I was looking for Mrs. Clarke,' Kevin began. 'I don't suppose you've seen her about?'

'She lives two doors down - number fifty-nine. Sorry, you've got the wrong house.'

'I know - but I have called at her house and a young man answered her door. He said she'd gone away a few days ago but I saw her on Tuesday. It just seems odd to me and...' he paused. 'I don't suppose you know where she might have gone?'

'No dear, I'm sorry. But I did see her on Tuesday morning too. She walked past on her way to the shops. I was in the garden and she asked me if I needed anything. She always does bits of shopping for me but I didn't need anything that day as it happens and I don't remember seeing her come back this way.'

'Are you sure it was Tuesday?'

'Of course,' she snapped. 'There's not a lot wrong with my memory you know.'

'I'm sorry... I do believe you. I know I saw her on Tuesday too. It's only that the man said she'd gone away a few days ago.'

'Well she couldn't have. He must have been mistaken. Now, if you don't mind, I have things to do.' She pushed the door to as she spoke.

'Thank you for your time, sorry to intrude.' But the door was already shut. Kevin stood for a moment - staring at the door, took out his handkerchief and wiped his hands as he turned back down the path. Soon he was at the corner with Gem.

'Well? What did she say?' Gem asked.

'I was right. Joan was here on Tuesday - I knew it. The lady doesn't know where Joan went, or anything about her going away. She would have known, I'm sure, as Joan often would ask her if she wanted her to get anything from the shops. I'm sure Joan would have told her if she was going away. Now I think we should go to the police.'

'No!' Gem realised as soon as she opened her mouth her voice was too loud. 'Sorry - I'm sorry Kevin but I think we shouldn't do anything hasty yet. The police won't be interested - the man might have been mistaken - he probably meant Wednesday. We just don't know.'

'But she might be hurt - or worse,'

'Don't be silly, things like that don't happen in real life,' Gem said. 'You've been watching too many tv cop programmes. Look, I'm sure it will be alright. Just leave it with me for a bit - please,' she added.

Kevin didn't look convinced, but he nodded. 'Very well, I won't go to the police yet, but I don't see what you can do.'

'Trust me - I know what I'm doing,' Gem said, unconvincingly.

'What shall we do now then?' Kevin asked.

'Just go home and do whatever you usually do in the evenings.' Gem said impatiently. 'Now I have things to do. See you tomorrow.' And she walked off down the street before he could say anything else. At the end of the road, she glanced back but Kevin was nowhere in sight.

Chapter Thirteen

Gem

It wasn't the morning sunlight that woke Gem up. Nor was it the annoying sound of early morning birdsong making all that row outside her window. She'd been awake all night, worrying about what the hell was going on in Joan's house. She tried not to think about what she'd seen through the window last evening. She couldn't tell Kevin that she knew one of the two men who were in there. It was her Billy - she recognised him even though it was only a glimpse. To be honest, she was quite scared. Scared of getting involved with him again and scared of what he was up to. She didn't think he could possibly be related to Joan - or could he? Maybe it was quite innocent and the old dear really was away. Perhaps he was looking after her house and the cat whilst she was having a nice break away with her friend or a relative. But it didn't feel right somehow.

These and many more thoughts had kept Gem awake. Before she'd even gone to bed, she'd decided to try and find out. When they'd split up Billy told her he was going to move into his old aunt's house and had given her the phone number. She should have thrown it straight in the bin but something made her shove it in the drawer by her bed instead. It was still there, under a load of crap. She took out the paper and sat looking at it for a while before phoning. At first there was no reply - it went straight to voice-mail and there was no way she would leave a message. She was only half expecting him to be there anyway. He'd probably still be in Joan's house doing God knew what. When she did get through and heard his voice actually speaking she lost her nerve and hung up. Then she was so annoyed at herself because he obviously guessed it was her ringing and within a few minutes he was calling her back. Her phone rang six times before she unplugged it. She couldn't face him yet. The longing for the drugs was too strong. No - she wouldn't trust herself not to go there again. But that didn't solve the problem of what Billy was up to.

Without further hesitation she went into the kitchen, plugged the phone back in and began to punch his number in before stopping again. She stared at it, thinking. The last thing she wanted was to be involved in all that stuff again. The phone glared back at her. She slammed it down and reached for her cigarettes. Another bad habit, she thought as she lit one up and took a deep drag. Her hands were shaking as she sat down at the small kitchen table. Breaking up with Billy was both the hardest and the best thing she'd done for a long time. She'd talked about him a lot with Karen and splitting with him had been one of the few things they'd both agreed on as being for the best. The thought of him being back in her life was worse than awful. She was terrified.

'I should just go to the Police,' she spoke the words out loud knowing she would never do that. It was "grassing" and she wasn't a grass whatever was going on. The thing she was most afraid of was getting tempted to use again. Late evenings were the worst time when the Methadone was starting to wear off. 'Nothing worse than coming down from Methadone,' she muttered to herself. 'But if they've done something stupid and hurt the old lady...' She picked up the phone once more and dialled before she could change her mind again. It rang five times before he picked it up.

'Billy?' Her voice cracked. 'It's Gem.'

'Hyah, babe.' He sounded pleased to hear her voice anyway. 'I didn't think it would be long before you'd be in touch. You want to meet? I've got some good stuff.'

'No. I mean, yes. Can we meet up? I don't want anything though - just a chat.'

'Oh, yeah? What about?' His voice sounded hopeful now. 'You want to get back together?'

Gem hestitated. 'I just need to talk to you about something. Can I come round?'

'No - it's O.K. - I'll meet you in town. In the Railway Pub.'

'Right.   In about half an hour then?'

'See you there.'   And he hung up.

The Railway - that's the pub just around the corner from Station Road. Gem's thoughts were racing. She decided to go and meet him but had no idea as to how she was going to get to the bottom of what he was up to. In the end she decided that she'd ask him outright and if he didn't come clean and give her a reasonable explanation, she'd follow him and see for herself what was going on.

Chapter Fourteen

Billy

My name is Billy Jackson. I'm 24 years old and a mess.

My childhood was OK, I suppose, except for having to watch my dad and all his mates when they came round to our flat to shoot-up. It didn't really bother me even though I had to be careful not to step on the needles they sometimes left on the floor. My mum loved me in her own way but she was a bit of a mess too. Dad called her a slag but he didn't seem to care when she took his so-called mates into the bedroom while he sat on the sofa getting out of his head on heroin. Sometimes there'd be a knock at the door and Dad would let in men I'd never seen before. Then Mum would disappear with them into the bedroom too. I didn't understand what was going on at the time. Dad said they had a bit of business with Mum. I used to sit and watch the telly and try not to listen to the noises coming from behind the door. Once I got upset and tried to go in the room after Mum but my dad belted me around the ear. I didn't try that again.

When I was twelve my dad let me try some of his gear. He said it would make me feel good and it did. I remember floating and feeling really loved, so much so that I didn't care when one of his friends took me into my bedroom and started touching me. I don't remember if I liked what he did or not, but I liked the floaty feeling and was up for it the next time that man came round.

I didn't do so well at school and used to scive off all the time. I failed my GCSEs. Well, I didn't actually even sit them to tell the truth. My parents didn't care.

What makes me tick? I don't really think anything does - I spend all my time ducking and diving for the next fix of heroin. I've been addicted since I was a kid and it's taken over my life - it is my life. Even though I moved out of Mum and Dad's when I was sixteen and moved in with Nan it was too late for me to get out of the drug life-style.

I lived with my nan for a few years and they were the best years of my life so far. Nan would listen to me without shouting back when I ranted about stuff that was getting to me. She used to sit me down and let me talk while she cooked my tea. I can't remember Mum or Dad ever cooking my tea. For a while I stayed in with Nan in the evenings and she would tell me stories about when she was young. Stories about Granddad and how he used to spend time on his allotment with Dad when he was little. She said my dad was alright then but he got into trouble with some lads when he was in his teens and that was when he started on the drugs.

What do I look like? I'm not very tall, about five foot ten I suppose, skinny because I never eat very well. I suffer quite a bit from bad skin and get spotty at times. My hair's ginger. I've shaved my head but sometimes it grows out if I can't be bothered to shave it. Same with the facial hair. I only shave every few days or so. When I lived with my nan I looked much smarter - she used to wash and iron my clothes but I don't bother much these days and haven't bought a new pair of jeans or t-shirt for ages. My favourite thing is my leather jacket. It's black and a bit battered now but wearing it makes me feel good. Nan got it for me from a charity shop - it didn't cost a fortune - but it reminds me of better times.

Nan made me feel good about myself and I stopped using for a few months. It wasn't easy though and I slipped back into it, bit by bit. I thought I could handle it but life got so boring. I tried to keep busy and even went looking for work but it was too hard. I started back on the dealing, just a bit now and then to pay for my own use at first. Then it began to take me over and I was out all the time, day and night. Nan tried to talk to me, she tried so hard, too hard really. She pushed me into using more with her nagging - it was her fault and then she told me I had to leave. I was gutted but didn't let her know.

It was at this time I went into rehab. Nan chucking me out was what did it. I went into this drop-in centre one day and asked for help. That was one of the hardest things, walking through that door. They got me the place in the detox and rehab centre - I got off the drugs completely while I was in there. But then Nan died and I went off the rails again for a while but being in treatment got me through it I guess. That's when I met Gem. When we got out of the place I lived with her for a while, but it was too hard. It's hard enough in rehab but much harder when you're outside in the real world again. I was soon back into it and messed Gem about so much eventually she chucked me out too. She got fed up with me bringing people back to her place to use. I wasn't very good to her to be honest. I can't seem to trust women after what Mum was like and Nan throwing me out. Then her dying didn't help. I admit I did hit Gem sometimes but she used to drive me to it. I'd be different if she'd only take me back.

When I left Gem's I told her I was going to be at my Aunty Joan's house. I didn't want her thinking I had nowhere to go. I've been sleeping on a mate Dan's sofa up until about a month ago but he got into trouble with his landlord and got thrown out. I managed to talk old Aunty Joan into letting me move in there for a while, seeing as I had nowhere else to go. She was my mum's Aunt really but a bit like a second nan to me. She still wasn't that happy though and said no way could Dan stay. She was easy to fool and I used to sneak him in late at night. Not every night, mind you, just when he had nowhere else. Now everything's gone wrong and I don't know what to do. If only Gem and me could get back together I know it would be alright. Yeah, I've got a good feeling about today 'cos this morning she got in touch so things maybe are looking up after all.

Chapter Fifteen

Gem

Walking into a pub at eleven in the morning is an experience few people should make by choice. The morning sun illuminated the seediness of the place, the light catching on the dust being breathed in by the few customers. There was the aroma of last night's beer spillages and as she walked to the bar and looked around the room, Gem felt the stickiness of the carpet under her feet. Two men sat in one corner, hunched over their pints of lager, a woman in overalls wiped the tables, and the landlord was re-stocking the shelves behind the bar. Otherwise The Railway was empty. She ordered a coke and found a seat near the window.

It was nearly eleven-thirty before Billy came through the door. He spotted her straight away and sat down opposite, grinning inanely. She felt her stomach churning in trepidation.

'Hello Babe, it's good to see you,' he leaned back in his chair, seemingly full of confidence.

Gem smiled, blushing back at him, trying to think of what she could say.

'So, what did you want to see me about?' He looked over his shoulder glancing around the room. 'I've got some good stuff.'

'Yes, you said on the phone. I'm not after anything like that. I'm in treatment now.'

'Well, good for you.' He sounded ever so slightly sarcastic. There was a pause. 'OK, so, what do you want? You made it effin' clear the last time I saw you that we were finished.'

Gem looked out of the window, not sure how to broach the subject. The sky was filling with dark clouds. She took a breath and faced him again.

'It's about this old lady I know - Joan - Joan Clarke. Do you know her.'

The smile wiped from his face. 'How do you know her?'

'She's a volunteer in the shop I work in. So, what do you know about her?'

'Don't know what you're talking about. Why would I know some soddin' old woman.'

'Look, Billy - I've seen you at her house. Just tell me what's going on. You haven't done anything stupid have you?'

'Why do you always think the worst of me?' He looked around the room, avoided her eyes.

'Probably because I know what you can be like. I don't trust you. I used to but not any more.' She felt the hurt of past bad times.

'I'm not like that any more, Gem.' He reached out and touched her hand. 'We were bloody good, weren't we?'

Gem snatched her hand away, frightened by the feelings his touch ignited. 'Don't,' she snapped. 'Just don't!'

'Come on Gem, just give us another chance. I'll even go back into treatment if that's what you want.'

He's whining. 'I don't think so.' She sipped her coke.

'Let me get you a drink.'

'I've got one thanks.'

'What is it? Rum and coke?'

'No. Just coke and I don't want another one.'

'Don't you want a proper drink?' Billy smiled. 'At least have one with me.'

'No thanks.'

'Well, I'm going to have one anyway.' He stood up impatiently. 'Don't go sodding off, will you?' And he strode across the nearly empty space to the bar.

She watched him go and tried to understand the emotions pushing their unwelcome way into her guarded self. This was stupid, she knew it'd been a mistake to come. She still felt so vulnerable around Billy. Whatever he'd done to her there was still something there, something about him she couldn't leave alone. I've got to get out of here. Then she remembered Joan. Maybe if she went along with what Billy wanted, she could find out what had happened to the older woman. So against her better judgement she stayed and soon Billy was back.

He sat down again in the seat opposite her. She looked at him, wondering what to say. He raised his glass to her and took a swig of beer. 'So, you've brought me here just to ask if I know some effin' old dear that you know. I can't believe you've suddenly started caring about some old bag you've only just met. You sure you don't want something else?'

'No, I really don't want anything. I've not used drugs for a couple of months now. I'm on Methadone - I've been getting my life back together. I'm sorry Billy, I don't want to go back to all that.' She paused and took the plunge. 'But I guess I thought it would be nice to see you again if I'm honest.'

'You know I never wanted to split up with you, don't you?' His face lit up.

Gem was cringing. 'Yes, I know. If it could have been any other way...'

'Give me another chance, Gem, please.'

She looked at him. 'Oh, God, what am I doing?'

'You're doing what you've always wanted. Come on Gem, things can be bloody good between us again.' He smiled and reached for her hand. This time she forced herself not to pull it away.

'I'm not promising anything,' she said. 'Let's just be friends.'

'Better than nothing,' he grinned.

'But no drugs. Not for me and not when I'm around.'

'You're the boss. So, what have you been up to lately?

Chapter Sixteen

Karen

Karen shut her front door and walked to the car, parked just outside in the street. She'd never really stopped counting her blessings. Lucy, happy at school, setting off on the school bus at eight, leaving Karen that precious half an hour to tidy the house before going off to work. She looked forward to being at work, loved the team - the feeling of working with such a great bunch of people. She even had a fondness for the patients, clients as they were called now. It was so different from working on the wards. Yes, they were more like clients than patients, living in their own homes, each one with their unique problems and situations. You had to remember you were the guest of the client. It was a totally different way of working. And working with people with substance misuse issues was very different to working with those with severe mental health problems. Sometimes it could be very frustrating work - then at other times it could be so rewarding. More than anything, Karen loved the feeling when one of her clients started to get their life back on track, not necessarily being drug-free but being able to live a decent life, taking care of themselves and their families and looking to a better future.

Take Gemma for instance, she was such a mess when she first started on the Methadone programme and look at her now. Yes, she was still struggling with the reduction of her script but she was getting up in the mornings and going to work in the charity shop. Maybe not every day, but three shifts a week was a good start. Getting away from Billy was a good thing. Karen couldn't help comparing her old life with Peter to that of Gemma and Billy. Of course, Peter wasn't using drugs like Billy so it wasn't quite the same but he was abusing her in the same sort of way that Billy had abused Gemma. Thinking about those days still made her feel sick inside. She would do her utmost to help Gemma stay away from Billy.

She stopped herself. Look at me, getting over-involved again. She'd done that before when she first started nursing, going off to search for her patient Evelyn's lost Mother, against all the rules. Still, it had worked out well in the end with Evelyn and her mum being re-united and Karen becoming almost like a member of their family. Without them in her life things could have been very different. She thought about old Mrs. Chapman. She missed her, her dry sense of humour and sensible approach to life's problems. Evelyn was always there though if ever she wanted to spend some time talking over things. Karen still found it hard to believe how much Evelyn had changed since leaving hospital after so many years. Now she was like a wise aunt to Karen although sometimes she seemed to drift back into her shell.

Karen pulled into the car park at the clinic, locked her car and went into the building. The office was buzzing. Sharing with seven other workers, most of whom were nurses like Karen, was fun, challenging at times, sometimes hilarious. Decisions were all made at team level. It was not only a team of nurses though - there was a social worker, medical officers on a rota and the Consultant Psychiatrist as well as three admin support workers who typed all the letters, covered reception and produced the prescriptions for over two hundred clients.

Each morning there was the Methadone clinic when those on the early stage of the treatment programme came in, daily at first, then as they became stabilized on the Methadone, they reduced to three times, then twice or once a week. Eventually, most clients progressed to picking up their prescription from a local chemist and only came in to see their key worker once a week or once a fortnight. A good part of the work was visiting people in their own homes which sometimes meant travelling as far away as Liss, north of Petersfield.

The clinic was already underway by the time Karen reached the group room. The door was always open and the room was filled with clients waiting for their daily pick-up.

She was greeted by several of them as she sat on the window-sill, opening a window a few inches to let in some fresh air. The room was filled with tobacco smoke. Most of the drug users were also addicted to tobacco and denying them a cigarette in the building was, for many, one step too far. She looked around the room and even after so much time of working in this field wondered what could bring someone to this. What makes one person become addicted and yet another can experiment with drugs and never get into this state? She remembered the amount of people she'd known who'd used drugs when they were younger and most of them had moved on, grown out of it, she guessed. In fact, she couldn't think of one of her friends who'd not stopped using drugs eventually.

She dragged her thoughts back to the room. The early morning clinic was one of her favourite times of the working day. The clients came in at the start of their treatment, often in a complete mess, having not eaten properly for months or even years. Once they started, most of them gradually settled down to a routine of getting up in the morning, the relaxed atmosphere of the group room making it easier for them to talk about things. Karen's role in the room was to try and keep the conversation on a positive note, to help the clients see how well they were doing and to offer suggestions on how to improve their lives. Sometimes things would get a bit volatile, especially with those who were struggling with the change of lifestyle and were at the beginning of their treatment. However, often it was the clients who had been on the programme longer who helped the new ones through their problems. Karen loved seeing people moving on, doing well for themselves and helping each other.

Of course, there sometimes were clients who could be disruptive and some who even saw the group as an opportunity to connect with dealers in the car park outside. Karen knew there were always risks in working with drug users but this was no reason to deny them the opportunity to get clean. Most worked hard to do just that. Their chaotic lifestyles were never easy to leave behind, but when they did succeed, it was a great feeling for Karen that she may have helped them, even just a little bit.

The group was soon over and Karen made her way back through the reception area to her desk. The post-it note stuck on her desk phone greeting her made her feel anxious. She recognised the number - it was her past mother-in-law's. She hadn't seen Margaret for some months - it wasn't easy to keep up her visits since Peter's release from prison even though Margaret assured her he was living in Salisbury and had no interest in making contact as he was happily settled with a new woman in his life. Even so, Karen felt the old panic from all those years ago. She sat at her desk, staring at the message, mulling over what she should do. Margaret and she had drifted apart naturally since she'd been working in the community team and not having so much time during the week to meet. But Karen couldn't help remembering all Margaret had done for her when she was younger, taking her in as a teenager with no-where else to go and no family of her own. After Peter had attacked her, Margaret had been there, staying loyal even after she learned Karen was pregnant with another man's child.

After Peter's arrest, and the divorce, Margaret still supported and helped her with the new baby as much as she could. It was once he'd come out of prison things had changed. He'd only stayed at Margaret's for a short while before moving to Salisbury, but Karen found it too difficult to visit Margaret at her home any more. That was quite understandable, Margaret told her. Sometimes Karen had wondered how the older woman could be so laid back. She wasn't used to people caring for her, that was certain.

She looked at the post-it again and dialed the number. The phone was answered straight away, Margaret's familiar warm voice on the other end of the line.

'Hello, Margaret, it's Karen,' she said. 'I got a message to phone you.'

'Oh, Hello, Karen. Thank you for getting back to me. How are you, Karen?'

'I'm alright. You know - life's busy as ever. Work's great.'

'And what about Lucy? Is she OK?'

'Yes, she's fine. Doing alright at school. She moved up from Brownies last week and has started Guides now. She loves it. What about you?'

'I'm fine.'

'Good.'

Karen waited for Margaret to fill the silence. 'Are you sure you're OK?' she asked finally. 'I'm not being funny, but you never phone me at work unless there's something wrong. Has something happened?'

'No, nothing.' Karen heard the catch in Margaret's voice. Strained. 'I just wanted to invite you over for tea - or lunch. Are you busy this weekend?'

'Well, I can do Sunday lunch.'

'Great. Both of you, of course. Come over at twelve and we can have a good old natter.'

'OK. We'll see you there. Is there anything I can bring?'

'No. Just bring yourselves. I'll see you on Sunday then.'

Karen put the phone down, wondering about what could be going on. She's not phoned me at work for ages. There must be something going on. Something on her mind. Why do I feel so uneasy? It's only an invitation for lunch. I know I haven't been to her house for a long time and have never stayed for longer than a short visit for a coffee when I have been. It wasn't that she didn't get on with Margaret or that she didn't trust her. It was just the memories of the years she'd lived there before she'd married Peter, of the early days of their relationship and of how he'd behaved towards her once they were married. She still couldn't believe she'd been so naive to have fallen for him. The last thing she needed in her life now was to be reminded of those things. Still,

Margaret was a good woman and Karen knew she owed her so much. Anyway, I've already said I would go so I can't get out of it now. Bringing herself back to the present, she checked in her bag for her notebook, diary and keys and left the office for her home visits.

Chapter Seventeen

Kevin

All night he'd been awake, wondering what on earth was happening in Joan's house. After Gem left him yesterday Kevin didn't go home and do whatever he normally does in the evenings. He did go home but he couldn't settle to anything. He sat with his mother trying to watch TV, only she kept talking to him - asking him how his day had been and she wouldn't take a simple 'fine' for an answer. It was very frustrating when you were trying to think and your mother was talking all the time. In the end he'd gone to bed early, just to get away from her questions. Then he lay in bed, staring at the ceiling, still trying to work out where Joan was and if she was really alright, as Gem seemed to think she was.

By the time the dawn was breaking, he'd given up trying to sleep and got up. He showered and tidied his room. Well, it was already quite tidy but he'd been lying there looking at his things on the shelf and decided it was time to sort them out again. Every summer since he could remember he'd gone on holiday with his Mother and everywhere they'd gone, he'd brought home a souvenir. Egg-cups with a little picture of the town, just to remind him of the lovely times they'd had together.   And there, in the middle of them all, was the jade rabbit. Seeing it there made him feel guilty. I should really take that back to the shop, he thought as he placed it on his bedside table. He put everything else on his bed in a neat row and wondered if he really needed to keep them all. Now that he was grown up it seemed silly to keep things from his childhood. He decided, yes, it was time to pack them all up and take them to Charlie's Choice. Someone will want them. But first he'd have to dust them all. He fetched a duster from the airing cupboard and sat down to clean them, one by one, trying to keep himself occupied until it was time to go to work.

His mind kept drifting to thoughts of Joan. Had she really gone away? He looked down and saw he was holding the egg-cup from Whitby. That was a long way away from here, right up in the North of England. He could imagine Joan having a holiday in Whitby, or somewhere like that, but she would have let them know if she was going away and she hadn't told anyone, that was what was bothering him. He suddenly decided he wouldn't give away his collection yet. The gap on the shelf was too big, too empty. What could he put there instead of them? He carefully replaced the egg-cup from Whitby back on the shelf and put the rest of them all back in order of how long ago he'd bought them. One for each year going back over fifteen years. He stood back to admire them and felt that everything was in its place again.

Except for Joan. She wasn't in her place. She was still missing, or had been last night. He knew he couldn't leave it at that. He decided he should go to work and maybe she'd be there. That was what he was hoping anyway. He made his way to the bathroom to shower again and prepare himself for the day ahead.

Chapter Eighteen

Catherine

She walked into the empty shop, locking the door behind her. She loved this place first thing in the morning - the calm peacefulness that was there every day before anyone else came in. It was tidy last evening when she'd gone home and it was just as she'd left it. She smiled to herself and went into the back room to take her coat off and put the kettle on. Soon Kevin would be in, then Joan. Remembering that Joan seemed to be missing, she frowned, hoping perhaps she would be back today. Kevin was right, it wasn't like her to let you down and although they could probably manage without her, Catherine wasn't looking forward to hearing Kevin fretting away about her all day again. She would have to give him something practical to do to keep him focussed on his work. A tapping on the back door brought her back to the present. It was Kevin.

'What are you doing, coming round the back way?' She was surprised that Kevin would change his routine. He always came to the front door, the most direct route from the bus stop.

'I was checking to see if there were any clues.'

'Clues? What do you mean?'

'For Joan. I need to find out why she's disappeared.'

Catherine tutted. 'You don't know that she has disappeared. She'll most probably be in shortly, so you can stop worrying.'

'I went to her house, Catherine, and she wasn't there. Her cat was there and two young men who didn't look like they belonged there. It was horrible and Gem came back with me so she can tell you I'm not imagining things.'

'Slow down, Kevin. You went there yesterday? And went back again with Gem? What were you thinking?'

'I was worried about Joan so I took her address and went and looked for myself. I tell you, Catherine, there is something very wrong about this.' He paused. 'I know I shouldn't have taken the envelope but I had to find out what had happened to her.'

'Yes, you were wrong to take that envelope and you were wrong to go to her house without asking me first. She may not have wanted people to go knocking on her door.' Catherine sighed.

'Well, I'm sorry, but I had to do something and now I have been there I'm even more sure that something bad is going on. You should have seen how her cat was with me - like he was trying to tell me something. It was very strange.'

'You've got a vivid imagination, Kevin.'

'We'll see.' He took his coat off and hung it in the cupboard, next to the one which he said was Joan's. 'There's no point in talking to you about it. You just won't believe me.'

'Well never mind all that now, we've got lots to do here this morning. You'd better start with this lot.' Catherine lifted one of the black bags from the pile in the corner and tipped it onto the table. 'It looks like there's some nice things in here.' She began sifting through the clothes. 'I'll leave you to it.'

Walking back through to the front of the shop and unlocking the door, Catherine turned the closed sign around. She looked at the clock - already twenty to ten and Joan wasn't in. It's not like her to be late, but I'm not going to get caught up in Kevin's fantasies. She'll be in soon, I'm sure. She looked down the street but there was no sign of Joan so she shrugged her shoulders and went to the counter, turned on the till, then remembered she'd not made the coffee - the first thing she always did before opening up.

'Can you make the coffee, please,' she called out to Kevin. 'I'm sorry, I forgot, what with all the fuss about Joan.'

'Of course, white, two sugars for you, isn't it?'

Ten minutes later he brought the coffee through and placed the cup on the counter. 'She's still not in, is she?' he said.

Catherine bristled. 'No. I can see that. Yes, she's late.'

'Not late - missing.' Kevin mumbled.

'Well I don't see that we can do anything about it. If Joan doesn't want to come to work here then it's her choice. She's not here under any contract of employment, we don't pay her, after all, so if she choses to go away for a few days then it's up to her.'

'But she wouldn't do that without letting us know. And she's not done it before. Gone away I mean.'

'Nevertheless, it's not any of our business.'

Chapter Nineteen

Billy

I knew she still liked me. You can tell, can't you? Even when you're stoned most of the time like I've been over the past couple of months. I was really chuffed when Gem phoned me and even though she pretended she wasn't interested in seeing me again, she still turned up, didn't she?

I'm glad we've got the chance to get back to how we were. Well, not how we were at the end, of course, that was effin' shit. But it wasn't my fault - she shouldn't have pushed me to the limit. OK, maybe it was my fault. I suppose I can blame it on the drugs but that would be just another cop-out. Now I've got another chance I'll make sure I don't screw it up this time. Because, well, I bleedin' well love her I suppose. She makes me feel safe. At least, she used to. I can't remember when it all started going tits-up.

I'm determined not to let it go wrong again though. As I walked away from The Railway pub I made up my mind I was going to sort things out. But how do I do that? It's all a soddin' mess now. It's about my Aunty Joan, see. She was good enough to let me stay, but, as I said before, there was no way she was going to let Dan stay. She didn't even like him coming round and although she'd make him a cup of tea, she always gave him the crappy old mug I'm sure she got from that charity shop she works in. And then she would scrub it clean as soon as he'd finished with it, like he was some sort of scab or something. I tried to talk her round but she'd just give me one of her looks, turn her mouth down and sniff. 'You choose your own friends, Billy. But don't expect me to like them.'

Sometimes I'd let him in after she'd gone out but always tried to get rid of him before she got home. A couple of times I let him in through my window at night - only if he had nowhere else to doss down. Well, he is my mate and he'd do the same for me.

Me and Aunty had a bit of a row when she found out I'd sneaked him in one night. There was a tussle and she fell over. It was an accident. I only gave her a bit of a shove but I was desperate.

Dan was threatening me so I had no choice when he said to me that I had to put him up. Trouble is, he had stuff on me - like he knew I'd been in trouble before and would have grassed me up - not to the police. He wouldn't do that, but there are these big shot dealers who were after me for working their patch. They carried bleedin' guns. I would never stoop that low. And anyway, I owed him one from when I was in a really bad place and had got me out of trouble more than once. I don't like thinking about all that. Now I need him even more. He said he'd help me sort it all out. I have to trust him.

And now Gem's back in my life. I think that this could go either way. Gem is the best thing that's happened to me in my skank life. I just want all this to go away and for it to be just me and Gem again, like we were in the beginning. I would stop using drugs for her, I really would.

So, what to do? Try and sort out this mess, tidy up the house a bit and think about getting together with Gem again. She said she would see me just as a friend but I know she wouldn't take much persuading to get back like we were before. I just need to work on her a bit.

I reached the house and her manky cat was waiting on the doorstep - Aunty Joan's cat I mean. I tried to stroke him but he just hissed at me. I made to kick at him but he darted away out of reach. The house was quiet. It's always too quiet since Aunty went. I guessed Dan'd gone out to do a bit of wheeling and dealing as usual. As I made my way to the kitchen I passed the cellar door and I was feeling a bit spooked. I never liked cellars and always had dreams when I was little about things being down there, waiting to jump out on me. I hurried into the kitchen and put the kettle on but I couldn't shake off the cold feeling that came over me.

Chapter Twenty

Gem

Another afternoon in the shop ahead of her. She felt as though her future was looming over her like a black ominous cloud. Looking around her flat, she wondered yet again what she was doing. Not about going to work in the shop, she was quite looking forward to that. No, she was wondering about Billy and seeing him again. She could just about bear to be with him, to keep him at arm's length if she was with him in a public place but she knew she would have to go back to Joan's house with him at some stage if she wanted to find out more about what he had been up to.

'I don't think I can do this,' she said out loud. 'But there's no choice really.' She convinced herself as she brushed her hair that it would have to be alright.

Kevin was already in the shop working in the back room when she arrived. Catherine greeted her as she entered through the front door. It was a busy lunchtime rush which she knew would go on until well past two.

'Hi Catherine. Has it been like this all morning?'

'It was quieter earlier but Joan didn't come in so there's plenty of sorting out to do. Can you take over from Kevin and send him out here. We both need a break.'

Twenty minutes later, Catherine left for her lunch break, leaving Kevin in charge. Luckily it was still too busy in the shop for him to pester Gem. Relieved, she got on with pricing up the stock ready to take onto the shop floor, knowing that it was only a short reprieve. She wondered what she could say to Kevin when he asked her about Joan's disappearance again.

It wasn't long before Catherine was back and Kevin was sent on his break. At last they were alone in the back room. Gem braced herself.

'Gem, I've not been able to stop thinking about Joan being missing. I've spoken to Catherine about it and she says

I should leave it as it's not my business but I can't just leave it. I'm sure there's something wrong and I think you agree with me, don't you?'

Gem shook out a shirt that she was holding. 'Why do you say that?'

'It was the way you said I had to leave it, after we'd been to her house yesterday. I wondered if you knew something you were keeping from me. About the man who answered the door when I knocked perhaps.'

'No! Why would you think that?' Gem snapped. 'What do you think about this shirt? Do you think it's any good?'

'Don't change the subject. This is important Gem.'

'I don't know what you mean. Why would I be keeping anything from you?'

'It's just a feeling I have. I'm right, aren't I? Is he someone you've met before?'

'No, of course not. I'd have said at the time if I thought I knew him. Anyway, I didn't see who answered the door. I wasn't there with you then, was I?'

'I know. But you looked through the window at the back and something frightened you. You didn't want to be recognised, did you?'

'I didn't want to be seen! If we'd been caught creeping around the back of the house, peering through the windows, we'd have been in big trouble. Trespassing for one thing, Peeping Toms for another. And they might have thought we were checking out the place to break-in later. No, Kevin, I don't know any more than you about what's going on in Joan's house. I just didn't want you to get into trouble, poking about there. Those men might be dangerous. I know what people like that can be like, that's all.'

'Then why were you so sure that we shouldn't go to the police?'

'Because - well because I've only ever had bad experiences with the police in the past.'

'What do you mean? The police are there to help us, aren't they?'

'Of course.' She paused. 'Look, I'll tell you the truth. I haven't always been on the straight and narrow. There was a time when I did some things I'm not proud of. I was caught and arrested. I've been to court and now I'm on a Probation Order. I can't afford to be found messing about in any way.'

'Oh, I thought there was something about you, something you were hiding.' Kevin thought for a moment. 'But you've changed now. You're paying back by working here, aren't you? I still don't see why you can't let the police help us though.'

'I just can't face being around the police, OK? It's too much. And I thought if I made some enquiries through my old friends I could sort this out without the police having to be involved. Joan wouldn't want all that fuss, would she? Suppose one of those two are her grandson or something and she is just away on a holiday, she would hate the police to be called, wouldn't she?'

'I suppose you're right. It's just I can't stop thinking about her and wondering. I've been worrying all night about it.'

'Well, I'm sorry about that and I will ask around today, after I've finished my shift here. I know some people I can get in touch with who'll be happy to help me.'

'I don't know. I still think we should do something more. It might be dangerous.' Kevin looked pained.

'Just trust me, Kevin. Give me another couple of days before you do anything more about it. It'll be alright. I promise.'

'Two more days?'

'Yes, just two more days.' Gem looked over his shoulder at the clock on the wall. 'You'd better go on your break, Kevin. You won't have time to get to the park to eat your lunch if you don't go now.'

She watched as Kevin collected his sandwich from the fridge, then went back through the shop and out of the front door. She made a decision. She'd phone Billy after work and arrange to see him that evening. She was determined to get to the bottom of this little mystery even if to do so she had to go back to a world that she'd hoped she'd left behind.

Chapter Twenty One

Kevin

Kevin sat in the park, eating his sandwich and thinking.

Just two more days. That was what Gem said. Trust me. He wasn't sure whether he could trust her though. What if she was one of the gang - in on it all. It seemed odd to him that all this had happened after Gem started working in the shop. Before she came along everything had been just right. Everything in its place and everyone turning up for their shifts on the right days at the right times. Then she'd come along and Joan had disappeared. It was definitely something to think about.

But what could he do about it? Well, he could go to the police, or go back to the house to investigate further. But he was a bit scared to do that. He didn't want to get caught out and end up in a bigger mess. Those men were definitely unwelcoming. And as for going to the police, well, he was a bit like Gem in that he was uncomfortable around the police. His mother had always said they were there to help us but he remembered the time when he had been trying to see that old lady across the road and she had got a bit confused and shouted out for help. He had only been trying to help her but she thought he was after her handbag and her shopping. Alright, so he had taken hold of her bags but it was only so she could get across the road easier. And the police officer who had heard her shouting had come along and taken him quite unnecessarily brutally by the arm and dragged him away from her. It had taken him quite a long time to explain that he was only doing the lady a good turn.

Ever since then, he'd tried to stay away from police officers and anyone else in uniform. You never know who they are, do you?

So, back to the problem in hand. What to do about Joan Clarke being missing? Gem could be right about the young man being her relative. It would be very embarrassing if she had genuinely just gone away to stay with a friend or a relative for a few days and had left her house to be looked after by that young man. Although he didn't look very nice. But then, you never know about people and their relatives. They may not look nice but they could still be a loving grandson or nephew. Or even a not-so-loving grandson or nephew but if you got involved sometimes they might not like it. His mother had told him that once. Oh, dear. He was truly worried about all of this but just didn't know what to do for the best.

Kevin looked at his sandwich. I think I'm off my food, he thought. I just can't stomach eating when I don't know what's happened to Joan.

He wrapped the sandwich up in its greaseproof paper and put it back into the carrier bag. Then he stood up and walked smartly out of the park, making his way to Station Road before he could even think again about what he was doing. A few minutes later he arrived at Joan's house. He glanced at the windows - the curtains were still closed and it was well past two o'clock in the afternoon. Kevin still had a bad feeling about this. He walked to the end of the road and back, looking again at the house as he passed. I'm going to go in, he said to himself. As soon as he had made the decision and had placed his hand on the gate, the front room curtains twitched apart and a man's face peered out at him. Kevin lost his nerve, turned away and walked swiftly back down the road towards the town centre. He was almost running by the time he reached the shop door.

Catherine was behind the counter. She glanced at the clock as he entered. 'Sorry I'm late,' he gasped as he ran through to the back room.

Gem looked up from her work as he entered. 'Are you OK? You look like you've been running.'

'I'm alright,' he panted. 'I just lost track of time, that's all.'

'Did you enjoy your sandwich?'

'No. I didn't eat it.' He screwed up the bag and dropped it into the rubbish bin. 'I've gone off tuna.'

'Are you sure you're alright? Has something happened to upset you?' She looked at him pointedly.

'I told you. I'm alright.' The last thing he wanted Gem to know was that he'd been snooping about again at Joan's house. She would only be cross with him and he didn't like it when people were cross with him. Still, he couldn't help feeling he should have handled himself in a better way. That he should have gone up to the front door and insisted he get into the house so he could find out what was really going on in there. As the afternoon wore on, Kevin became more and more convinced that he should go back to investigate again sometime soon. He decided he would do as Gem had suggested and wait a couple of more days, but then, if Joan hadn't come back, he would make plans to get into the house come what may. He just needed to get through the next two days, that was all.

Chapter Twenty Two

Gem
She finished work and made her way home, still arguing with herself about whether to see Billy or not. She knew she should stay away from him for her own sake but had to find out what was going on. Kevin had come back from his break in a right state and she was convinced that it was to do with Joan and Billy and all that. She knew what she had to do, as much as she hated the thought of it, so as soon as she got home she phoned Billy before she could change her mind and arranged to meet him at seven in the pub.

The Railway was a different pub in the evenings. Busy, noisy, with loud music and people shouting to be heard above the din. She spotted Billy as soon as she entered the room - standing by the bar, watching her make her way through the crowd towards him. He was smiling at her and yes, against all her better judgement, Gem felt something as she smiled back. Soon they were sitting together at one of few small tables that were unoccupied. It seemed safe to Gem, being in such a crowded place with people jostling all around them. She relaxed.

Billy raised his glass to her. 'Here's to us, - getting back together, I hope.'

Gem looked at him. 'Let's not get too ahead of ourselves. I said I only wanted to be friends, nothing more. It's just a drink.'

'OK. Here's to "just a drink" then.' He grinned as he clinked his glass against hers.

Gem smiled back and sipped her drink. 'Yeah, whatever.' She sat for a moment then continued. 'Just one thing - friends or not friends, I haven't got any room in my flat for you. My life's on track again now and I don't need any complications. Whatever happens, wherever this goes, you're not moving in with me again. I value my space too much to share it again. There's no way...'

'Don't worry,' he bristled. 'I don't need to stay at yours, or anyone else's place. I've got my own place now.'

'Really? Where's that then?' Gem looked surprised. 'I thought you were staying at your aunty's place.'

Billy looked uncomfortable. 'I was, I am. But she's not there at the moment and she said I can stay as long as I like. She won't be back for ages so it's like my own soddin' place. I've got free run of it.'

'Where's she gone then? Your aunty, I mean.'

'To stay with a friend on the Isle of Wight.'

'Really? She's gone to the Isle of Wight and left you on your own in her place?' Gem stared hard at him. 'So, how long's she gone for then?'

'I don't know, a few weeks,' Billy bristled. ' Why are you being like this? Don't you believe me?'

'I don't know. It seems a bit far fetched to me - that your aunty would let you live in her house when she's not there. I know what you're like. Does she?'

'Well, she is my bloody auntie so I should think she does know me. Why are you making such an issue about this? I would have thought you'd be glad that I'm settled in my own place.'

'But it's not your own place though, is it?'

'Oh, for fuck's sake! What's the matter with you? Why are you so hung up on whether it's my own place or not? It never bothered you before what I was doing or where, come to that.' He took another swig of his beer and wiped his mouth with his hand. They sat, looking at each other, the silence drawing out between them.

Finally, Billy broke the tension. He grinned at her. 'Look, Gem, let's start again. I don't want to fall out with you before we've even got going. I'm staying at my aunty's house, she's gone away for a long visit and asked me to look after the place for her, to feed her cat, cut the grass and that. She just wanted someone to be there so the house wasn't empty, that's all. There's no big deal.'

Gem looked at him. 'OK. You don't have to get upset about it all. I believe you. Where is this place anyway?'

'Just round the corner, in Station Road.'

'Not far, then.' Gem wondered whether he would invite her back to the house.

'No. Come on then, Gem, tell me what you've been up to. Been out much?'

'Not really.' He obviously seemed uncomfortable talking about his aunty's place so Gem decided to let it go for the moment. 'I've been doing some charity work. After we split up I started on a programme - I'm on Methadone now, a reducing script, and I have to work in a charity shop as part of my probation deal. I've been doing a few days a week in that shop in the precinct, Charlie's Choice.'

'Charlie's Choice! What's Charlie's Choice supposed to mean?'

'It's to raise money for helping teenagers stay away from drugs - legal highs mainly. Some kid called Charlie died after taking something - her first time apparantly. I sort out all the stuff that people donate, price it up and put it out in the shop. It's dead boring actually, but it keeps me busy and off the streets.' She laughed, then went on. 'A bit ironical, isn't it? Me working for nothing in a shop after being done for shoplifting.'

'It must be effin' boring. That's the trouble with going into treatment - you end up having to do things like that, just to keep people off your backs. I suppose it's better than prison though.' He thought for a moment. 'I think my aunty was working for a charity shop in the precinct. She talked about it sometimes. Kept going on about the people she worked with.'

'You talk about her as though she's dead.' She looked straight at him and noticed that his face was quite red. He looked away.

'No, not dead, but she has gone - to the Isle of Wight, I mean.'

Gem was sure that he was lying. She knew that flustered tone in his voice, that shifty look about him. She watched as he drank his beer, his eyes meeting hers over the rim of the glass. She shook her head slowly as she looked back at him. He looked away and took a deep breath before looking back.

'Billy...' she began, then stopped, waiting for him to speak.

'What?' He put down the glass. 'Why are you looking at me like that? You don't believe me.'

'Why are you saying that?' Gem asked. 'I only wondered why you were talking about your aunty as though she wasn't around any more, that's all. Of course, if she's only on the Isle of Wight, she could come back at any time, couldn't she? It's only just across the Solent. Maybe you could go over and visit her. We could go together, have a great day out. What part of the island is she staying? I like Sandown but it's right across the other side. Still, you can get the train across, or the buses are really good, aren't they?' She stopped, realising she was gabbling.

Billy was staring at her. At last he spoke. 'There's no way I'm going to the soddin' Isle of Wight,' he said. 'Let's talk about something else.'

'OK. What about you, then. I've told you what I've been doing,' Gem took a sip of her drink. 'What have you been up to lately? Got a job yet?'

'There's nothing out there, is there?' he said. 'I've been trying to find work. I go to the job centre and look in the papers but there's nothing. It's just a fuckin' waste of time.'

'Still doing smack, then?'

'Only now and again. It's under control.'

'How do you get the money together for that?'

'I sell a bit. Only to people who ask for it. It's not every day.'

'So, nothing's changed with you then?' Gem knew that would be the answer, but still, she felt disappointed.

'It's easy for you to say that. You've got it bloody easy, always have.'

'I don't know how you can sit there and say that. I actually think you believe it, too, don't you.' She looked at him, a feeling of disgust rising. 'It's never been easy, Billy. I just work hard at getting it right, that's all. You could do the same if you wanted to. If you really wanted to.'

He looked back at her. 'I could if you were here to help me.'

Gem was thinking to herself - I've been here before with him and it didn't work then. In fact it nearly destroyed me, dragged me down. I should leave now before I get sucked into something I won't be able to get out of. Then she remembered why she was there. Poor old Joan, his Aunty Joan. God knows what's happened to her, she thought. I would bet a hell of a lot that she's not having a nice time away on the Isle of Wight. This was what was in the forefront of her mind as she sat there opposite Billy whilst he waited for her to smile back and say she would be there for him.

'What do you want from me?' she asked.

'Can't we just start again? I'd get myself clean and we could have a good life together.'

Gem took a deep breath. 'OK. We'll make another go of it. If you really mean it, about getting clean, I mean.'

'I promise.' His face lit up.

'But I don't want you coming to my flat until you can prove you mean what you say. You'll have to go to the clinic and get on the treatment programme. I'm not having any drugs near my place, or near me. It's just too much. And no violence either. The first time you raise a hand to me I'm off. Do you understand?'

'Of course. I never wanted to hurt you before, you know.'

'It's easy to say that now.'

'I mean it. That was the last thing I wanted to happen.' He reached out to hold her hand. 'I'd do anything to take it back, what I did then. It won't happen again, I mean it.'

'OK. I'll take your word for it.' Gem wanted to move the conversation away from the troubled past. 'You going to take me round to your place, then? Or is it full of drugs and your druggy friends?'

'No. Why do you think that?'

'Because I know you. Shall we go round there then? I'd like to see where you're living. I bet it's a nice house isn't it? If your Aunty Joan lives there. Is it all flowery wallpaper and crocheted covers on the cushions?'

He laughed. 'It's a bit like that I guess. And she's got an old cat I have to feed.'

'Come on then, let's go round now. I can't wait.' Gem drained her glass and stood up.

'Wait up,' Billy remained seated. 'There's just one thing first. My mate Dan's staying with me at the moment so we won't have the place to ourselves.'

'Dan? No druggie friends, you said.' She shook her head. 'You're not still hanging out with him, are you? He's the last person you need to have around you.'

'He's my effin' mate. He put me up when I had nowhere else to go. What was I supposed to do?'

'What happened to his place, then?'

'He fell out with his landlord and I said he could come and stay for a bit.'

'But he's bad news. He'd beat you up as soon as look at you.' Gem knew Dan had been staying with Billy but she still felt she had to say her piece and pretend she didn't know. 'I don't know whether I want to come back with you if he's there. Maybe we should leave it.'

'No. It'll be alright. I'll tell him to stay out of the way if you don't want to see him.'

'I don't know.'

'Come on, Gem. You said you were curious about the place. It'll be like old times, you and me. I'll tell Dan to go out for a bit and we can have the house to ourselves.'

101

'Alright,' Gem said as she made for the door. 'Just keep him out of my way, that's all.'

Chapter Twenty Three

Billy

Things are taking a turn for the better. Gem got in touch with me again and we went for a drink. She was acting a bit weird though, but I put that down to her being off the gear and on Methadone. That drug does wierd things to you, I know from when I was on it myself. It's supposed to be a substitute for Heroin but it's nowhere near as good a feeling. They say it's meant to keep you stable, to stop the craving, and it lasts for 24 hours but it's not true. You still get the shakes and feel sick every night. A dose never lasts the whole time it's supposed to and it makes you feel like fuckin' shit. Then if you can't get to the chemist in time you really suffer. Being on Methadone means you have to go to the clinic and give clean urines so there's no way you can cheat and have a little bit of smack in between. I think that's a bit friggin' unfair personally, as a little bit of smack now and again can't do you any harm, can it?

Anyway, back to Gem and me. We're getting back together. It's going to be great again, I just know it. I bloody love her, always have and this time I'll do my best to make it work. She wasn't very happy when I told her about Dan staying with me though. Still, I can get around that. He'll just have to stay out of the way when she's with me. Luckily for me Dan was out when we got to the house last night. Gem wanted to have a look at where I'm living now. I can understand her not trusting me after what happened before with us but I think I've persuaded her that I can change and I really meant it when I said I'd get off the drugs and go to the clinic. It won't be easy though, I know that.

When we went into the house I showed Gem around the place. It was in a bit of a mess what with Aunty being gone now for a few days and I've never been one to clean up. Gem wanted to go into all the rooms so I took her around the house. Aunty's bedroom was still as she'd left it. Gem looked a bit surprised when she saw the bed was unmade and

Aunty's clothes were draped over the chair looking like they were waiting for her to put them on. I wished I'd tidied up in there but I told Gem that she'd got called away suddenly like.

I made us some coffee and when I went to take them into the front room, Gem was in the hallway by the door to the cellar. She wanted to know what was behind the door but it was locked. I told her that Aunty always kept it locked. I said it was a cupboard and that I didn't know what she kept in there but it must be something she didn't want anyone to get at as she'd taken the key with her when she went away. I couldn't let her go down into the cellar. Cellar's are fuckin' horrible places.

We had a nice time, although it was a bit bloody odd sitting on my aunty's sofa with Gem. I kept thinking about all the times we'd had in the past and couldn't get some things out of my head. Thoughts of Aunty kept popping up too, making me feel a bit sick, to be honest.

Dan came in just after Gem had left which was handy as I didn't want them to meet up yet. I can't really blame her for not wanting him to be around but Dan's a good mate and I need him to help me sort out this bloody mess, don't I? I know it wouldn't have happened if he hadn't been here in the first place, but still, I have to take the soddin' blame for pushing Aunty Joan over and if I hadn't done that she'd still be here, wouldn't she? My head is in a real friggin' mess and only Dan can help me.

When he came in he said he needed money to pay off the scum that were after me. I told him I didn't have any money and he knew I didn't so why was he asking. The only way I could think of was to go out on the rob again and I'd always tried to avoid that since I nearly got caught once in someone's house. It had been that close - I still have nightmares about it. He said I'd find a way - didn't have any choice really. And then he said that he'd got an idea of how to sort out my other little problem, as he called it. But he'd need more money for that too. I didn't want to think about that and said I'd leave it to him. So that was my next fuckin'

105

problem - how to get together some cash. Dan said I should use my brains and look around me and how come I was so bloody thick. I don't think Aunty would like it but I had no choice.

I felt a little better going into Aunty Joan's bedroom this time. After all, I'd already been in there with Gem earlier in the evening. There wouldn't be any ghosts hiding behind the door, would there? I riffled through her dressing table drawers. They were mostly filled with a load of old junk - old ladies' junk, jewelry worth nothing, rubbish mostly, a few old photos in frames which had once been in pride of place on the mantle piece in the front room. At the back of the drawer on the right hand side was a small box. This looked a bit more promising. I pulled out the box and opened it. Inside, coiled up, was a pearl necklace. I carefully took it out and looked at the clasp. It was gold, 22 carat. So this meant that the necklace was probably worth a few quid. That'll do, I thought. I rummaged about a bit more and in the bedside cupboard I found an old watch, and wrapped in tissue paper, a gold brooch, set with what looked like emeralds. So I bundled them all together and took them downstairs where I found a carrier bag. I wrapped the lot up seperately in pieces of kitchen roll and put them into the carrier bag. Soon I was off down towards the town to the old jeweller on the corner of the street. Surely I should get a good price for this little lot.

Chapter Twenty Four

Karen

Lunch at Margaret's. Something she used to look forward to. She thought back to those times when Peter was safely behind prison bars. When although going back to Margaret's house reminded her of Peter, she was able to put thoughts of the bad times out of her head and enjoy watching Margaret play with Lucy. Unfortunately for Karen, Peter was only in prison for a couple of years and once he was released, she'd found it impossible to relax in their old home, just in case he decided to turn up and visit his Mum. Margaret tried to reassure Karen and said he'd promised her he wouldn't do that but Karen couldn't believe it and stopped visiting as often as she used to. It was much easier for her to invite Margaret to her own home. Even these visits became less and less since she'd worked in the Community Drug Team. Life was so busy, with less time for keeping up with visits. She wasn't sure how she felt about going there today. Still, she said she would go and Lucy was looking forward to seeing Margaret after all.

She knocked on Lucy's bedroom door. Ten years old now and quite grown up in many ways. She always insisted on Karen knocking on her door before she entered. Where's my little girl gone? Lucy called her in and she entered the brightly decorated room, photographs of Lucy and her friends plastered to the walls.

'Are you ready to go? We should be leaving in five minutes'. She watched as Lucy pulled her blonde hair into a scrunchy and tightened up the pony tail, finishing it all off with a sparkly hair clip on each side to hold the loose hairs in place. 'You look pretty,' Karen smiled at her daughter, dressed in pink pedal pushers, a purple t-shirt, pink trainers and white ankle socks rolled down to her heels.

Karen smoothed down her own red top, worn over black trousers, a change from her usual jeans. She tutted at the unruliness of her auburn hair which always seemed to stick out at the wrong place these days, picked up her bag and they were off.

Margaret's house was small, one of a row of terraced houses in a street off Forton Road in Gosport. Soon they were standing on the doorstep, ringing the bell. Margaret opened the door, beaming at them.

Lucy leapt into her arms for an enthusiastic cuddle and a 'Granny!' Margaret swept her into the house, kissing her several times before letting her go.

She turned to Karen. 'Come in my dear girl,' she said and reached out to hug Karen too.

Margaret, dressed in a knee length tartan skirt and a blue tee-shirt, always looked comfortable to Karen, her short cropped brown hair now showing flecks of grey, her brown eyes were twinkling. Karen felt that familiar feeling of love, of being welcomed home. After all, this was the first real home Karen had ever had - Margaret was actually her foster mother for a few years before Karen and Peter married. Every time she came here, Karen had so many regrets. Perhaps if she hadn't married him in the first place her relationship with Margaret would never have become so strained. Still, it was pointless thinking like that. She had married Peter, he had tried to kill her, and that was that. She was just grateful she'd got through it in the end and Margaret still seemed to care for her and her beautiful daughter. She thanked God that Peter wasn't Lucy's father although she still felt a little guilty about sleeping with her colleague John whilst she was still married to Peter.

Thinking about all of this brought back to her the day when she'd told Peter she was pregnant and how he'd reacted when he found out it wasn't his child. How could I have been so stupid? And cruel too, although things between us were pretty bad at the time, I should have finished with him first. Then she remembered how controlling he'd been, not letting her out of the house, feeding her sedatives to keep her drowsy. He'd told lies to his Mother and the Doctor and had tried to get her sectioned under the Mental Health Act.   Karen shuddered.

'Are you alright?' Margaret was asking her. 'You look like someone's walked over your grave.'

'I'm fine.' Karen smiled. 'It's so nice to see you. What's new? How's your job at the Co-op? I've been looking forward to seeing you again. It's been a while.'

The next two hours were filled with gossip, laughter, sandwiches and cakes which left Karen feeling over full with food and love. After they'd eaten more than they needed, they went for a walk to the local park and watched as Lucy played on a swing. Karen remembered doing the exact same thing all those years ago when she was recovering from an operation, with Margaret fussing around her. That was the start of my new life. It was from then things started to change for her. She smiled to herself thinking about how far she'd come since that day.

Then it was time to leave. They bundled back into the car after many more hugs and promises to see each other more often in future and soon Karen was driving to the end of the street. She paused as she waited to turn back onto the main road to Fareham and glanced into the rear view mirror, lifting her hand to wave to Margaret. That was when she saw him. Peter, standing behind Margaret, staring down the road after her.

Fear washing over her, she looked at Lucy who was busy gazing out of the side window. Looking back into the rear view mirror again, he was gone. No Peter, no Margaret either. Just a street empty of people. I must have imagined it. He can't have been there - I would have known - Margaret would have said something, surely. Her thoughts tumbled about, convincing herself that she'd been mistaken. She had to get away from there. She checked the traffic, pulled out and drove in a daze back to Wickham and their home, checking in the mirror all the way, wondering if he was following her.

Chapter Twenty Five

Karen

She had been awake all night worrying. Wondering if she'd imagined seeing Peter outside Margaret's house. Back in the early days after the attack, she'd suffered these imaginary things that she called visions. Everywhere she went, she'd seen him, hiding from her, waiting to pounce. But it was all just part of the Post Traumatic Stress Disorder apparently. A new diagnosis for post trauma jitters which included depression and anxiety. She'd got over it some years ago now although she would always be afraid of him, of coming face to face with him. But there's no reason for him to want to see me. Lucy isn't his child so he has no claim on her. And he surely knows he couldn't come back into my life and take control of me like he did before. Standing up to him was what broke the spell in a way, although it had nearly cost her her life.

She got out of bed and made herself a cup of tea, called Lucy to get up for school and started getting ready for work. Think about something else, she told herself.

Soon she was in her car and thinking about work. She had to meet up with Gem later today. Thinking about Gem lifted her mood a little. Karen felt good about how well she seemed to be doing. It was not always easy to get someone as messed up as Gem back on track and her working in the charity shop was a big step towards normalising her life again. Yes, Karen had a good feeling about her.

Parking her car, she walked through the precinct away from the clinic, towards the supermarket to pick up a few things. On the way she passed Charlie's Choice. It was closed, dark and quiet inside. Peering through the window, a light came on in the back room and there was the outline of a man standing in the doorway, looking back at her. Her heart was thudding in her chest, suddenly she was afraid. It took a few seconds to see it wasn't him. It was not Peter. Just a man in a suit. He was shorter than Peter and as he moved into the shop she could see his hair was wrong - the wrong colour and the wrong style. In fact, he looked nothing like Peter. Karen was shaking. She took a step away from the window, looked about, feeling silly, wondering if everyone was looking at her. There were a few people in the precinct, walking this way or that, on their way to their places of work probably. No one was looking at her. She glanced back at the shop window and noticed that the man was watching her from inside. He looked concerned as she turned and walked briskly away. It was only when Karen reached her office that she remembered the groceries.

Karen's appointment with Gem was at 10.30 after a couple of other appointments. It was already after 10.30 and Karen was running late. She came out of her session with the second client, dashed to the reception to apologise but Gem wasn't there yet. It had already been a hell of a morning. Her first client, Andy, had been coming to the clinic now for two years. He was only 19 and started using drugs when he was 12 years old. Drug taking was so ingrained in his behaviour and lifestyle that he couldn't see a way out of it. Stopping drugs would mean him changing his home life, his friends, even moving away from his parents to get away from it all.

Karen felt overwhelmed sometimes with the issues facing her clients. It's all very well, sending people away to rehab, but what do they do afterwards? Some programmes included re-settling people away from their families and friends and those they grew up with. This seemed to work for a lot of users but you had to be so motivated to make decisions like that and a lot of the programmes believed you had to hit "rock bottom" before you were ready to make big life changes. Then there was the "Twelve Steps" programme, where the addicts, as they labelled people with drug problems, had to give themselves over to a "Higher Power" and admit that they were suffering from a disease. Karen personally could see although there were different ways of working for different people she favoured a model where the client was empowered to change. Of course, it was always hard, whichever way you looked at it and trying to keep someone motivated to make good life choices when they were living in a mess was difficult to say the least.

Then there was her second client, Lisa, a young mum, struggling to keep her kids whilst on a Methadone script. She seemed to be doing well, but it was always a battle to help her stay positive about life when she had little money coming in and Social Services were holding regular child protection meetings to monitor any potential abuse or neglect of her children. Karen had been supporting Lisa through this but had to be honest with her - a part of Karen's role was to watch how she interacted with her kids and to write a report for the next meeting which was looming up in a week's time.

Karen started writing her notes on Andy and then the report on Lisa and left them ready to be typed up. She looked at the clock and realised another half an hour had passed. So Gem hasn't turned up, then. Damn! She was doing so well. There must be a good reason. She looked at Gem's notes and dialed the phone number on the front page. It rang several times with no answer. Karen had a bad feeling about this. Don't be ridiculous. She's probably just out shopping, or working in the shop in the precinct. But something was niggling at her, telling her to go and check. She grabbed her bag and got up to leave.

It's only a few minutes walk to Gem's flat and soon she was ringing the bell. She waited only a short while before the door opened.

'Oh, God! I was supposed to come in to see you this morning,' Gem was still in her pyjamas and dressing gown. 'I'm so sorry. Come in.'

Karen followed her up the stairs and into the little sitting room. She glanced around the room. It was neat and tidy, furnished with a sofa and one easy chair. In the corner there was a small table and a couple of dining chairs. A few pictures decorated the walls. Pictures of poppies in fields, three of them, one on each wall. There were no photographs but a small bookcase full of books, mostly paperback novels, she noticed.

'Please, sit down. I'll make some coffee.' Gem moved towards the door into the kitchen.

'Don't worry about the coffee. I was concerned about you. Are things OK?'

'Sorry, I should have let you know I wasn't coming this morning. I had a headache and decided to stay in bed - I've only just got up. I should have phoned you earlier but I fell asleep and the next thing I knew, you were ringing the door-bell.'

Karen smiled. 'It's alright, really. It just wasn't like you not to turn up and I had a bit of time spare so I thought I might as well come round. I did try phoning but there was no answer.'

'Are you sure you don't want a coffee? Or tea? I'm making myself one anyway.' Gem went into the kitchen.

'No thanks, really, I'm OK.' Karen followed her into the small room. Like the sitting room, it was tidy and clean. 'You keep your place nice,' she said.

'Thanks. Yeah, I like to be tidy.' Gem was pottering about getting a cup from the cupboard and spooning some coffee from a jar. She turned to Karen. 'Look, I hope me not turning up this morning won't mess with my Methadone pick up. I won't miss another appointment, it's just I was feeling unwell. It's alright, isn't it?'

'Don't worry, I'll turn a blind eye this time, but you'll have to come in tomorrow and give a urine specimen. Just to make sure your records are straight, not because I don't trust you. You know that, don't you?'

'Yes, OK. I get it. I'll come in tomorrow.' She took her coffee through to the sitting room. 'Come through and sit down for a bit then.'

Karen wondered if there was more going on with Gem and wanted to confront her but there was something holding her back. Maybe the best way forward was to leave it open for Gem to tell her when she was ready. The last thing Karen wanted was to ruin her relationship with Gem. It had taken her weeks to get to the point where she felt Gem trusted her.

'So, things are OK with you, then Gem? Everything alright at the charity shop?'

'Yes, it's all good,' Gem sipped her coffee.

'What about away from your voluntary work? Anything happening in your social life at the moment?'

'No. Nothing at all.'

It was the way she snapped back at Karen that made her wonder whether Gem was actually telling the truth or hiding something. If she was doing something she felt Karen would disapprove of, something like maybe seeing Billy again, or getting into the drug scene, then Karen would be worried. But there was no way she would find out that easily. She sighed and picked up her bag.

'I should be going.'

'That was a quick visit,' Gem looked uncomfortable.

'I know, but I've got other people to see today. I wanted to make sure you were OK, that's all.'

'I am. Just had a headache.' Gem put down her coffee and stood up.

'Well remember, I'm here for you if you need to talk about anything.'

'Yeah. And I'll come in tomorrow to do a pee.'

'Good,' Karen made her way towards the door. She turned. 'Only I won't be able to see you in the morning. You'll have to wait and see the duty worker. I can see you tomorrow afternoon if you want but otherwise it'll have to be the duty worker.'

'I'll be OK with a duty worker, I'm alright.'

'I'll tell her to expect you then. In the morning?'

'I'll be there, don't worry.'

'And I'll see you next week. Same time.'

'Thanks for coming round.'

Karen hurried back to the office, passing Charlie's Choice on the way. She glanced into the shop but it was

116

empty. She shook her head and kept on walking.

Chapter Twenty Six

Gem

She breathed a sigh of relief as soon as the door closed behind Karen. Although feeling bad about not telling her about seeing Billy again, she knew exactly how Karen would have reacted. And she would have been right of course. Billy was bad for her, even though there was still something there between them - that spark she ought to ignore. Gem knew she had to be very careful with how far things would go before she got in too deep.

The truth was she didn't have a headache. The truth was she'd been awake all night again thinking about everything that was going on, about all the things in the past she'd walked away from, mulling over in her head about what to do next. In fact, she'd been worrying about it all weekend, wondering whether she was actually doing the right thing agreeing to get back with Billy at all. After Friday evening, she'd managed to persuade him that she needed a bit of space to think things through. It was all too much for her to take in, her feelings were so confused. She'd finally agreed to see Billy again later today and was hoping she'd find out a bit more then about what was going on with Joan but didn't want to face up to her own emotions yet.

First she needed to go to Charlie's Choice. Catherine had phoned and asked her to do an extra shift as Joan wasn't back and apparantly Julie had let her down again. Gem had hesitated as she wasn't looking forward to working with Kevin again as he would probably be going on and on about Joan and how she'd disappeared. Now that Gem knew for sure Billy was Joan's nephew and now she'd actually been inside the house herself, it was likely that she'd find it difficult to keep anything from Kevin.

Thinking about Kevin made her think about the house. She had a weird feeling about Joan's bedroom. It looked as though the woman had just left in a hurry without packing anything. Even though Gem had never met Joan, from what

Kevin told her, she didn't seem like the kind of person who'd go out leaving yesterday's clothes still draped over a chair. Gem wished she could have another look in that bedroom to see if there were signs of clothes and stuff missing from the wardrobe. She wished she'd taken time to look in the bathroom, to see if Joan's toothbrush or other toiletries were still there. And there was that door in the hall. It certainly looked like it was a door to a cellar. The house was old enough to have a cellar and why would anyone want to lock a cupboard door. More likely to lock the cellar to stop people from going in and falling down the stairs. It would have been good to have a look in there, especially considering how Billy reacted in the way he did - as though he was afraid she'd found him out. She remembered that look from before.

Gem shook her head. I've just got to put it out of my mind for now and get to work. I'll try and find out something more tonight.

Charlie's Choice was quiet that afternoon. Catherine was dusting the shelves of bric-a-brac; Kevin was behind the till. Gem said hello to them both and went into the back room. She was already sorting through some books when Kevin appeared in the doorway. She looked up, dreading what was coming.

'Another two days have passed and still nothing heard from Joan,' he paused to look over his shoulder and waited until Catherine was back behind the counter out of earshot. 'We agreed to wait two days before we called the Police and now the two days are up. I think we should call them today.'

'We can't do that yet. Joan might be back at her house as we speak. We can't contact the Police without being sure she's actually missing.'

'I have tried phoning her again. She's not answering her phone and I'm worried about her cat being left without anyone to feed it.'

'But there's those two young men staying there. We saw them. You saw them. They must be looking after the cat and taking care of the house whilst she's away.'

'I've got a bad feeling about them.'

'What do you mean?' Gem felt sick.

'We don't know who they are, do we? I mean, I can't imagine Joan letting two people like that stay at her house. Not without her telling us. She didn't tell us she was going away, did she?'

'No. But she must have had to get away in a hurry and not had time to let you know.'

'She would have let us know. I know she would. Even if she'd telephoned from wherever she's supposed to have gone to.'

'Maybe she just forgot. Maybe she got caught up with whatever it is she's gone away for. We're not the most important thing in everyone's lives you know.'

'I am aware of that.' Kevin glared at Gem. 'I just have a bad feeling about this and want to get to the bottom of it. I went past her house again yesterday.'

'When?' Gem wondered if he'd seen her with Billy.

'Don't worry, no one saw me. There didn't seem to be anyone there. I didn't do anything, just walked past the gate and back again.'

'You shouldn't keep going back there, Kevin. You don't know those people...'

'Neither do you, and I was worried about Joan.' He looked at her in surprise. 'Or do you know them? Is that it? You know who they are, don't you? That's why you told me to leave it to you. You didn't want me to find out who they are because you already know. That's what it is, isn't it?'

'You've got a great imagination, Kevin. Of course I don't know them. I'm just concerned about you, that's all. I know what those sort of people can be like.'

'What do you mean, "those sort of people"? How do you know what sort of people they are? If you think one of

121

them is related to Joan why would they do any harm to me?'
He paused. 'I think you know more than you're letting on.'

'Well, I don't. Let's just leave it. I said we should go
to the Police in a couple of days if she doesn't turn up and I
still stand by that. It's only just two days now and if she's not
back by tomorrow, we'll do something. She'll probably be on
her way back today. We can't waste Police time. We just
need to be sure she isn't back home first.'

'Shall we go round to her house this evening, then?'

'You don't need to go,' Karen said hastily. 'I'm
walking past her house this evening to meet my friend so I can
pop in on the way.'

'Are you sure you don't want me to come too?'

'No. Don't worry. I'll let you know how I get on.'

Kevin didn't look convinced but the shop door opened
and two customers came in. He hurried out of the back room
and went to his post behind the counter. 'Good afternoon,
ladies,' he said. 'Can I interest you in our raffle?'

Gem cringed. Then, feeling relieved she was let off
the hook, she turned back to sorting out the books. Her mind
was full of thoughts about what to do next. She'd have to get
a look at Joan's bedroom as soon as possible. And then there
was the cellar.

Chapter Twenty Seven

Catherine
Well, that was certainly a strange shift. She was sure there was something going on between Kevin and Gem. All that whispering in the back room. It wasn't like Kevin to chat when there were things to be done in the shop. In fact, it wasn't like Kevin to chat at anytime, unless it was to tell you how to do things properly or when he was doing his thing with the customers, saying "good morning" and "would you like a raffle ticket". Kevin and Gem seemed a very unlikely pair to be friends although she had seen some strange things in her time. It was surprising what working closely with someone could bring out in a person.

Then there was Joan. She still hadn't been in contact and Catherine had to admit she was getting a bit worried. She was sure she heard Kevin mentioning Joan's name and he'd sounded quite agitated at the time although when she'd asked him if anything was wrong he'd denied it. It was simply the way that he'd hesitated and looked towards the back room where Gem was working that made Catherine wonder. She'd tried Joan's number again but there was no reply. It was definitely a bit worrying but the nature of working in charity shops was that people dropped in and out, sometimes without letting you know they were leaving.

Catherine sighed, wondering how much longer she'd have to work in the shop before a decent job came up. She knew one thing, she wouldn't hang around for any longer than she needed. She wanted to work in a proper business where the staff were committed to making the place successful, not somewhere where you had a load of volunteers who were either well-meaning do-gooders, or people who were struggling to get into the real world of working. 'Like me,' she said to herself.

At one point in the afternoon Gem had come into the shop with some books to put on the shelves. Kevin was making the tea. Catherine decided to tackle Gem whilst she was on her own with her.

'How are things between you and Kevin?' she asked. 'You seem to be working well together.'

'Fine. He's alright, I guess. We get on alright.'

'Is there anything I need to know?' Catherine felt a bit awkward but ploughed on. 'Things seemed to be getting a bit intense in the back room earlier. I could hear you whispering and it sounded to be a bit heated. Is everything really alright?'

Gem blushed. 'Of course. We were just arguing about these books. Kevin said they should be priced at £2.00 and I thought they should be less, that's all.'

'Are you sure?' Catherine continued. 'Only Kevin's quite upset about Joan not coming in and I thought I heard him mention her name.'

'Well, he did mention her to me but I said she was probably just away on holiday so he shouldn't worry. I don't know why he gets so involved in every little thing that happens. It's stupid letting things upset you.'

'I know,' Catherine smiled. 'But that's part of the way he is I suppose. We have to be patient with him.'

'I do try to.'

'Anyway, I've decided I'm going to drop in at Joan's later today to see if I can find out what's happened to her so Kevin can relax again once we find out.'

'No. No, I don't think you should do that,' Gem said urgently.

Catherine stared at her in surprise. 'Why ever not? It can't do any harm. Whatever's the matter with you?'

'Nothing, nothing. I'm sorry, I'm a bit jumpy today. I didn't mean anything. It just seems a bit hasty. I wouldn't like my employer coming round my house if I was taking a few days off. Joan might not want to see anyone from here. She obviously doesn't want to speak to you if she's not picked up the phone. She probably just wants some space.'

Catherine was a bit taken aback at the way Gem blurted out her opinion but it did make her begin to doubt going round to Joan's would be the right thing to do. Maybe she should wait a few more days. After all, I wouldn't want any of this lot knocking on my door if I was feeling the need to be alone for a bit. Catherine knew what that felt like.

'Maybe you're right,' she said eventually. 'I guess we should let things be for a while. But if I haven't heard from her by the end of this week, we're going to have to get someone else to take on her shifts on a more permanent basis. We can't go on like this indefinitely.'

Gem looked relieved although Catherine couldn't work out why. The younger woman went back to putting the books on the shelf and Catherine went into the back room to see how Kevin was getting on with the tea.

Chapter Twenty Eight

Billy

So I went into town on Monday and got a bit of cash from the bits and pieces I found in Aunty's bedroom and the next thing was to sort out a time to get the job done. Dan said that it would take a few days to set up. He knew some people who would do it without asking any questions. They couldn't just drop everything and do a job like that without working out a bit of a plan, he said. I didn't really want to know the details - just wanted the effing job done so that I could get on with my life. After all, things were starting to look up for me, with Gem coming back to me. It was finally agreed that they would come just after midnight on Wednesday, that was just in two days time. The sooner it was all over, the better, to be honest.

Gem was coming round later so I tidied up a bit, put clean sheets on my bed - well you never know, do you - and did the washing up which, to tell the truth, had got to the stage where there weren't any clean cups left to drink out of. I felt a bit better when it was all done and sat down to wait for Gem.

She was late. I was expecting her at seven and I sat there looking at the clock, wondering what was going on, thinking that she'd stood me up. She'd been a bit weird on Friday, after all, and I thought she'd cooled off when she said she didn't want to see me over the weekend. Then at a quarter to eight she finally arrived, standing on the doorstep looking sheepish. I thought to myself, there's something going on with her, but when I asked her she denied it and just said she'd fallen asleep after work and woke up late. I'm not sure I believed her but she just gave me that smile that always melts me so I started to think it was alright after all.

When she was here on Friday I thought she'd suspected something. It was the way she looked when I found her standing by the door to the cellar. I watched her as we passed the door this time and noticed that she didn't even look at it, or pause when we passed it. We went straight through into the kitchen and she sat down at the table so I felt I'd got away with that.

I made some coffee and we went into the sitting room. I was glad I'd made an effort to tidy up. The place did look a bit more homely. We were sitting there with me wondering what to talk about when Aunty's cat came in, making a load of fuss, yowling at her like he was trying to tell her something. I was about to say something like, bloody cat, and shoo it away out of the room, when Gem started fussing over it, cooing and stroking the skanky thing. She was asking it if it was hungry and I told her I'd just fed it but the cat kept going backwards and forwards to the door and meowing at Gem. I felt like giving it a good kicking but didn't think that would go down very well with Gem. Then Gem got up and followed the cat out of the room. It seemed like it was going straight into the kitchen where its dishes were but it stopped right outside the bloody cellar door and sat down like it wasn't going to go anywhere soon. It just looked up at Gem and yowled at her.

'What's the matter with you,' she said. 'What are you trying to say?' She started to stroke the cat then looked at me. 'He's trying to talk to me. Is he usually like this?'

I told her the cat was just fuckin' greedy, always wanting more food. To show her I was telling the truth I went into the kitchen and started opening a tin of cat food. Of course, the cat, who does love his food more than effing anything, dashed into the kitchen and was dancing about in front of me. I filled his dish up again and put it down on the floor. The cat starting gobbling up the stuff straight away. I thought to myself it was another close shave but when I looked up Gem was standing in the hall staring at that damned sodding door again. She looked at me in an accusing way and asked me what was going on. That pissed me off. It seemed like she was never going to take my word or trust me so I just told her nothing was going on and if she didn't trust me she should effin' well go. She soon changed her tune then and was all sweetness again.

'Don't be like that,' she'd said. 'It just seemed a wierd way for that cat to behave, but it seems to be happy now.' She'd looked down at the little bastard who was still eating as though it was his last meal.

'Like I said, he's just greedy,' I said.

So we went back to the sitting room and I put the tv on.

Chapter Twenty Nine

Gem

She had been feeling jittery after Catherine said she'd drop in at Joan's house and Gem spent a lot of time at her flat afterwards, wondering whether to forget about going to see Billy at all. Finally, she got herself together and made her way there but she was quite a bit late. Knowing he'd probably be pissed off with her, the bad feeling about it still hung over her as she walked to Station Road.

When she arrived at Billy's - or rather at his Aunty Joan's house, things seemed to be alright. The place was cleaner, like he'd made a bit of an effort and there was no sign of Dan. The kitchen was tidy and neat now, and they went into the sitting room with their coffees. It was when the cat came in and started on at her that she began to feel uncomfortable again. It was as though the cat was trying to tell her something and when she followed him into the hall, he was sitting outside that locked door, looking at her and making a lot of noise, meowing. Billy made out the cat was hungry and even gave it some food just to make a point but she wasn't convinced.

They went back into the sitting room and she tried to relax into being with Billy again. It wasn't easy as she had all these bad memories but he'd always been a smooth talker and knew how to make her feel good. When he leant in to kiss her she didn't even have to pretend. It was what she wanted deep down. It's only a kiss. It can't do any harm, she thought. Before long he was leading her up the stairs to the bedroom. He had the room at the back of the house and she noticed that he'd tidied up in there too. And there were clean sheets on the bed.

Being in bed with Billy felt good. She was surprised at how much she'd missed him, the feel of his warm body against hers. He could be so gentle and she relaxed as he stroked her hair and held her close. He kissed her again, softly on her lips and she felt herself longing for him. Not wanting to think about what she was getting into, she floated along with the moment, drifting as if in a dream, enjoying the intimacy of their love-making. Afterwards, lying in the warmth of his arms, she had no regrets.

Gem woke up in the dark. Confused, it took her a moment to remember where she was. She could feel Billy lying next to her, his body still comfortable against her skin. Wondering what the time was, she thought it must be early as the windows were still pitch black - no dawn light showing through the curtains yet. She groped for her clothes, and slipping out of bed, dressed herself and crept quietly to the door. Pausing to make sure Billy hadn't stirred, she opened the door as slowly as she could, hoping it wouldn't creak.

She paused outside Aunty Joan's room and decided to have a look inside before she tried the cellar. The room looked different. There were no clothes on the chair now and some of the drawers were open. She wondered to herself whether Billy had been in here tidying up, hiding the evidence, maybe. Then she told herself not to be so dramatic. She was obviously imagining things. How could that same man who was so tender towards her last night do anything to an old lady? Still, it did feel a bit odd.

Touching the wardrobe door, it swung open revealing a neat row of clothes. It didn't look as though anything had been taken but Gem couldn't tell for sure. Joan may have taken a couple of things with her. You wouldn't be able to tell from looking in a wardrobe full of clothes. She pulled open drawers which were stuffed full of clothes, underwear, woollen jumpers, t-shirts, socks and tights. It was impossible to know whether Joan had taken anything or not. Gem wondered how one old woman could have so many clothes.

She was sitting on the bed, just about to look into the bedside table drawer which was slightly open, when she realised she was being watched. Billy was at the door, looking furious.

'What the hell do you think you're doing?' he seethed as he moved towards her.

'I couldn't sleep,' she stammered. 'I went down for a drink of water and I got lost coming back to bed.'

She could tell he didn't really believe her but his glare slowly turned to a smile as he moved closer, taking her hand.

'Well, let me take you back to bed, then. We've got unfinished business there.'

She let him lead her back into his room and they sat on the bed. He kissed her tenderly but she moved away from him.

'I'm sorry, Billy,' she said. 'I'll have to get going. I've got to go to the clinic this morning. I can't miss it today or I'll lose my Methadone script. And then I have to get to the shop.'

'Just stay for a bit. There's plenty of time. It's still dark outside.' His persuasive voice and his gentle way made her pause. She decided to go along with it, at least until she could find out what had happened to Joan. Before long, they were making love again. Gem felt herself slipping into a place she thought she'd never go to again. As soon as it was over though, the same uneasiness grew within her. She lay there waiting, still unsure that she ought to be getting in so deep with Billy.

Soon he was fast asleep again, snoring gently beside her as she slid out of the bed, gathered up her clothes and this time she crept down the stairs. Once in the kitchen she quickly got dressed. That was when she noticed the key beside the clock on the shelf. She took it up and held it in her hand, turning it over and thinking. Hesitating, and frightened at what she might find, she decided she had to do it as she made her way into the hall. The key fit and turned easily. The door was unlocked! But before she could open it Billy was behind her again, clattering down the stairs.

'What are you doing now?' He rushed towards her and grabbed her arm. With his free hand he smacked her hard against her cheek. If he hadn't been holding her she would have hit the wall. Pulling her towards him he shouted in her face. 'You bitch! What's going on with you? Can't you just keep your fuckin' nose out?'

He dragged her down the hall and threw her into the front garden. Her bag came flying out after her. He stood over her as she struggled to her feet. She turned to him, her face red with tears and stinging from his slap.

'I'm sorry,' she stammered. 'I was just curious, that's all. I didn't think it was a bit deal.'

'Well, it's not but it's none of your business. Why can't you be happy with me without having to know every bleedin' thing?'

'Please, I'm sorry,' Gem moved towards him. 'Let's try again, please. It was so good last night, and this morning.'

Billy just stood there and looked at her. 'I need some time to sort out my head. I'll give you a ring.'

And he went into the house, slamming the door behind him.

Chapter Thirty

Karen

Only Tuesday morning and Karen was already looking forward to the weekend. She planned to take Lucy shopping and then see a film. They were sitting at the table in the kitchen, having a quick breakfast before her daughter went off on the school bus. Karen watched Lucy as she ate her cereal and marvelled at how much love she felt for this girl and how grateful she was at having such a beautiful daughter. Lucy's blonde hair was caught up in a pony tail and she was dressed in her school uniform.

'Can we go to MacDonalds for a burger on Saturday, Mum?' she asked.

'Of course, we always do, don't we?' Karen laughed. 'But first we need to find you some new trainers and then we need get your summer clothes sorted out. You've grown out of all your nice clothes, even the ones I bought just a couple of months ago.'

'Which shopping centre are we going to? I like the MacDonalds in Fareham best. There's a good play area there.'

'You're getting a bit too big for that play area, though. They might not let you in for much longer.' She smiled at her daughter. Although she was only ten years old, she was tall for her age and seemed to be growing far too fast for Karen's liking. 'Don't pull that face, Lucy. Everyone has to grow up.'

Karen got up and cleared away the dishes. 'Come here and give me a cuddle,' she said. 'You'll always be my little girl, however big you get.'

'I love you Mum,' Lucy said, her arms wrapped around her mother.

There's nothing like the feel of your child snuggling into you.

'Now, you'd better get your school bag. I'll walk you to the bus stop.'

Karen waved at the school bus as it disappeared around the corner, and turned to walk back home. She was passing the telephone box when she noticed the silver car parked on the opposite side of the road, about twenty feet away. There was someone in the car, watching her, she was sure. The car wasn't one she had seen before but that wasn't unusual as many people stopped there to use the local shops. She just had a bad feeling about it. Taking a few steps towards the car, she tried to see who it was sitting in the driver's seat but whoever it was turned his head away to look behind him. The engine was running and before she could see clearly, he pulled out and drove away. There was no doubt about it though - she recognised that curly hair. It had to be him. Karen could feel herself shaking all over. She stopped and leant against the wall, trying to calm her breathing. Eventually she felt strong enough to walk away and hurried back to her house.

But she was afraid to go into the house until she was sure he'd really gone. How could he know where I live? Has he been following me and Lucy? Did he follow us home from Margaret's the other day? Did Margaret tell him where we lived? All these questions and more were reeling through her brain. Why would he want to follow me? It was eleven years since she'd seen him, and he'd not been in touch before. Even though he had only spent a few years in prison and had been out for quite a long while, this was the first time anything like this had happened.

She made up her mind to go and see Margaret again to ask a few questions about what could be going on. But first she had to go to work. Only Karen's mind was in such a state of turmoil she wasn't sure she could get through a day at work. Deciding to take the afternoon off, she'd cancel her appointments and go and see Margaret as soon as possible. After all, Margaret wouldn't be working this afternoon and it would be a good idea to drop in on her unawares. If Peter was trying to get at Karen, she wouldn't put it past Margaret to cover for him. She went into the house and gathered up her work things. Soon she was in her car and driving to the clinic.

Even though it was only early in the afternoon, the road to Gosport was as busy as ever and this gave Karen time to think about what she was going to say to Margaret. After her fright that morning, her determination to face up to Peter had waned, but if he was playing mind games with her she would never let him win. A part of her was even hoping he would be there at Margaret's house so she could speak to him face to face. He'd soon see he couldn't frighten her any more.

She pulled up outside the house and knocked on the door. With no time to think any more about what she was going to say, the door opened immediately, almost as if Margaret was waiting just behind the door. Karen was a little taken aback for a second, then before Margaret could say anything, Karen pushed past her into the house. As soon as she was inside, Margaret closed the door and turned to face her.

'Whatever's the matter?' she asked. 'You're upset. What's happened?'

'I just want to ask you something. When I came here the other day with Lucy, I saw Peter speaking to you in the street after we drove away.'

'What? Peter wasn't here. He hasn't been to see me for ages. At least a couple of months.' Margaret answered hastily, looking flustered.

Karen looked at Margaret. 'I'm sure it was him.' She didn't know what else she could say in the face of Margaret's denial. 'It was him, wasn't it?'

Margaret just shook her head and went into the kitchen. 'I'll make some tea,' she said. Karen followed her, unable to let her go without getting the truth out of her.

'Look Margaret, I don't know why you're not telling me the truth. It was him I saw, I know is was.'

Margaret sank into a chair at the kitchen table and looked up at Karen. 'Alright, it was him here. I didn't want to upset you. I know what you went through with Peter and how much it affected you - and still does, so when he turned up the other day, I thought it best not to say anything to you. There's nothing to worry about though. He wanted to come and see me, that's all. It happened that you had just left. I didn't think you'd seen him.'

'Why did he want to see you? I mean, did he want to see you about something in particular? He hasn't been for ages. What's changed to make him suddenly want to see you?'

'Nothing. Why shouldn't he see me?' Margaret snapped. 'I am his mother, after all.'

'I'm sorry. You're right, of course.' Karen sat down, deflated.

'Although he did have some news.' Margaret paused. 'He's broken up with his girlfriend. You know he was with her for four years. I always thought they would get married one day, but it seems that she's gone.'

'I'm not surprised,' Karen said under her breath.

'I know. He's never been an easy man to live with.'

Karen gave a cynical laugh. 'That's an understatement.'

'I'm sorry.' Karen could hear the sadness in her voice.

'Look, Margaret, I think he's been following me. I'm sure I saw him again, near my house. Have you told him where I live?'

'No, of course not. I wouldn't do that.'

'Then how did he find out?' Karen glared at her.

'Are you sure it was him? You know before, well, you thought you saw him before and it wasn't him then. It couldn't have been, could it? He was still in prison.'

'I know all that, but this was different. This was really him, I'm sure of it.'

'Well, he didn't find out from me. I wouldn't do that.' She reached out for Karen's hand. 'You do believe me, don't you? I know he's my son, but the last thing I want is to hurt or upset you in any way.'

'I know. He's not moving back here though, is he?' Karen asked.

'No. He's definitely not doing that. I've told him I'll always be here for him but he can't live here again. No way.'

'I think he must have followed me home that day. Did he leave straight away after us?'

'No, he didn't. We had a coffee together first.'

'Oh? Then how did he know where I was? It was definitely him I saw.'

'I don't know. Really.'

Karen left Margaret's house and started to make her way back home, watching in the rear view mirror at every turn, wondering if she was being followed. That must be how he found out where I lived, surely. He must have followed me in the past, maybe not the last time I was at Margaret's house, but perhaps on a previous occasion. She wouldn't put anything past him.

Chapter Thirty One

Kevin

Tuesday evening already after another day in the shop and Kevin couldn't bring himself to go straight home. He wandered about the town. He was trying not to go down Station Road again but Gem's insistance they leave it another day was making him feel uneasy. He was confused at why she was so sure Joan would come back if they left it any longer. Eventually he made his way back to his home. His Mother's worried face greeted him as he entered the house.

'Where have you been?' she asked, raking her fingers through her perfectly coiffured hair. 'Your dinner's nearly completely dried out. I'll get it on the table. Now go and wash your hands before you sit down.' She didn't even notice how upset he was. Kevin smiled at his Mother and hurried upstairs to the bathroom.

Sitting at the table a short while later, he struggled to eat his shepherds pie. Yes, dried to a crisp - his stomach was churning in anxiety as he wondered what to do about Joan. Something was wrong, he was sure and he didn't understand why Gem had stopped him from going to the Police.

'Come along, eat up Kevin.' His Mother's voice invaded his thoughts. Kevin looked up.

'I'm sorry Mother. It's been a busy day and I have lots on my mind.' He carefully lifted a forkful of food and struggled to finish his meal, aware of his Mother's watchful eye. Finally, after forcing the last portion of food into his mouth, he carefully placed the knife and fork together on the plate and adjusted them to make sure they were exactly in the centre of the plate before his Mother swept it all away to be rinsed and stacked in the dishwasher.

Kevin sat with his Mother, watching Emmerdale on the television. Well, his Mother was watching Emmerdale but he was not. He couldn't stop worrying about Joan. He couldn't help thinking that waiting another night would be wrong. She could be hurt, or worse. If anything had happened to her he'd not forgive himself. He looked out of the window. It was still light outside and would be for another hour or so. Deciding he was not going to wait any longer he got up from the sofa.

'Where are you going?' his Mother asked. 'Emmerdale's not finished yet. You'll miss the end.'

'I'm going out for a walk, Mother,' he said as he stood by the door.

'Whatever for?' His Mother sounded surprised. After all, it was not like him to go for walks in the evenings. Usually he would spend the whole evening sitting with her and watching television.

'I just want to go for a walk. I won't be long,' he said as he put on his jacket to go out.

'But you haven't had your shower. You always have your shower after Emmerdale. I've recorded Countdown so we can watch it together.'

'Pardon. Sorry, Mother, I wasn't listening.'

'Don't say "pardon". Say "excuse me." I said you should have your shower now, then we can watch Countdown.'

'No. I've got to go out again.' He looked at his Mother's surprised and slightly worried face. 'It's alright Mother, I just need to get some air. I won't be late.'

'Well, take care, then,' his Mother said and she turned her attention back to the screen.

Station Road was quiet with only a few cars passing him as he almost ran down the street to number 59. Kevin stopped outside the gate and looked about, suddenly aware he had no idea about what he would do next. There were a couple of people a few gardens down, the man mowing the grass and a woman pottering about. There was no-one else about. He could feel the sweat on his face and there was a rancid smell in the air which he quickly realised with horror came from his own armpits. Cursing quietly at his hurry to leave the house, he wished that he'd done as his Mother suggested and had a shower at least before he'd rushed out again. And now there was a stain on his pullover - dried shepherd's pie. Fumbling with his jacket buttons, he felt a little better with it done up. 'Out of sight, out of mind,' he muttered to himself. Now, who used to say that? An image of his Father, now long gone, flashed into his memory. He pushed it away - too painful to let it stay. Mind over matter, he told himself and without further thought he opened the gate and walked purposefully to the front door. He rang the door-bell and knocked the knocker as well, just to make sure he was heard, determined not to be fobbed off this time. Briefly, he wondered what happened to the cat.

The door opened and it was the tall young man who looked to Kevin like he was a bit of a thug. Still, this was not going to put Kevin off as he asked to see Mrs. Clarke.

'She's not in,' said the young man. Then, recognising Kevin, he added, 'I know you. You came knocking on the door here the other day. Didn't you understand what I told you? Mrs. Clarke's gone away - now you piss off too!'

'I'm not going anywhere,' Kevin said and he pushed his way past the tall man before he could think about what he was getting himself into.

The front door slammed and the man knocked Kevin over, punching and kicking him wherever he could land a fist or foot. He tried to fight back but it was impossible.

'You'll regret coming in here, you little shit!' Kevin heard before everything went black as he passed out. He remembered seeing the front door open again just before he lost consciousness and heard a voice in the distance calling out a name, 'Dan, Dan, you bloody idiot.'

Kevin woke up in the dark. It was cold, cold beneath him and it appeared that his face was flat against a stone floor. He pushed himself up to a sitting position which was difficult because his hands and feet were tied. He tried to get his bearings but it was too dark. The air felt damp.

Kevin didn't like the dark. he always had the bedroom door slightly open at home so the hall light could shine through the gap. He would never admit he was afraid before, but now he saw that he probably was - a bit. He took some deep breaths and tried to calm himself but the fear was too much. He started to panic, feeling his heart beating loudly in his ears. He closed his eyes, hoping it would subside and tried to imagine himself at home in his room. No. That wouldn't help. He needed to get out of here. He tried to remember what his father would have said if he'd been here. Mind over matter, mind over matter. He opened his eyes again and tried to keep calm.

Eventually his eyes became accustomed to the darkness and he could see a faint light across the room. It was a green light, the kind you see on the front of fridges to show they're working. Just a tiny spot but in the darkness it gave out quite a bit of light and Kevin could make out it was coming from a chest freezer, or something looking like a chest freezer. His Mother had one in her garage and she kept ice-cream and frozen vegetables in it.

He could also make out the outline of a staircase. It looked like it might be brick but he couldn't be sure. Brick staircases in houses usually meant a cellar, so he thought he might be in a cellar. His mind was racing - he could feel the panic forming again like a hard lump in his stomach which made him feel sick. I can't be sick, my clothes will smell. Should I call for help? No. He held back, realising no-one would hear him apart from that man and the other one - the one who'd come into the house before. What was his name? Billy. That was it. 'Keep calm,' he told himself in a whisper.

Slowly his heart steadied as he tried to put together what had happened - how he had got into this place? He remembered that he'd got into Joan's house and there was a fight with that man but he couldn't remember going down any stairs so someone must have tied him up and dragged him down here. His body felt as though it was covered in bruises but he was tied up very tightly and couldn't move his arms or legs otherwise he would have tried to stand up. He closed his eyes again and began to count. Counting had always helped him in the past if he was ever in a difficult situation. He felt himself becoming calmer and eventually he drifted off to sleep.

Some time must have passed because when he opened his eyes again he could see more light coming from a window high up on the wall above the freezer. Not really a window but a barred opening which had been boarded up from the outside with a bit of light seeping through small slits between the boards. This gave him a little hope that maybe someone might hear him if he called out. Someone in the street. But he was still afraid of doing that in case those two men heard him and came down to sort him out again. Then again, if they did come down, that could be Kevin's chance to escape.

'I wish I'd never come here,' he said to himself. 'This was not one of my better ideas.' He realised his only hope was probably Gem. 'She'll come looking for Joan soon. I'll just wait until she comes and then shout as loud as I can.'

He waited.

Chapter Thirty Two

Karen

All that worrying about whether she was being followed was getting to her. She'd not gone home but headed towards the coast instead and found herself parked at the sea front in Lee-On-The-Solent. This had always been where she went when she was troubled. She had good memories of times at Lee, walking with Lucy when she was a baby, the sea always seemed to calm her. She got out of the car and walked across the shingle beach until she found her favourite place - a concrete block, left over from the war, perhaps, but the perfect place to sit and watch the waves.

It was at times like these when she almost wished she had a man in her life. But after Peter she'd not wanted to be in any sort of relationship and although she had a few friends, she'd always been a bit of a loner and any boyfriends that had come along, well, as soon as they'd started to get serious, she'd finished with them pretty smartish.

Lucy's Father, John, a student nurse she'd had a one-off fling with, hadn't wanted to know when she'd told him she was pregnant, and although Karen had tried to contact him after Lucy was born, she'd heard nothing back from him. He'd gone to Plymouth not long after she'd told him she was pregnant and being a single parent wasn't all bad. Lucy was the centre of her world.

Karen sat and allowed the sound of the sea to calm her. Alright, Peter may be back, trying to mess her head with following her but he had no legal right over Lucy. Besides, why would he want to get at Lucy who was nothing to do with him anyway.

She couldn't understand why Peter would want to start following her after all this time but supposed it might be something to do with his girlfriend finishing with him. She wondered what had happened there and was relieved in a way that another woman had escaped from him. Then Karen started looking at it from his side, as always. Maybe he's changed. In prison he would have had anger management and other therapies. She caught herself - why are you always making excuses for him? This conversation had occurred over and over again in the early years after he'd gone. Now he was back - in her head, if not in her life. She wanted, more than anything, to be rid of him once and for all.

Karen walked back to her car. She was starting the engine when she saw him. Standing on the other side of the road, watching the traffic as if about to cross over to the car park and far enough away for her to get a good look at him before he turned and looked straight at her. She stared back at him in the mirror, then turned around to face him as he walked across the road. Karen was unable to move for a moment, then, realising he was coming towards her, she slammed the gears into reverse, spun backwards, and sped away out of the car park heading for home. She drove too fast along the sea-front but once she was at the bend of the road to Stubbington, she slowed down, turning towards Hillhead. She stopped the car and waited. In her mirror she watched the cars pass the end of the road. After twenty minutes, and no sign of Peter's car, she carried on making her way through Hillhead to Titchfield, the long way home, her heart still pounding.

Chapter Thirty Three

Billy

So I came back in and walked right into seeing Dan attacking that twat who was snooping around here the other day. I was shouting at Dan to leave it but it was too late. The bloke was already on the floor and unconscious. I don't think he saw me before he passed out but obviously he got a good look at Dan so he's a fuckin' liability now. I was all for dragging him out into the street and leaving him there. With a bit of luck he'd come round and get himself as far away from here as possible. Dan and I had a bit of an argument but in the end I agreed we should put him in the cellar, just until later.

Dan had been in touch with his mate and they were coming round that night. I wondered if they could take this bloke away with them at the same time. Dan said they'd probably want more money so we decided that we should leave him then move him ourselves afterwards. It would have had to be later anyway; there were too many people about in the street that early. We'd have had to wait until dark.

I'm still not sure what to do about Gem. I feel bad about throwing her out and really do want to get back with her. I know she's good for me but I was in such a bloody mess at that moment I thought it'd be better to keep her away from this place - at least until things were sorted. I was still thinking about her when there was a knock at the door. It was about eight o'clock - too early for the lads. I opened the door and it was Gem standing there, looking at me with those eyes that make you melt. I knew that I shouldn't have let her in, it was too effin' risky what with everything going on. Only there was something about the way she looked at me - so I invited her in, thinking that I could maybe make some excuses and get rid of her quickly. For a start, Dan was in the house and that was one of the things she said she wouldn't like - having Dan around when she was here.

I took her into the kitchen and offered her a beer. She said she'd rather have a coffee and put the kettle on. I told her Dan was in the front room. She didn't like hearing that and said she wouldn't stay long. She started to tell me she'd been having second thoughts about getting back together with me. I told her I was sorry for the way I'd been when I chucked her out before and I hadn't meant to hurt her but I was having a bad time and things had been a bit frought between us so what did she expect? She didn't like hearing that so I said I was sorry again and we sat down with our drinks.

Then in the silence between us I heard someone calling out. I tried to disguise it by starting to talk again. I asked her how her job was going, hoping she hadn't heard it. I silently cursed Dan for not gagging that soddin' bloke down in the cellar. Gem gave me an odd look and said 'What was that?' Then she got up from the table and went into the hall. Of course I followed her and tried to make out it was Dan watching tv in the front room. I wasn't sure if she believed me but there was no way she was going into that room to talk to Dan. She really friggin' well hates him - I can't think why, he's not so bad.

Anyway, she came back into the kitchen with me and she seemed to relax a bit more so I asked her to come upstairs to my room, thinking it would be better to get her away from the cellar. I know I ought to have got her to leave at that point but I just couldn't let her go. She was happy enough to come upstairs with me and soon we were relaxing on the bed. After a while, though, she started looking a bit uncomfortable, sweaty, like she was withdrawing so I said, 'How are you getting on with the Methadone script?' She just shrugged and said it was alright most of the time but the late evenings were pretty bad. The Methadone never seemed to last long enough. So I offered her a bit of smack to help her sleep.

That's when she turned on me. I said I only wanted to help her. I know how hard it can be.

'Don't you realise if I give a dirty pee I'll lose my script?' She started shouting at me and looked at me like she was going to kill me. 'Of course you know, that's why you're offering it, so that I can fail again and you'll win. No thanks.'

I tried to calm her down but she was totally off her head. She was shaking so I backed off until she'd cooled off a bit. I said I wouldn't hurt her and only wanted to help. Eventually, she stopped shaking and we ended up cuddling each other. It was all going really well until Dan started shouting up the stairs.

'What the hell does he want?' Gem said to me, struggling to get up out of my arms.

'Stay here, I'll sort it.' I went out of the room and left Gem sitting on the bed. Dan said his mate would be coming round in a bit and I'd better get Gem out of the way. So I told him to stay out of sight and I'd get rid of her.

I went back up to my room and Gem was standing by the window, looking out. 'I'm sorry, Gem, but something's come up and you'll have to go home now,' I said. 'I'll phone you tomorrow though and we can meet up again.'

'What's going on?' She turned on me with a sort of accusing look in her eye. 'I know you, Billy. What are you up to?'

'Nothing,' I held her close and gave her a kiss. 'You've got to trust me. Nothing's going on. I'm just doing something with Dan. I know you don't like him but he's been a friend to me and I owe him. I can't tell you what we're doing but it's nothing to worry about.'

I knew she didn't believe a word I'd said, apart from Dan being my friend but she did leave and I watched her walking down the street until she was well out of sight.

Chapter Thirty Four

Gem

Of course she didn't believe him, so as soon as she was out of sight, she made her way to the back lane behind the row of houses and walked along to the rear of number 59.

She stood there for a moment, still not sure she was in her right mind, then shrugging to herself, she crept through the overgrown garden to the back door. That was when she noticed the cellar window, down by her feet. It was boarded up but the boards were old and split so she reached down and tried to pull the board away so she could see inside. It was far too dark down there and although she managed to pull some of the board away, she could see nothing. Underneath the boarding there were metal bars. She tried to twist and wrench at the bars and they were definitely a bit more loose but she was not strong enough to pull them free.

A light coming on in the room above the cellar startled her. She stood up and peered through the small gap in the curtains. It was Billy and Dan, standing there, looking like they were arguing. She couldn't quite hear what they were saying though and as she stared through the window, Dan turned and looked straight at her. With a shout he dashed to the door. Gem was terrified but couldn't seem to move to run away. Before she could come to her senses she was being grabbed by Dan and dragged in through the back door.

'What the hell do you think you're doing?' she shouted. 'Billy, get him off me!'

'What were you doing out there, Gem?' Billy's voice was quiet, quieter than she would have liked. 'I told you to leave.'

'I know,' she said. 'I was half way home when I realised I'd left my keys here. I took them out of my bag. They must be upstairs.'

'Then why didn't you come to the front door? What's with the fuckin' snooping around the back?'

'I wasn't snooping. I was near the back alley when I remembered and it was be the quickest way back here. I certainly didn't expect to be jumped on by that thug!' She glared at Dan.

'I don't trust her,' Dan said. 'Now what do we do?' He gave Billy a hard look. 'You'll just have to get rid of the bitch!'

'Don't call her that' Billy was sticking up for her now but he turned to her and the look in his eye frightened her. 'Why didn't you just go home?' he said.

'I told you, I left my keys here. Let me go and look upstairs and I'll go.' She shook Dan off and made a move to the door.

'I'll come with you,' Billy said. He glared at Dan. 'You stay here.'

'Just get rid of her,' Dan growled.

Billy followed Gem up the stairs and into his bedroom. Gem looked around the room, pretending to look for her keys. They were in her pocket and she wondered how she could fake finding them but Billy was watching her like a cat waiting to pounce on a bird. After moving a few things around on the chest of drawers she turned to him, holding her hands out in submission.

'OK, I'll come clean. I didn't leave my keys here.' she smiled sheepishly and moved towards him. 'I just wanted to be with you. It was so good the other night and the thought of going home to my empty flat was just awful. Please let me stay again. I'll keep out of Dan's way.'

'You can't.'

'Look, I don't care what's going on with you two. I'm OK with whatever you were going to do this evening. I just want to stay with you tonight, that's all. Please.' She reached out and touched his face, put her arms around him and drew him nearer for a kiss. She could feel him melting under her lips. She wasn't sure whether it felt good or not. For a moment, she was lost in something stirring deep inside her. But he was pushing her away.

'Look Gem, I want you too, but not tonight, OK? There's stuff I've got to do and you can't be here, believe me.'

'Alright, I'll go, in a minute,' she sat on the bed. 'Just come here for a while. I need you.'

So Billy sat next to her and before long they were at it again under the covers. Gem knew that he wouldn't be able to say no to her for long.

Afterwards, they were laying there, relaxed and sleepy. Gem was feeling a mixture of emotions. She still felt some kind of love for him but there was that other, darker side to him and she didn't like what she might find out. She wondered how low he may have sank this time.

As she was lying there, thinking these thoughts, she gradually drifted off to sleep. She was dreaming about past times with Billy, he was putting a tournique on her arm, smiling down at her and drawing some smack into a syringe. She was waiting for the warm feeling to flow through her when suddenly it was the sharp jab of a needle in her arm that woke her up. She struggled to move away as soon as she realised it was more than a dream and Billy was really there, holding her down whilst he injected her.

'No! Don't, Billy! I don't want this.' But the heroin was already coursing through her veins. It was too late. She sank back down, tears starting to flow, helpless now to do anything else other than go with it. 'I hate you, Billy,' she said, her voice more of a whisper now, as she drifted into a stupor.

'I'm sorry,' he said. He kissed her gently and left the room.

Chapter Thirty Five

Kevin

It was much later. He had waited and waited for someone to come so he could call out for help but no-one came. He must have fallen asleep. He was angry with himself for falling asleep. Suppose someone had come and he'd missed the chance to call out?

There's only one thing for it, he thought. I will have to somehow get my hands free and try to escape. I can't stay down here any longer. It's too dark, and damp and cold and I don't like it. My clothes must be very dirty. Mother will be very annoyed with me. It's making me feel so bad. I can't keep counting all the time. I thought it would help but it doesn't. He started to move his hands about to try and loosen the rope that was binding them. His hands were very sore and he was sure that all that rubbing was making his wrists bleed but he could see no alternative.

His eyes were becoming accustomed to the darkness and that was when he noticed there seemed to be more gaps in the wooden slats at the window. It looked as though someone had been pulling at the wood from the outside. This gave him something to think about. Had someone been trying to find him? It would have been Gem probably, although she wouldn't have given up unless she'd been disturbed. This made him feel worse. Suppose she'd been found out by the two men. Kevin could hear them moving about above him in the house. Knowing they were still up there frightened him even more. Mind over matter, mind over matter.

He worked harder on trying to release his hands. Eventually he could feel the ropes were becoming a little looser. Not quite loose enough to free his hands yet. He carried on wriggling and tried to look about the room - it would have been great if there was a sharp edge somewhere that he could cut himself free. That's what would have happened in a spy film on television but the room was to dark so even if there had been something, he wouldn't have been able to find it.

He had a very bad feeling about this. What was going to happen to him? Were they going to leave him here indefinitely? Did they plan to kill him? These thoughts were too much for him so he decided not to think along those lines any more. He had almost given up all thought of getting out of there when the rope suddenly became much looser and his hands were free! Quickly fumbling with the knot holding the rope around his feet he managed to untie it even though his hands felt like sausages and he had pins and needles in his fingers.

Getting up was difficult too. His feet were numb. Eventually he managed to stand and leaned against the wall for a while until he felt ready to move. He didn't think he had the energy to do any more and if it hadn't been so nasty in that cellar, he would have been happy to wait there until he was rescued. A noise above him in the house brought back his motivation to get on with escaping from that awful place. That, and the thought of Gem being in trouble too.

The little window was high up on the wall which would mean climbing on top of the freezer to reach it. He managed to reach the freezer and looked up at the window. A couple of the bars were set into ancient brickwork. He didn't know what made him do it, perhaps it was him thinking of what people could hide in them in the stories he'd seen on tv, but he found himself opening the lid of the freezer. He stared at the contents before slamming the lid shut and he quickly climbed on top in sheer panic.

The bricks around the window were loose and after a bit of a struggle he managed to shift one of them out of place. Soon he had pulled two of the bars completely out. They dropped with a clang to the floor of the cellar. The noise was so loud he was sure the men would hear and come down to catch him at it before he could escape. He stopped and listened but all he could hear was the thumping of his own heart and his heavy breathing. He found another loose brick lower down and pulled it out. It was perfect for a place to put his foot to climb high enough to reach out. Hauling himself up he managed to squeeze himself through the gap between the bars. Then he was stuck. Wriggling about he realised that his jacket was caught on a nail! He panicked for a moment, worrying about what his Mother would say if he ripped his clothes. Then he heard his Father's voice in his head, telling him to "Man Up!" Blast it, he thought. Then sorry Mum, as he wrenched at his jacket, tearing himself free.

At last he was out in the night air. He couldn't believe what he'd seen and couldn't believe how good it felt to be free again. He peered back down into the cellar one last time and saw there was a light shining into it from the open door at the top of the stairs. Someone was coming! He'd managed to escape just in time. Kevin scrambled to his feet and made his way swiftly down the garden path, past the overgrown shrubs and out through the back gate to the alley beyond. He knew they'd be after him as soon as they realised he was gone so he didn't waste any time hanging about and was soon back at his own house and safely inside the door.

'Is that you, Kevin?' his Mother called. She came into the hall, a look of shock on her face. 'I was so worried about you. Where on Earth have you been?'

This was the point when Kevin should have told his Mother everything - to have called the Police and put the whole affair into their hands. Why didn't he do that? Kevin wasn't sure, but he just had the feeling that his Mother wouldn't believe him - he did have a history of making up adventures in the past, which had ended badly. Only this time it was real and he didn't quite know how to deal with it.

She was waiting for him to explain.

'Kevin,' she said. 'Kevin, your clothes are filthy!'

'I went for a walk.' Kevin thought he'd got away with it. He just wanted to get to the safety of his room.

'You had better go and have a bath. Take off those dirty clothes and I'll put them in the wash. We'll talk about where you've been tomorrow. I'm going to bed.'

Kevin looked at her in amazement. She would never have believed that he'd spent half the night stuck in that cellar, tied up like a turkey at Christmas. It was all too much for him.

'I'm sorry, Mother, I'm very tired. It's been rather a difficult day,' he said as he pushed past her and went upstairs. It was only once inside the safety of his room that he realised she hadn't noticed that his jacket was ripped.

Chapter Thirty Six

Billy

He hadn't want to hurt Gem, but what else could he have done. He'd had to get her out of the way before Dan's mate came round. It would have been too complicated if she'd been around asking awkward questions. And then there was that idiot who'd come snooping around and got himself locked in the cellar. Billy was feeling bad about that and still wasn't happy about him being down there. He wasn't sure either, about what they would do with him.

Billy was just leaving his room when he heard Dan shouting. He rushed down to see what was happening. The cellar door was ajar.

'Billy, get down here!' Dan was shouting up at him. 'The stupid bastard's gone!'

Billy stood at the top of the stone steps, feeling sick. 'How could he have fuckin' gone? You tied the bastard up tight enough and there's no way out. The door was locked.'

Dan indicated towards the window. 'That's how he got out,' he said. He must have smashed his way out. Those bricks are fucked. I knew we should have got rid of him. I told you we shouldn't have left him without checking.' He glared at Billy.

'Don't blame me. You're the one who hit him on the head and had to tie him up. If you hadn't been so bleedin' heavy handed, he could have been persuaded to just go away again. You're too effin' hot headed. You never think before you act.'

'Don't turn this on me! You're the one who killed his own bloody auntie, so don't have a go. I'm only trying to help you sort it out.'

'You always think with your fists. You're a bleedin' liability.'

'This is stupid. He could have gone anywhere. He could have seen the body. And now you've got that bitch upstairs as well. We're stuffed.'

'She won't do anything. I've sorted her out. She'll be out of it for a while and when she comes round it'll all be over.'

'What have you done? Don't tell me you've tied her up, too.'

'I didn't tie anyone up, you did.' Billy said. 'She's just having a bit of a chilling time - I gave her some smack if you must know.'

'Well I suppose that's one way of keeping her out of the way. Just as long as she doesn't come out of it too soon.'

'It'll be alright. Keep cool. What time are your mates supposed to be here with the van?'

Dan looked at his watch. 'They should be here in about an hour. But what about the other one? The one who escaped - what if he goes to the Police and tells them what he's seen?'

Billy couldn't think any more. 'I don't know. It's all a bloody mess. You'll have to sort it out. I can't do it.'

'I can't do it on my own, and it's your problem, Billy, not mine. We'll have to move her into the shed down the bottom of the garden. Then when the boys get here they can drive round the back and pick her up from there. If the Police come, they won't be looking out there, will they.'

'It's a bit fuckin' risky, isn't it?' Billy said. 'What if they have sniffer dogs?'

'They're not going to have sniffer dogs, are they?' Dan snorted. 'They don't know we've got a bleedin' body - they've only got the word of that idiot that we locked him in the cellar. We'll just deny it, let them look around and then they'll most probably go away again.'

'What about Gem?'

'You said she'll be asleep for a while yet. Stop wasting time and get moving!'

It was harder work than they thought it would be, lifting Aunty's body out of the freezer and dragging her up the stairs. She was still wrapped in the blanket so they didn't have to look at her face which was just as well as Billy was feeling very sick and if he had to look at her it would have been too much. He was sweating by the time they got her into the hall. They stopped and listened. The house was quiet but Billy was nervous. He went upstairs and put his head round the door into his bedroom. Gem wasn't stirring. She looked so peaceful, laying there asleep. He felt a slight regret about what he'd done and hoped she would forgive him.

'What are you doing up there?' Dan called. 'Let's get this job finished, shall we?'

Billy shook his head to himself and soon they were carrying the body out into the back garden. They stopped to check none of the neighbours were outside and glanced at the windows overlooking the back of the house. It seemed as though there was no-one about and no sign of anyone watching.

'Carry her as though we're moving an old carpet,' said Dan.

'How do you do that?'

'I don't know. Just act as though it's a fuckin' carpet. Think about it being a carpet. It'll just happen if you believe it.'

'You're effing mad. How can I act as if my aunty's body is a carpet?'

'Just get on with it! We're running out of time. If the Police are coming they could be here any minute now.'

'Well stop saying daft effing things then.'

'OK!'

They reached the shed and opened the door. It was filled with clutter - an old bike, a rusty lawn mower, boxes of junk and loads of cobwebs. There wasn't much room to get a body in there but somehow they managed to balance it on top of a pile of boxes, just behind the door.

'That'll have to do,' Dan said. 'Now we need to go back to the cellar to clear up any evidence that we had that bloke down there.'

It didn't take them long to clean up the cellar. Billy looked in the freezer at the frozen food and shuddered. *I won't be eating any of that lot.* They pushed the bars into the gaps on the window, balanced the loose bricks into place and swept the floor around the freezer. They removed the rope that was used to tie up Kevin and went back upstairs to the kitchen, locking the cellar door behind them.

Billy checked on Gem again. She was still out of it. He was starting to feel a little better now. Once the body was gone, he knew he'd be in the clear and then he could start making plans for his new life, hopefully with Gem.

There was a knock at the door. He ran down to the hall.

'It's the boys,' said Dan. 'I'll deal with this.' He answered the door and went out into the front garden with them. 'We need to drive round the back,' he said to them as he closed the door behind him.

Billy waited in the house. He felt bad about letting his aunty be taken away by those two but would rather they just got on and did it without him having to see. *Anyway, she's dead so she can't feel anything, can she? Once they've got rid of her, I can clear her stuff out of the house. But I'll have to think up something to tell Gem. I could make out Aunty's decided to stay with her friend on the Island and wants me to send her stuff over to her. She's asked me to look after her house indefinitely, like. I'll say that Aunty Joan plans to leave me the house when she dies and wants me to have the benefit of it now. I wonder if Gem would believe that?*

Dan coming in through the back door burst into his dreams of the future.

'She's gone,' he said. 'I showed them where she was, gave them the money and left it up to them to get rid of her. She'll be buried a long way from here in some woods.'

'Don't tell me that!' said Billy. 'I don't want to have that in my mind when I think about Aunty.'

'Well, you should have been more careful with her then, shouldn't you. If you hadn't shoved her so hard, she'd still be alive now.'

'Alright, I know. Do you think I don't feel like shit about what I did? Now can we just move on?'

'Whatever, I was just saying,' Dan sniffed. 'You'd better check on that bird of yours upstairs. Is she still out of it?'

'Probably, I'm just going up now.'

Gem was sitting on the edge of the bed when he entered the room a few minutes later. She was looking at him accusingly. He wasn't sure whether she'd heard anything of what was said downstairs or whether she was just pissed off with him for giving her the fix. He smiled at her and sat down, taking her hand but she snatched it away.

'Don't touch me!' she snapped. 'How could you do that?'

'Do what?' he still wasn't sure what she meant.

'You know what,' she turned and looked straight at him. 'You drugged me! How could you, after all I've been saying? You knew how important it is for me to be clean. Now I could lose my script and my Probation Officer'll be onto me. I could go to prison if I don't stay clean.'

'You won't go to prison,' he shrugged. 'Your drug worker'll write good reports on you. It was only one friggin' hit, after all. When's your next pee test, anyway?'

'They can ask for a test whenever they want. It's sometimes weekly, sometimes twice weekly. It's random.'

'Well, keep your fingers crossed then, that you don't have to give one for a week. The heroin'll be out of your system by then. Even if it's not, you'll be able to blag it by saying you've taken codeine or something.'

'I know, but I don't want to lie!' Gem was furious. 'And I don't want to get hooked on smack again. I'm really having a hard time keeping off as it is. The Methadone is bloody awful but I'm well on my way to reducing off, at least

I was until now. I could have been drug free in a couple of months. You've messed me up again, Billy and I hate you for it.'

'Don't say that,' Billy said. 'I only meant to give you a treat.'

'A treat! You call messing up my life, a treat?' She was shouting now and moved to the door.

'Look, I'm sorry. I won't ever try to give you a fuckin' treat again, OK?' he reached for her. 'Look, please, Gem, let's start over again. I promise it won't happen again. Please.'

'I don't know,' Gem said, calmer now. 'I've got to get home. I need to do some thinking.'

'Don't go like this,' he pleaded.

'I'm going. I don't know what to do about us. I'm not sure what I want any more. You've just got to give me space to think.'

She made her way down the stairs and glanced at the cellar door as she passed it. She looked back up to him to where he was standing halfway down.

'I don't know what's going on, Billy, with you or with us. It all feels weird and I can't get to the bottom of it. I know you're not being honest and I need to get my head together to work out what I want and what's going on. I hope you'll respect that.'

'Phone me, please,' was all he could think of to say in reply as she went through the front door and out into the garden. She walked down the street without looking back.

Chapter Thirty Seven

Karen

Getting to work was a relief. Keeping busy where she didn't have to think about her fears was the best thing for her. She had so much on her mind at home, worrying about what Peter might be doing. She was starting to see him almost everywhere she went. The doctors had told to her to expect this but she really thought she'd got over all of that long ago. But since Margaret had told her he was actually around that day, the fear of meeting up with him was real, not imagined. Karen was beginning to wish that she'd stayed and confronted him instead of running away.

Turning her mind to her work, she had a bad feeling things weren't as they should be with Gem either and decided she should get in touch with the young woman as soon as possible. Picking up the phone she dialled the number on Gem's casenote folder. No answer. Damn, another home visit then, she thought as she made her way to the flat.

There was no reply there either so Karen waited outside for a while, thinking about what may have happened. Then she remembered that Gem would probably be at the charity shop.

But Gem was not at the shop. Karen looked in through the window and could see a woman behind the counter. There was another assistant coming out of the door at the rear of the shop. Karen went in and spoke to the woman at the till. 'I'm a friend of Gemma Wylde,' she said. Is she working today?'

'Not this morning,' said the woman. 'But she'll be in this afternoon.'

'Oh, I thought she might be here now. She's not at her flat.'

'Sorry. She only does a few half days. I'm afraid I can't help you. I don't know where she might be. You can come back this afternoon.'

'That's OK. Thank you. I'll just have a quick look around the shop if that's alright.'

'Of course,' the woman smiled. 'You're welcome.'

Karen made her way to the book shelves and was looking through the titles, trying to think. Was she making too much of Gem not turning up this morning? She had also missed her appointment two days ago but it may be that she was struggling with having to keep to appointments. It wasn't easy always being on the straight and narrow and it may be that Gem was just sick of being under the spotlight. It could be very wearing. All the same, she had seemed to be doing so well up until now. Karen brought herself back to the moment, picked out a paperback and took it to the counter to pay. It was at times like this when she wished that she didn't have to be so aware of confidentiality. This woman looked to her like she might be a good ally for Gem, someone to support her in her recovery. If only Karen could confide in her and ask how Gem was getting on, whether she'd noticed any changes in her. Finally she decided that although she wasn't able to divulge their relationship she could ask a few questions.

'Has Gem been alright?' she asked. 'I'm a bit worried about her. Has she been coming in regularly?'

'She's been fine,' the woman answered. 'Always turns up on time - every day that she should be here, she comes in. She usually works with Kevin. He could have confirmed this but he didn't turn up today. It's him I'm worried about.'

'Kevin?' Karen wondered. 'Gem mentioned his name. She told me about him. Said that she works with him.'

'It's not like Kevin not to turn up. He's most particular about being here on time and always dresses smartly. He has a good work ethic. Almost too good sometimes, I think.'

'I see, thank you.' She wondered where this could be leading. Was Kevin somehow mixed up in what may have been going on with Gem? The woman was speaking again.

'I didn't think that they would get on, to be honest, but the other day I noticed Gem and him talking in the back room. They were whispering. Worrying about one of my other workers, Mrs. Clarke, who strangely enough has also gone missing. It's all a bit odd, isn't it? Kevin had got himself into a state wondering what had happened to her and I think he was talking to Gem about it. I'm pretty sure I heard her saying that he shouldn't worry about it and I could have sworn she'd said that he should leave it to her but I couldn't be completely certain.'

'It all sounds a bit strange, don't you think?' Karen asked.

'Exactly. I said that I would go and visit Mrs. Clarke if we hadn't heard from her by the end of the week. She only lives around the corner in Station Road. I'm afraid I haven't had time to do anything about it yet.'

'I'm sure there must be an explanation for all of this.'

'I'm sure too. Anyway, I'm sorry I couldn't help you with Gem. If I see her, I'll tell her you were looking for her. What is your name, by the way?'

'Karen. Just tell her Karen was looking for her.'

As Karen left, she wondered whether she felt better or not.

***

She was still worrying about where Gem could be as she made her way home from work that evening. She hadn't been back to the shop in the afternoon - other clients had taken all her time. She decided that she'd check again in the morning if there was no sign of her.

As she drew nearer to her house, she started to think about Peter. In fact, she'd been thinking about him on and off all day. It was really worrying her and she felt she had to find out what he was playing at. She decided that enough was enough - time to do something about it.

An hour later, Lucy was settled in front of her homework with the babysitter. 'I won't be late,' Karen said as she left the house and got into her car. She wasn't really sure where she could start with this but began by driving to Gosport, to Margaret's house. It was a sunny, warm evening and the traffic was busy through Fareham, people still making their way home from work. She was glad that she'd moved out of Gosport, battling to work every day through all this would have driven her mad. The job was stressful enough without a long drive there and back every day.

She parked at the far end of the street from Margaret's house and sat in her car to wait. What am I waiting for, she thought. Images flitted across her memory of herself coming home from work to Margaret's house when she was younger and the warm feeling she'd had at finding herself in a loving, safe place at last. Her childhood had been difficult being passed from one foster family to the next when things hadn't worked out. Margaret had been the only one who'd coped with her and life could have been perfect except for the times when Peter came home from university. But gradually they'd got to like each other, eventually marrying when she was still only a teenager. What a big mistake that had been! Still, it was a long time ago now and she'd made herself a good life on her own with her little girl and Margaret was still a Mother figure to her, even now, after all that had happened with Peter.

She was sitting there watching Margaret's front door when she noticed a car passing hers. It was Peter. He pulled up outside the house and let himself in with a key. Before she could think any more about it, Karen got out of her car and walked briskly to the house. She was knocking on the door before she could think.

He opened the door almost immediately. He smiled.

'Well, Karen, come in,' he said. 'I was wondering how long it would be before you got here but didn't think it would be this soon. Couldn't wait to see me?'

She swallowed the lump in her throat.

'I shouldn't have come,' she stuttered, then immediately hated herself for showing her fear. She took a deep breath. 'I don't want to see you at all,' she continued. 'I just want to know what you're playing at, following me around. Are you trying to frighten me? Because if you are, it won't work. You can't scare me any more.'

He laughed. Towering over her, his curly hair, once a light brown, now grey at the temples. His blue eyes pierced into hers. She held his gaze, feeling a shaky kind of bravado as she did so. 'I asked you a question. What do you want with me?' She perservered.

He took a step towards her, his laughter turning to a fixed sinister smile. 'You ruined my life,' he whispered. 'I hate you for that.'

'I didn't ruin your life, you did that yourself,' she said. 'Now just leave me alone. What happened to your girlfriend? Carol, is that her name? What happened to her? You were settled down pretty quickly after you came out of prison, weren't you? You couldn't have been bothered about me then.'

'She's gone.'

'What do you mean, gone? Did you attack her too?'

'Shut up! It wasn't like that. And I didn't attack you either, you made all that up. Go on, admit it!'

This was completely unexpected. Karen could not believe he was so much in denial with what he'd done to her. 'You kept me prisoner, drugged me and then beat me until I was unconscious. How can you not admit that. You even pleaded guilty at court.'

'I only did that because that stupid solicitor told me it would reduce my sentence,' he explained. 'I didn't do any of what you're saying. Carol believed me.'

'So what did happen to her, then?'

'Someone told her about you, you bitch! Someone sent her some old newspaper cuttings of the court case and she started asking questions. Then she said she couldn't live with me. She said she was going away to think about things

176

but she cleared all her stuff out of the house when I was at work one day.' He started to pace the room then turned to face her again. 'It was you, wasn't it?' he spat.

'Why do you think I would want to do that? I moved on from you the day you went into custody. I've got a good life now, a good job and a nice home. I don't need you in my life. All I want to do is to forget you.' She looked at him. 'The only thing I wish is that I'd never met you, never had to go through that awful time with you. I can't believe you're saying it never happened. The worst years of my life they were.'

'Don't say that!' he shouted at her. 'We were good - at first we were anyway, until you started to change. I still blame that job at the hospital.'

'I'm not even going to listen to this, Peter. You are not in my life any more. I don't care any more about what you think about my job or about anything else in my life. You've got to back off and leave me alone. I mean it.'

'You don't really think that's true,' he said. 'Anyway, I don't want you back. Oh, no, don't think so highly of yourself. Why would I want you? Damaged goods with a bastard daughter!'

'Don't you dare say that! You just keep Lucy out of this, and keep away from us both.'

'I can still ruin your lives,' he said. 'You'd better be careful, remember that.'

'Just keep away,' she repeated. 'I can still go to the Police. It won't be good for you if you keep following me, or if you do anything to me or Lucy. You've already got a prison record remember.'

'We'll see. You shouldn't threaten me, that's all I'm saying.'

Karen had an overwhelming need to get away from him. She turned to leave. 'You're unhinged.' she said. He grabbed her wrist and pulled her back round to face him.

'Don't you dare say that!' His face was close to hers.

She felt a real fear rising from her belly. Resisting to close her eyes, she glared back at him and wrestled herself free. Before he could say any more, she heard the sound of a key in the door. It was Margaret.

'What's going on?' Margaret looked at Peter then at Karen.

'I'm just going,' Karen pushed past her and went out into the street. Margaret called after her.

'Karen. Are you alright? Don't rush off yet, please.'

But Karen kept walking away and didn't look back until she reached her car.

Margaret stood watching for a while then went back into the house and closed the door.

Karen was still shaking with fury by the time she arrived home. She sat in the car to allow herself to calm down before going indoors. She looked at her watch - it was only seven thirty. She'd only been out for an hour and a half but it seemed like hours since she left to go to Gosport. He's not right in the head. She resolved to keep away from him and keep him away from Lucy.

Thinking about Lucy reminded her she'd promised they would spend a bit of time together this evening. These times with Lucy were so precious. Karen knew what it was like to be neglected. She'd never known her own Mother and until living with Margaret had little experience of a loving family life. She'd vowed that she would give her daughter what she'd not had in her own life.

Lucy leapt from her chair as soon as Karen came through the front door.

'Hey Mum, you're home early,' she said. 'Come and look at my drawings.'

'OK, just give me a chance to get in,' said Karen. She paid the babysitter and made herself a cup of tea. She could feel the tension dropping from her shoulders. This was her own safe haven, a secure home for her and her daughter and Peter could not hurt her any more.

Lucy opened the sketch book and showed her Mum what she'd been working on. Karen turned the pages, looking at pictures of horses, horses and more horses.

'They're very good, Lucy. You like your horses, don't you.'

'I want to have my own horse, Mum,' she said. 'I know we can't afford it but if I draw horses it's almost like I've got one of my own.'

'That's lovely. Maybe we can see if you can have riding lessons.' Karen said.

'Can I?' Lucy squealed. 'Really?'

'I don't see why not. I'll look into it. There are riding schools all over the place. We'll see how much the lessons are. I'm not promising anything though.'

'Oh, thank you Mum!' Lucy hugged her Mother.

Lucy was soon settled in bed and Karen made herself another cup of tea, before sitting down. She couldn't stop thinking about Peter. What should she do about him? She'd been hoping that after confronting him he would get the message and leave her alone. There was nothing she could do about him feeling so angry towards her. She knew he was deluded and possibly was quite dangerous though and she wondered whether she ought to get in touch with the Police, or maybe the Probation Service. They would know what to do about him and his threats, wouldn't they? She remembered they were in touch with her just after the attack when he went to prison. They'd told her then they would keep her informed of when he was going to be released. They hadn't though - she'd assumed they were too busy and she'd found out from Margaret a few weeks after he'd been let out. That hadn't given her a lot of confidence in them at the time. Still, I ought to give them the benefit of the doubt.

Her mind on to Gem. What was happening with her? She was sure her gut feeling was right and Gem was off the rails. She'd have to go and check on her again tomorrow. This time she would make sure that Gem was alright and if she wasn't she'd try to get her back in line. It wasn't too late to stop her from getting herself into big trouble again. Karen thought probably the other assistant in the charity shop might be able to help, maybe give her a clue as to where Gem was if she wasn't in the shop again. What was his name? Keith? No, Kevin, that's it. She made up her mind to ask Kevin. Of course she would have to be careful with the confidentiality issue and wouldn't be able to disclose who she was or anything about her relationship with Gem. She would have to do some thinking on to how to handle this.

Telling herself not to worry about all these problems, Karen picked up the telephone directory and looked up "Horse Riding", jotted down a couple of numbers into her diary and got herself ready for bed.

Chapter Thirty Eight

Catherine

Another day gone and still no sign of Joan. And now Catherine was worried about Kevin as well, who was never late for work and hadn't come in yet. After speaking to Gem the other day about visiting Joan, and what Gem had said about people not wanting their boss coming round to check up on them, Catherine had decided not to worry too much about it when Kevin hadn't turned up. But she couldn't stop herself from worrying.

She looked at the clock on the wall - eleven o'clock already and still no sign of either him or Joan. She was just wondering whether to phone Gem and ask her to come in early when the door opened and Kevin walked in. There was something about him that seemed different. She couldn't quite work it out, he just seemed not quite himself. Then she noticed his jacket had a small tear on the elbow. She knew how particular he usually was with his appearance and was going to mention it then thought perhaps it would be best to say nothing. So she just wished him a good morning and let him go into the back room without getting into conversation. Standing for a moment, staring after him, she purposefully walked across the shop floor to the doorway.

'Are you alright?' she asked.

'Yes, yes, I'm fine,' he answered. 'I was rather unwell and slept in. I hope it wasn't too inconvenient for you.'

'No, not inconvenient at all. I was just worried about you. It's not like you to be late. Are you sure everything is alright?'

'I said I was,' he snapped and went to put the kettle on. 'Are you having tea or coffee?'

'Oh - coffee, please,' she answered. 'Have you seen Gem?'

'No. I haven't seen her. I don't know why you think I would have seen her.' He frowned at her.

'I just thought, when I overheard you two talking, you seemed to be quite - thick with each other. I wondered if you were arranging to meet up after work maybe.'

'No. We weren't. We didn't. I don't remember that occasion.' Kevin picked up the kettle and took it into the cloakroom.

'No?' Catherine wasn't convinced. She stood in the doorway, watching him. 'Well, if you're sure there's nothing going on - nothing to do with Joan not being around?'

'Why? Why would you think that?' He looked at her sharply. She noticed a bead of sweat on his temple.

'Because you seemed concerned about Joan going missing, and when I talked to Gem about going round to her house to check up on her, she got upset. She made a good job of talking me out of it.' She looked at Kevin. 'Are you sure there's nothing you want to tell me?'

Kevin squirmed under her gaze. She knew he hated any kind of confrontation. He pushed past her and walked across the room to put the kettle on. She waited whilst he put coffee in two cups. Finally he took a deep breath and his shoulders slumped.

'I do need to tell you something,' he began. 'I've been very worried and don't know what to do for the best. My brain is all confused about things.'

'Well, perhaps it will help if you tell me what's happened. What's on your mind?'

'I went to Joan's house yesterday evening and got inside when the man opened the door. It wasn't Joan and she wasn't there. He was very angry with me and we had a fight and the next thing I knew I was in the cellar all tied up with rope. It was cold and damp down there and my jacket got dirty. I hate the dark and was very scared but then I could see some light coming from a window but it was barred and boarded up. I was there for a long time. I waited for someone to come so I could call out for help but no-one came and I fell asleep. When I woke up the window boards had been broken. I managed to get my hands free and escaped through the window and ran away. I looked in the freezer and saw something horrible in there. I was going to tell Mother when I got home but I didn't think that she'd believe me so I didn't tell her anything but I was very tired and went to bed. When I woke up it was very late - I was going to go to the Police but I didn't think that they would believe me either.' He paused. 'I have made up stories before, but it was a long time ago and I wouldn't do that now.'

Catherine stared at him, her mouth slightly open. She didn't quite know what to say.

'You don't believe me either, do you?' he asked.

'I want to,' she said. 'But it all seems a bit unlikely. Who was this man who hit you?'

'I don't know his name. He was at Joan's house the other day when I went there and there was a cat, too.'

'Well, if all of this is really true, then we must tell it to the Police.'

'No! I don't want to talk to the Police. You don't understand.'

'No I don't understand. Kevin, we must tell the Police. What exactly did you see in the freezer?'

'I think it was a body, rolled up in a blanket. I wanted to phone the Police. I was very frightened in that cellar.'

'Are you sure? A body? Now come on, Kevin, surely you must have been mistaken about that?'

'Well, I thought it was, but I might have imagined it. I was very scared down there. I wanted to get home more than anything.'

'Perhaps we'd better phone the police then? And then I'm going to phone Joan.'

'No. You can't do that. You mustn't. Because they will answer the phone and then they'll know where I work.'

Catherine sighed, frustrated. 'Alright, we must give this a bit of thought. What about Gem? What's her part in this? I do think that she's involved somehow. She is, isn't she?'

'Only that she came with me after the first time I went there and we sneaked round the back and she looked in the window. She seemed a bit shocked and said we shouldn't do anything for a while. I thought she knew more than she was letting on but I trusted her. She said she would sort it out and didn't want me to go to the Police yet. I don't know whether she's found anything out since then as I haven't seen her. She'll be in later today so she might know something more about it all. What do you think we should do? Wait and speak to Gem before we phone the Police, or just phone them anyway? They shouldn't have put me in the cellar, should they?'

It all sounded hugely far fetched to Catherine who wasn't one to want to waste the Police's precious time. Kevin's story, if it was just a story, seemed like a pure fantasy to her. 'Perhaps we'd better wait until we speak to Gem, then,' she said finally. ' A few hours more can't make much difference.'

Chapter Thirty Nine

Billy

He's running through the woods. It's raining hard and dark, so dark and he hasn't got a torch. He keeps stumbling over roots and dead branches that have fallen from the trees. He doesn't like the rain on his face. It's running down his neck, icy and cold. He can feel the rivulets down his back, sending shivers through his body, even though he feels hot and sweaty from what he's trying to get away from. Or is he trying to find something? Or someone? He realises that he's lost. Lost himself and lost someone. He's lost his Aunty Joan. She's here somewhere but he doesn't know where. He knows he's got to find her before it's too late. She can help him. She's the only one who can save him from himself.

Finally he reaches a clearing in the woods. It's still raining and the ground is muddy. The mud sticks to his shoes. He looks down and sees he's wearing Aunty Joan's slippers and they're caked with mud. He stops and tries to get the mud from his feet. He's scraping the slippers against a rock. The rock starts to move and as he watches, he sees that it's not a rock at all. There's a face looking up at him. Aunty Joan's face, her eyes are dead but still stare at him accusingly. He reaches down to help her up but as he takes a hold of her, she melts into mud in his hands. Now he's screaming and trying to run again but his feet won't move. They're completely stuck in the mire. He feels something gripping his ankles. It's Aunty Joan's hands. He can't get away. The screaming gets louder and louder.

Suddenly, he was awake. It took him a moment to work out where he was. The bed was damp from his sweat and the sheets were twisted around him, holding him down as he tried to sit up in panic. The feeling of relief that it was all a dream was short as he soon remembered Aunty Joan was, in fact, dead and really was buried in the woods somewhere. A feeling of desolation washed over him. I've got to get over this. There's nothing I can do about it now it's done. He got out of bed and staggered into the bathroom.

He leant over the sink and splashed water on his face. That was when he heard it for the first time.

'Murderer. You murdered Aunty. Murderer.'

It was quiet, almost a whisper and he was not really sure that he actually heard it or whether it was his own thoughts. He felt so much guilt anyway, so it probably did come from himself. Still, he found himself answering back.

'It was an accident. It wasn't my fault,' he said.

'Murderer,' came back the voice.

He stopped himself from looking around the small bathroom. No-one else could possibly be in there with him.

'Go away,' he pleaded.

'Murderer.' It was louder now. 'You murdered Aunty. Murderer.'

Billy was a bit scared but with all the drugs he'd taken in the past, stranger things had happened to him. He tried to ignore his feelings and made his way down to the kitchen. He put on the kettle and looked in the larder for something to eat.

'Murderer. You murdered Aunty. Murderer.'

'Shut up!' He looked around the room. 'Where are you?' He ran into the hall and then the sitting room. There was no one there. He bounded up the stairs and into Dan's room. It was empty. He looked into his own bedroom, opened the wardrobe and looked under the bed. No-one there either. Hesitating outside Aunty Joan's door, he was too scared to enter.

'What am I afraid of?' he shouted out loud as he made himself open the door. This room was empty too. He was just turning to leave the room when he heard it again.

'Murderer. You murdered Aunty. Murderer.' And it went on and on, a constant babble of words getting faster and faster until they were all muddled up and he could make no sense of them any more.

'Stop!' he shouted finally.

Silence.

The silence was so sweet that he laughed out loud. He sat down and waited for it to start up again. He was still waiting when he heard the front door. It was with great relief he realised it was Dan.

'Bloody Hell mate, you look awful,' Dan said. 'What you been doing? You had some bad acid?'

'No. I've had a bad dream, that's all. I'm alright now,' Billy said. 'What have you been up to?'

'It's not good,' Dan paused. 'I don't know how to tell you this, but we've been let down. I checked in the shed before I came in and she's still there.'

A cold chill shot through Billy. 'What do you mean? She can't be. She's in the woods. You said she was in the woods.'

'We've been stitched up mate. The bastards took our money and stitched us up. I don't know what to do about it now.'

'We can't leave Aunty out there in the fuckin' shed,' Billy said. 'She'll be going off already. She'll start to smell.'

'We'll have to put her back in the freezer until we can move her, then work out where to bury her ourselves,' Dan replied. 'We need to get some wheels but we'll have to move her back into the cellar for now.'

'Shit, shit, shit! The last thing we need is to be moving a body about in daylight. We'll have to do it tonight.'

'We can't wait until tonight. She'll be in a bad state by then. We'll have to do it now. It's Ok, we should be able to get away with it. She's still rolled up in that rug. There's some polythene out there, we can wrap her up in that too.'

After much huffing and puffing, they managed to get the body back down the cellar stairs and into the freezer. It was a bit more of a squeeze to get her in this time, what with the polythene wrapping but after some re-arranging of the vegetables below and the removal of some prime pieces of meat, they managed to stuff her in and forced the lid shut. At least this time Billy couldn't see her face as it was still wrapped up well in the carpet. He was trying not to think about his dream and the voice telling him that he was a murderer.

They took the frozen meat up into the kitchen. Billy dropped it into a carrier bag and left it by the back door ready to take to the bin. Then he locked the cellar door and shoved the key at the back of the cutlery drawer, out of sight.

'Right, Dan,' he said, feeling more in control now. 'You'll need to borrow us a van. Only - give me a bit of time to think. It's all too friggin' much for me at the moment. I need to think about the best place to put her.'

'What about the Bere Forest out at Wickham?' Dan suggested.

'Maybe. But a lot of people walk their dogs there. That could be a problem.'

'Not if you dig a deep enough hole - there are some quiet spots up there, away from the main paths. And you can drive in quite a way down through the woods.'

'Maybe. Just let me think about it.' Billy was feeling a bit sick. 'Come on, I've got to get out of the house for a bit. Let's go to the pub for a sandwich.'

'You got any money, then? I'm brassic.'

'I've got Aunty's bank card. She wrote her number down in her diary so I'll be able to draw some out.'

'Great! Come on then,' Dan got up and moved towards the door. He stopped and turned. Billy was still sitting there. 'What's up, mate?'

'Nothing. I'm coming,' Billy said. But it wasn't nothing. As he stood up he heard it again.

'Murderer. You murdered Aunty. Murderer.' Then there was a second voice. 'Thief. You're a thief.' And he knew that neither of the voices were Dan's.

Chapter Forty

Gem

There was a queue at the chemist. Gem was panicking without really knowing what she was panicking about. The chemist wouldn't know she'd used heroin just by looking at her and she only had to do the pee tests at the drug clinic, not here. She wasn't due to go to the clinic today anyway, although she had missed her appointment the day before so should have made the effort to see Karen today. Maybe I could drop in and see the duty worker, she thought. That way I could probably get away without having to do a test and it'll go down on my record that I did attend so Karen won't be on my case. If I can hold off from doing a test until after the weekend the heroin'll be out of my system and I'll get away with it.

She snapped out of her thoughts, realising she was about to be served. She could feel she was sweating and tried to look calm, smiling at the woman behind the counter as she asked for her script. The woman smiled back, asked her name before going into the pharmacy area. She seemed to take an age to find the bottle but it was probably only a few minutes later that she was back and handing it over to Gem.

Gem took the bottle and turned to leave.

'Wait,' the assistant said.

Gem turned. Her hands were shaking.

'You haven't signed the form,' the assistant thrust a pescription form across the counter and handed her a pen.

'Sorry.' She grabbed the pen and prescription form, and signed it quickly before passing them back. She was out of the door before the assistant could say anything more and hurried down the street and around the corner. She finally stopped and paused for breath, thinking about what an idiot she was, trying to calm herself before she walked swiftly home.

She started to feel a lot better once the Methadone was in her system and she sat in her front room, thinking about

Billy. Her thoughts were in a turmoil. But before she could think about what she needed to do next she was disturbed by a knock at the door. Reluctant to go downstairs, she looked out of the window and saw Billy down there, leaning against the door. He looked up and waved, mouthing to her to let him in. He didn't look too good, she could see that. She didn't really want to see him yet. There was too much going on in her head. But he was ringing the door bell again, persistantly, and knocking at the door. She ran down the stairs and quickly let him in.

'For God's sake!' she started at him, then saw his face. He looked awful - like he'd been tortured or something. 'What's up? You look terrible.'

'You gotta let me in, Gem. Can I come up?' He pushed past her and was already halfway up the stairs before she could even think of a reply.

'Be my guest,' she said to herself as she followed him up.

Billy was pacing the floor, from the window to the tv and back again. 'Come and sit down,' she said. Billy just looked at her and carried on pacing. She patted the seat next to her. 'Come on Billy, come here and sit with me for a while.'

Billy looked at her as though he'd only just noticed she was there. 'Sorry,' he said. He sat down but he wasn't relaxed. His legs were jiggling and he couldn't seem to keep his head still.

Gem took his hand. 'Talk to me,' she said. 'Tell me what's going on.'

'I'm not a murderer,' he looked straight at her. 'I'm not a fuckin' murderer, nor a thief. It wasn't my fault.'

'What are you talking about? What have you done?'

'Nothing! I didn't murder her.'

'Who? What are you talking about?' she repeated.

'Nothing.' He jumped up and started moving about again.

Gem got up too and moved towards him. She took his hand to try and stop him from pacing. 'Billy, something's not right. I don't know what it is, but you've got to let me help you. I can help you if you let me.'

'I don't know how to. I don't think you can. No one can help me. I can't talk to anyone about it, not even you.'

'Just sit down again and try to relax. You're so uptight.' She led him back to the sofa and they sat down again. Gem held his hand. Gradually he seemed to become less tense and leant towards her. She stroked his hair gently, trying to keep him relaxed. Finally she asked him again. 'Please, Billy, just talk to me.'

At last he started talking, not looking at her, just talking as though to himself.

'It was an accident. I bloody well loved my Aunty Joan. She was my last hope. She took me in when there was nowhere else to go and now she's friggin' well gone.' He started to sob quietly to himself.

'What was an accident?' Gem wasn't sure whether she wanted to hear this. 'What have you done?'

'I haven't done anything! I didn't do it on purpose,' he said, the agitation rising again in his voice.

'I'm sorry. I meant - tell me about the accident. What happened to your Aunty?'

'She fell over and hit her head.' He stopped, seeming to be listening to something. 'Alright, I pushed her, OK? Fuck it! Are you happy now?'

'What do you mean? How did it happen?' Gem persisted. 'You pushed her....?'

'She was getting bleedin' heavy with me about Dan being in the house and we had a tussle. She fell, I pushed her and she fell onto the fireplace. She was dead, Gem, I fuckin' killed her.' He was sobbing loudly now.

Gem held him, letting him cry on her shoulder and wondered what she could do now. A part of her was wishing that she didn't have this information, a part of her was glad that at last she knew what was going on.

'Where is she now?' she asked eventually.

'I can't tell you that,' he said.

'Is she in the cellar?'

He jumped up and glared at her. 'Yeah, you knew already, didn't you?' he said. 'That's why you were so interested in the friggin' cellar door. I saw you looking at it. You kept coming back to look at that door, didn't you?'

He sounded completely paranoid. Gem was feeling uncomfortable about him being there. She knew that things weren't right with him. Well, he's just told me he's a murderer, she thought, of course he's not right. But am I safe with him? She wasn't sure any more. He seemed to trust her one minute, then the next it was as though he wasn't listening to her, but having an argument - a conversation with someone else who was not there.

'I was worried about you, Billy, that's true,' she began. 'I don't like to think you've got into some kind of trouble. I know you love - loved your aunty, and that she was good to you. I don't believe you would have hurt her on purpose, but sometimes you get angry and do things you regret later, don't you? You've done it with me.'

'I know, and I'm sorry, Gem.' He sat back down, next to her.

'I understand that. You've got to tell me everything, though. I may be able to help you sort this out.'

He looked at her as though for the first time. 'Gem. I want you to help me. I want to trust you.' He paused, glancing over his shoulder. 'It was like I said. I was on my own with Aunty and she fell - I pushed her over and she hit her head. I'm not a murderer! She fell over. I was holding her and Dan came back in the room. I said that I'd killed her, she wasn't breathing. I ran out of the room - I couldn't stand being in the room with her being dead. A bit later, Dan came out to me and told me I was right, she was dead and we had to get rid of the body. We put her in the freezer down in the cellar. She was in there all that time. She's back in there now and I don't know what the fuck to do. We're supposed to be moving her, to bury her in the woods but I don't think I can do that. I gave some money to these bleedin' guys to get rid of her body but they screwed me for the money and didn't do the job. Now it's driving me effing mad thinking about it. What am I going to do?'

'I don't know, we need to think it all through,' said Gem. She knew the right answer was to tell the Police but this wasn't the time to say that.

'I don't think I can stand it for much longer, Gem,' he said. 'There's something else, too. This young bloke came round snooping and Dan bashed him and locked him in the cellar with Aunty. I think he knows what we've done. The only thing is, he escaped through the fuckin' window and now he's gone. I'm surprised the Police haven't been round yet to have a look.' He looked at her. 'Why are you looking at me like that?' he asked. 'Do you know him? Is that it?'

He jumped up and glared at her accusingly. 'You sent him, didn't you? You fuckin' well sent him to spy on me!' He dashed to the door.

'Wait,' Gem called after him. 'Don't be daft, why would I do that? Billy, please...' But he was already halfway down the stairs. Then he stopped and turned back.

'I can't leave you on your own now, can I?' he said as he came back up the staircase. 'You'll just be straight on the phone to the Police, won't you?'

'No, Billy, I won't,' she said, trying to reassure him. 'You can trust me.'

'I don't know any more. Just shut the fuck up and let me think.'

Billy sat down at the table, watching her. Gem couldn't think of anything to say so she just sat and waited. She was wondering how to deal with this situation as she watched him, watching her. Then he turned his head away and seemed to be listening again.

'What's the matter, Billy?' she asked. 'What is it?'

'I said to shut up!' he glared at her then turned away again. 'Yes, shut up! Shut up, I said! I'm not a murderer!' He turned his head the other way. 'I'm not a thief, either!'

'Who are you talking to?' asked Gem.

'No-one, just leave me alone!'

'There's nobody here but us,' Gem said.

'I can hear them talking to me,' he replied. 'They keep telling me I'm a murderer and a thief.'

'Who do?' Gem was feeling scared now. She'd never seen Billy in such a state before, even when he had been at his worst in the past.

'I don't know who they are but I can hear them talking to me. They just keep saying the same things. One says that I'm a murderer and the other one that I'm a thief. It's doing my effing head in, I can't make them stop and I can't get away from them. Can't you hear them?' He stopped, listened again, shaking his head. 'There! Did you hear that?'

'No,' she said. 'I didn't hear anything. Look, Billy, don't you think you need to get some help? Maybe you had some bad gear, or something. It may just pass off in time, but if it doesn't you should get seen by a doctor.'

'I don't want to see any doctor. I'm just stressed about all this shit I'm in.'

'OK, well, let's see if there's anything we can do to help you out of it.'

'I don't know what you can do to help.'

'What about if we just go back to your aunty's and see if we can sort it out.' She was thinking maybe he had imagined all of this and there was no body in the freezer. He'd been acting so weird and she knew what could happen with drugs sometimes. If only they could get to the freezer, have a look in it, then maybe Billy might snap out of this mood. 'Come on, let's go and do it,' she said.

'I suppose that could work,' Billy said. He didn't look very convinced but with a little more coaxing, they finally left the flat and headed off to Station Road.

Chapter Forty One

Kevin

Gemma didn't come to work today. I know that something bad must have happened to her but I can't talk to Catherine about it because she's already cross with me for worrying about Joan so much and she'll call the Police and they will tell me I'm wasting their time again. I don't want the Police going round my house either because I've still got that jade rabbit in my bedroom and that's stealing. I should have brought it back when I was thinking about it but I forgot. Everything is getting on top of me. I don't know what to do. It would have been alright if Gem had come in as I would have been able to talk to her about what's going on at Joan's house and she could have told me about everything she's found out.

What if Gem's been caught by that man? Perhaps he's locked her in the cellar like they did to me. I'm very worried about her. It's not nice in the cellar - dark and smelly and very cold and damp. And I don't like to think about that freezer and what might be in it. Did I imagine it? I might have done. No-one should have to go through that like I did. I was very brave though and managed to escape. Gem might be able to escape too, but she won't know how to because it'll be dark.

I've got to stop thinking like this. It's making me shake inside. Mother said I shouldn't let myself get stressed. I must stop thinking about it and do some work.

***

I've been trying hard not to think about it but I can't help it. I will have to talk to Catherine. It's the only thing left to do at the moment.

***

I did talk to Catherine. She listened to me and then told me to calm down. Mind you, I think she was as concerned as me when Gem didn't come in. She said that Gem would most probably be back tomorrow. I did remind her that she said that we should phone the Police about what happened at Joan's house but she said that we shouldn't do anything until we've talked to Gem. She didn't really believe me and I don't see how we can talk to Gem if she doesn't come to work though. I didn't tell her about the rabbit.

It's all too much isn't it? All the people who work here keep disappearing, including me. But I came back - I escaped from the cellar and got home and luckily my Mother hadn't noticed that I didn't come home that night. Maybe I should have told her at the time and she might have helped me. It's all getting rather difficult. I wish Gem was here. She'd know what to do.

Now I have to get on with my work. There's not a lot of stuff to do today. I sorted all the new stock that had been left at the door. There wasn't very much and it only took me an hour to clear all of the pile. There are lots of new things hanging in the shop now, all ready and priced up for the customers. I sorted through the books too and put them on the shelves in alphabetical order just as they should be. My mind kept wandering back to my problem though and now there's nothing much left to do I can't stop thinking about it.

***

Catherine let me go home early. It's only four-thirty now and I'm out in the street. I don't know whether to go straight home or not. I feel that I should try and find out if Gem's gone back to Joan's house but I must admit I am a bit scared to do that.

I don't want the fear to get the better of me so I make up my mind to go there anyway. I can't help feeling I'm going to regret this, but something draws me on and I turn into Station Road.

Chapter Forty Two

Gem

They turned the corner into Station Road, Gem still holding Billy's hand. She was hoping Billy had imagined all this stuff about his Aunty. She was thinking that yes, maybe they did have a tussle and maybe he had knocked her over but she would be alright somehow, somewhere. Perhaps she only went away to a friend's after all, just to get away from Billy. Gem couldn't imagine he could have put her in a freezer and just left her there.

They reached the front door and Billy let them in with his key. As soon as they had stepped inside the hall he turned to her.

'You've got to be strong, Gem,' he said. This isn't going to be nice.'

'I know,' she squeezed his hand. 'What about Dan? Where is he?'

'Don't worry, he's not here. He went to meet up with some mates and won't be back for at least a couple of hours.'

'Good. I really don't want to see him. I don't know why you hang out with him, Billy. He's bad news.'

'He's my mate.'

'So you keep saying, but I just don't trust him.'

'Whatever.' He let go of her hand and went into the kitchen, returning with the key to the cellar door. 'You coming then?' he asked.

The cellar was dark, even with the light on. The bulb was weak and there were shadows in the corners where the light didn't quite reach. It smelt damp and the air was cold, catching her throat as she followed him down. She could see the freezer, up against the wall under the window. She remembered being outside of that window, pulling at the wooden slats and shuddered at the thought that maybe Joan was inside this white, cold coffin all that time.

Billy moved to the freezer and opened the lid. Gem held back, not wanting to step any nearer.

'There she is,' he said. 'All wrapped up, just like I told you.' He sobbed and put a hand to his mouth.

'Oh my God!' Gem couldn't really tell if it was a body. All she could see was a rolled up carpet wrapped in polythene, but why would anyone put a carpet in a freezer? He must have been telling the truth. She didn't want to question him any more about this. What if he insisted they unwrap this gruesome parcel and she saw the dead eyes staring up at her?

'Now do you believe me?' he asked.

'Yes, of course I do. What are you going to do now?' She just wanted to get out of that place.

He turned to her, his eyes still glistening with tears but full of hope. 'It will be alright, if we can just get rid of her body. We're going to take her away and bury her somewhere. No-one will know. People just think she's gone away. I can sort this. If only the soddin' voices would go away. They will go away when Aunty's gone, won't they?'

'I don't know. Look, can we just go back upstairs? It's so cold in here,' Gem said. She could feel herself shaking. 'I don't like being down here. Please, just close the freezer and let's go upstairs.'

Billy gently shut the freezer lid and they climbed the stairs back up into the kitchen. Gem sat at the table, trying to stop the tremors.

'You're cold,' said Billy. 'It is cold down there.'

Gem was trying to think. What the hell had she got herself into now? She'd known getting back with Billy had been a mistake but she'd had no idea things were this bad. She had to get away, to go to the Police. It was time she handed this over to them. She felt like she was drowning, completely out of her depth. Kevin had been right all the time when he'd said that was what they should do. But she'd had to be sure and now it seemed as though things were even worse than she could have imagined. Billy's voice broke into her thoughts.

'Dan's going to borrow a van and then we're going to get rid of the body, just like I said. It'll be alright then. We can sort out all of Aunty's stuff and make this place our own. You can come and live here then. It'll be our own little home.'

'What?'

'You and me, Gem. Just like before only better,' he said. 'We won't have to worry about rent or anything. This house is all paid for, you know. We can make it lovely. You can make it lovely.'

'What are you talking about?' Gem was horrified. 'I can't come and live here. I've got my own place and you've got Dan living here.' She hesitated, realising Billy was not looking happy. She quickly went on. 'I mean, I couldn't live with you if Dan was staying here. I told you that already. And it's too soon for me to think about moving in with you again. I can't forget how things were with you before and you seem to have forgotten you smacked me again only the other day. You say you've changed but I'm not sure. Can't you see that?'

'I have changed, Gem. It's just the soddin' stress I'm under at the moment.'

'I don't know.'

'You don't know? You don't fuckin' know? Is that all you can say?'

'Well, it's the truth. And what about Dan? What do you plan to do about him - your so-called mate?'

'I'll get rid of him.' Billy said. 'I would have done before, but I need him to help me get rid of Aunty Joan. I can't do that on my own.'

Gem shivered.

'You're still cold. Come here,' he moved towards her and took her in his arms. She flinched. 'What's up now?' he snapped and pushed her away again.

'Nothing, I'm just upset, that's all,' she said. 'It's not everyday you get taken into a cellar and get shown a dead body wrapped up in a carpet.'

'Shut up!' Billy shouted. 'You're just like them.'

'Like who?'

'Them. Those ones who keep telling me I'm a murderer. I'm not a murderer. I'm not.'

'I'm not saying you're a murderer, Billy. It's just I can't get my head around what's happened here. I know sometimes you can get stroppy and you've hurt me in the past but I don't believe you would ever want to kill anyone, especially not someone you love. Only, the drugs you've been doing could have tipped you over the edge, maybe. I don't know what to think, that's the truth of it. And I can't believe you would bury your Aunty in the woods and just carry on as if nothing had happened. She'd dead, Billy - and you are responsible, however it happened. You should man up and face what you've done.'

'I'm in a fuckin' mess, Gem. You've got to help me, please.' He seemed to crumble in front of her.

'Don't you think you should get some professional help?'

'Go to a Doctor, you mean?'

'Maybe. We're out of our depth here, Billy.'

'Then I'd end up in prison, or in one of them hospitals, bleedin' loony bins. No thank you.'

'But you need help.'

'No I don't. I just want to get things tidied up here and everything will be fine.'

'Do you really believe that? Nothing will be fine all the while you pretend you're OK when you're obviously not. Listen Billy, you've got to let me help you.'

'I want you to help me. That's what I've been saying all along. I love you, Gem.'

'Don't say that. You don't love me, not really. You just think you do.'

'I do. You're the only one who can help me now.'

'What about Dan?'

'I'm just using Dan to get rid of the body. Once that's done, he's history.'

'I wish I could believe that, Billy,' Gem was thinking about how she could get out of there, frantically trying to work out a plan to get away.

'I mean it, Gem,' he said. 'Let's go upstairs and lay down for a while. You're still shaking. We could cuddle up under the covers. Come on.'

She sighed and stood up. That was the last thing she wanted to do but felt she should humour him. 'OK. Just for a little while then. But I'm not staying long. I've got things to do at home and need to be at work later. I know it's only a volunteering job but it's important to me and I've already missed one shift this week.'

'I don't know why you care so friggin' much.' Billy took her hand and led her up the stairs to the bedroom.

'I just do,' she answered, thinking she would get away as soon as she could. Hopefully he would fall asleep and she'd slip away without waking him. All of this was terrifying. He was a time bomb waiting to go off and she didn't want to be around him when he reached exploding point.

Chapter Forty Three

Billy

Everything's a bloody mess. I think I convinced Gem to stay with me but soon she'll want to go away again and those voices still keep telling me that I'm a murderer. I don't know how to get rid of them. They keep on and on at me all the time. Being with Gem has only given me a bit of breathing space but I've got to keep her with me. When she's here talking to me it's not so bad. I can deal with anything then.

After showing her the freezer and Aunty all wrapped up in that carpet and stuff, I thought she'd understand and know how to make me feel better but it just seemed to make her more distant to me, like she was scared of me. I've seen that look in her eyes before. I've got to make her see I won't ever hurt her again. I never meant to before. I bloody love her.

Gem's awake now and I'm holding her. I stayed awake all afternoon because I didn't really trust she wouldn't leave me once I fell asleep. It took her ages to settle down but she finally drifted off. I lay here just looking at her sleeping. When she woke up and it was nearly five o'clock she looked a bit surprised at first. I'm glad I stayed awake, watching her. We're still in bed and it's so nice. She makes me feel safe when we're here together like this. But she's telling me that she's got to go home - that she wants to be in her own place so she can think. I don't really want her to be away from me, nor to think too much neither. We need to be together all the time, I tell her, but she's adamant she wants to go back to her bloody flat. I don't want her to do that. I'm not sure I can trust her not to tell someone but I'm scared if I try and stop her, she'll turn against me. Because I promised not to hurt her again I hold back.

So I agree she should go to her flat but manage to persuade her I should come with her. She doesn't look very happy about this but shrugs her shoulders and agrees. As we leave the house I see her looking at the cellar door again. I nearly snap at her then to stop looking at it like that but I stop myself from saying anything and we're soon on our way to her place.

Chapter Forty Four

Kevin

There was a bench part of the way along Station Road which was half hidden by an overgrown shrub which leans over the fence of the garden it was next to. Kevin was still unsure of whether to go too close to number 59 in case he was spotted by that man - the one who hit him before, or even that other one. Neither of them were very nice to him, were they? His gut feeling told him he should be very careful so he decided to just sit on the bench and wait. He was not sure about exactly what he was waiting for but imagined that just like detectives in the tv programmes he watched sometimes, something would happen sooner or later and then he would get some answers. It was better than doing nothing, after all.

He must have been sitting there for at least an hour when he saw the front door of number 59 opening. He nearly fell off the seat in surprise when he saw who it was coming out. First of all it was that red-haired young thug, but he was followed very closely by a figure who was all too familiar to Kevin. It was Gem! So she did come back! He felt betrayed for a moment then he wondered if she had been taken hostage like he had been. Perhaps they would have thought twice about putting a woman into that cellar. It had been horrible down there. He watched for a moment, trying to see what her facial expressions were like. She certainly didn't look very happy. Then he realised if he stayed on the seat watching them, they were going to have to walk right past him and that wouldn't do at all. They were still far enough away for him to get away, he thought, but to make sure, instead of walking away, he ducked down behind the shrub. He hoped he wouldn't be seen by them if he stayed there until they had passed.

His heart was beating so loud that he imagined that they could hear it but they walked on past without looking round and soon they'd gone on down the road. Still, he stayed there for a bit longer, just to make sure before he crept out again. Before long they'd gone out of sight round the corner and into the High Street. He wondered whether he should have followed them but decided that this could be his chance to have a look through the windows into the house. He thought maybe he could look in the cellar again even though that was the last place that he wanted to go back to. It was important though, to find out what had happened to Joan. After all, why would they make him a prisoner if they had nothing to hide?

Rather than approach the house from the front, he made his way around to the back, along the street and through the alley into the garden. He remembered the shed at the bottom by the rear gate and noticed that the door was swinging open. There were a lot of things in the shed. He peered in through the doorway. It looked as though something had recently been moved - there were cobwebs across the back part of the shed, but none in the front and there were scuff marks on the floor in the dirt. There were boxes piled up, some of the contents spilling out, old clay pots, a pair of secatuers, some old rags. He wondered who may have been rummaging in here. This was surely a clue to something amiss.

He was just about to make his way towards the house when the back gate opened. He ducked into the shed and hid behind the door. It wasn't very nice in there, cobwebs swept across his face. He wanted to sneeze but was afraid he'd be found so he held his nose tightly between his fingers. He could just see out of the window and watched. It was the man who had hit him and put him in the cellar. Kevin held his breath as the man passed by. He waited, listening to the footsteps moving away and up the garden path to the house. He could hear a key in the door and then the man cursing as the keys fell to the ground, clanking on the concrete, then finally the successful opening of the door. The door slammed shut but Kevin waited for what seemed like a long time before he crept out from behind the door again.

He could see the kitchen window from where he was, so watched as the man's form moved about the room. Kevin was too scared to come out of the shed whilst that man was in the kitchen. What if he looked out of the window and saw me. He waited. After a while, he couldn't see the man any more. Hoping that he must have gone into one of the other rooms, Kevin tentatively moved out into the garden and quickly ran back to the gate. He was too scared to do anything else but get out of the place. He forgot what he even went back there to do as he opened the gate and ran all the way down to the end of the alleyway as fast as he could before he stopped to catch his breath.

Chapter Forty Five

Karen

After a restless night, her head full of worries and night demons, Karen tried to shake off her troubles and decided to make contact with Gem again. First she went to Gem's flat but there was no answer. There was only one thing for it. She would have to go to the charity shop. She thought that Gem maybe working there that morning. She wouldn't have been very happy at Karen turning up at the shop but it was the only thing that she could think of to try and make sure that Gem was still coping with things. She thought that perhaps meeting Gem away from her flat could be a better idea anyway.

The shop was quiet. Karen peered through the window, wondering to herself whether she would cope if she had to work in such a place. Shop work would be quite nice, she was thinking. Less stressful than working with drug users anyway - just sorting clothes and dealing with customers. The shop seemed empty apart from the young man, Kevin, who was standing behind the counter, looking through a pile of books.

Karen entered the shop and made her way towards him.

'Good morning madam,' he said, smiling brightly at her. 'How can I help you?'

'Actually, I was looking for Gem,' she said. 'Is she in today?'

'No, she isn't. She was meant to be but she just hasn't turned up. I'm a bit annoyed with her actually,' he frowned. 'I don't suppose you know where she might be?'

'She's not at her flat. I've just been there and it's all quiet.' Karen paused. 'Look, to be honest, I was hoping that you might be able to help me. She's my friend and I've noticed that she's not been so well lately.'

' She was very well the last time I saw her.'

'When did you last see her?' Karen asked.

'Only yesterday,' he answered. 'But I didn't speak to her. She didn't see me. I just saw her in the street.'

'Oh? Where was that?'

'You're very curious,' he was giving her a suspicious look.

'Only because I'm worried about her. I need to see her. Please, I don't mean to be so... I'm just her friend, that's all.'

'No. I'm sorry.' He paused. 'You look like a nice person. I will tell you. I'm worried about her too. It's not like her to let us down. She knew we would be here on our own this morning. I was just going to phone Catherine - she's the manager here. But I have to tell you something has happened and I'm not sure but I think that Gem has got in with some not very nice people.'

'What do you mean?' Karen felt uneasy.

'Well, Mrs. Clarke who works here has gone missing and Gem and myself have been doing a bit of detective work to try and find out what's happened to her. We went to her house but she wasn't there. I didn't like it when I knocked on the door and this young man came out. He was very rude to me and looked like a nasty type of person. Gem came with me when I went back and she looked in the window at the back of the house. She seemed upset and we left straight away. Gem told me that we shouldn't do anything and that she would sort it out. I felt uncomfortable about this and after a day of waiting I went back but the man locked me in the cellar and left me there. It was horrible.'

'Wait a minute! You were locked in the cellar?'

'No-one believes me. I was locked in the cellar, and tied up but I escaped through a broken window and ran away. I told Gem and she was going to try and sort it out but then she didn't come back. I went to look for her and I was watching the house when she came out with one of the men.'

'How many men were there? You only mentioned one.' This sounded all very confusing to Karen, and a little far fetched, she thought.

'Sorry, there were two men. One was tall and he was the one who hit me and put me in the cellar. The other one was short and had ginger hair. He came into the house after the other man had hit me. I was very scared but didn't tell my Mother as I know she wouldn't believe me and she didn't even notice that I'd been out all night.'

'So who did you tell?'

'I told Catherine but she wanted to wait until Gem came in. She didn't really believe me. She said we should wait and talk to Gem about it all before we did anything. But Gem didn't come in and now I don't know what to do.'

'You should have phoned the Police.'

'I wanted to do that but I've told stories to them a long time ago and they said that I'd be in big trouble if I wasted their time again and I would go to prison so I didn't want to trouble them.'

Karen looked at him, beginning to doubt his account of events. 'Maybe you're right,' she said. 'Perhaps Gem will turn up soon. You say you saw her yesterday with one of the men. How did she look?'

'She looked unhappy, that's what I thought at first. They came out of Joan's house and walked all the way down the road and into the High Street. Should I have followed them?'

'I don't know. What did you do?'

'I went round the back of Joan's house, down the alley and was going to look in the window but the other man, the tall one who hit me, came through the gate and went in through the back door. I hid in the shed. It was quite scary. I didn't want to be in the cellar again.'

'No, of course not. Look, you've helped me a lot. I think I'll go and check out this house. Where is it?'

'It's in Station Road, number Fifty Nine,' he said. But please be careful.'

'I will. It's alright. I'm sure there's an explanation for this, and if anything is going on, they won't know me, will they. I'll be perfectly safe.'

'Will you let me know?' Kevin asked. 'I'm very worried about Joan - that's Mrs. Clarke. I don't think she would have gone away without telling us. She's usually so reliable, like me. We're similar, you know. She works hard and is very conscientious. I know she wouldn't just go away.'

'OK. Don't worry about it any more. I will get to the bottom of it.'

'Thank you.' He sighed to himself. 'Now I think I had better telephone Catherine and see if she can get someone to cover for Gem. Oh dear, I hope Gem is alright.'

Karen turned to leave. 'Me too,' she said as she left. 'Me too.'

Chapter Forty Six

Peter

Everyone thinks I'm a violent man. Of course I'm not - I've only lost my temper once in my life and that wasn't my fault. I've always tried to do the right thing - take care of Mother - I always make sure that she never wants for anything.

When I was with Karen, everything I did was for us. All I wanted was for us to have a happy marriage, that we would be together, bringing up our children in the right way. Things would have been alright if only she hadn't changed. When we were first married, she was a good wife. She worked in an office, shopped in her lunch-hour and cooked nice meals for us every evening. We did things together. Things like walking on the beach, going to the pub for drinks, or to the cinema. We didn't need friends because we had each other. Well, I had a couple of mates that I used to go out drinking with after work, but she didn't. A woman doesn't need friends when there's a good man at home after all, and she was too shy and quiet really. I didn't mind. I liked having her to myself.

Then she got ill and had that operation. It was after that, she started to turn into another person. She got it into her head she had to be a nurse. Not just a normal nurse, that wouldn't have been so bad. No, she wanted to be a psychiatric nurse and got herself a job in the mental hospital. I couldn't believe she could have been so stupid. I told her so, too, but that only seemed to make her more determined to do it.

It wasn't long before things started to go wrong in our relationship. I tried very hard to make things good again but whatever I tried seemed to be wrong. She didn't want to be at home, that was the problem, started working long hours, was never home to cook any more, and then she even went off sex - she didn't want to know me any more.

Things came to a head when she told me that she was pregnant and that the baby wasn't mine! You can imagine how it was for me. Betrayed doesn't come close to it. I tried to tell her how I felt but she didn't want to know. I said the best thing for our marriage, if she wanted to save it, was to have an abortion. She went completely crazy when I suggested that and I had to restrain her in the end. She stayed a bit mad through the next few months, started to hit me, stopped eating - I had to feed her. I did get her to see a doctor and he gave her some tablets but she was refusing to take them. In the end I had to insist on it but after that she only got worse.

I decided that the best thing to do would be to take her away for a while and we stayed in a house belonging to one of my colleagues whilst he was away. I thought that this would help but it didn't. On the last night there, she attacked me and I had to hold her down again. This time, though, she wouldn't calm down and so I had to hit her. It was completely in self-defence and I was going for help when she managed to get out of the house and run next door. The lies she told about me!

The Police took me away despite me trying to tell them it was she who'd attacked me and not the other way round. They never believed me, not then, nor did the jury later in the court. It's so wrong, how women are always seen as the victim - surely they could see that I was only doing what I had to do.

Then I was sent to prison. A long time away to think about things. It would have been even worse except I was saved by Carol. She was a prison visitor. Well, it actually started with her just writing to me. She was one of those volunteers - a do-gooder, I thought at the time. After a few letters, I got curious and asked her to visit me. She was nice looking and very understanding. I told her all about how Karen had behaved and she gave me a lot of sympathy. She helped me a lot while I was in prison.

Prison wasn't all bad to be fair. They gave me a job in the library, a nice cushy number. I just had to make sure all the books were in the right places, to stamp the cards and the books when they were taken out, and to sort out the newspapers for the prisoners each day. The Governor liked me. They didn't often have university educated prisoners to deal with. He said that I was like a breath of fresh air in the place. I was glad to be in the library. Not all of the prisoners were nice people. I kept myself to myself as much as I could. I have to admit it was a bit of a culture shock when I first went in - they had to put me on medication to help me over the first few months. I don't really like to think about it any more.

When I left prison, I stayed with Mum for a few weeks but didn't have to be there for long because Carol was waiting for me. She had a nice little house of her own, semi-detached on the outskirts of Salisbury. She wanted me to move in with her straight away, to look after me. I did think that maybe it was a bit quick and considered staying with Mother for a while longer, but in the end I decided that I deserved a bit of happiness and Carol is an attractive woman. I hadn't been with a woman for a long time, after all. So I moved in and we started planning to get married. I didn't want to lose her, you see. But she kept saying we should wait a bit. I kept my patience even though being married would have been the answer and if we had been married, we would still be together now probably.

I think things started to cool off after about three years. It was the same old story. First flush of love and excitement, then after a time together, things start to get stale. She began complaining she was bored and wanted to go out more with her friends. She, unlike Karen, had friends, women who used to come to the house when we were first together. They were noisy, giggling women, always laughing at stupid jokes I never understood. I eventually managed to get Carol to agree with me they should meet somewhere else, which was a great relief. She still went out to meet them though, much to my annoyance. You would have thought that she didn't need all those friends when we had us.

Then one day, she confronted me. She said she'd heard that the reason I'd been in prison wasn't exactly as I'd described. I'd told her it was all a mistake and I'd only pled guilty to save Karen from having to go to court - which was the truth even though no one had believed me at the time. I asked her who'd she been talking to but she wouldn't say. She said she was disgusted with me and couldn't live with a wife-beater. I told her that I wasn't a wife-beater. We'd been together for years and I'd never so much as laid a finger on her or raised my hand even though I'd been tempted sometimes. She said it was true, that I hadn't physically hurt her. Then she started having a go at me for trying to control her life. She was shouting that I'd tried to make her give up her friends which is a downright lie. I've never done such a thing.

Anyway, we rowed for a bit longer about this, and about other things but in the end she seemed to calm down and backed off. I thought everything was going to be alright again after that - it certainly appeared that things were OK between us. She even seemed to be making more of an effort to be a good woman to me - cooking nice meals, pleasing me in bed without me having to ask - that sort of thing.

But then one day, I came home from work and she was gone. All her things were packed up and gone. There was a note on the table which said that she's decided that she couldn't do it any more and that she wouldn't be back. She'd gone to stay with her daughter who lived in Manchester. Manchester, of all places! I was devastated.

For three weeks I walked around the house, trying to find clues as to why she'd gone. Trying to work out who'd got at her and turned her against me. I think I nearly went a bit mad during those three weeks. Then I started to put things together in my mind. It had to have been Karen, I thought. She must have been in contact with Carol and poisoned her against me. I started to think more and more about Karen and how she'd betrayed me. Firstly by sleeping with another man, secondly for giving birth to that brat, and thirdly for all the lies she'd told that had ended with me going to prison for something I never did. And now, she's ruined my relationship with Carol. That was when I decided that enough was enough and it was time she paid for everything that she'd done.

Chapter Forty Seven

Gem

She was trying hard to think. They were walking back to her flat and she was panicking inside, desperately searching for ideas on how to get out of this situation. She wondered if she should just break away from him, run away and go straight to the Police. That was easier said than done, though. The Police station was just too far away. She could just give him the slip and dash into a shop. There weren't many people about though so that may not have worked. If she was honest to herself, she knew she was just too confused about her feelings at that moment. On the one hand she was sure she should try and get away while they were out in the open but something was holding her back. Before she could work out what to do, they were already at the flat.

She unlocked the door and they climbed the stairs. She turned to him, hoping to persuade him to leave.

'Look, Billy, I need some time on my own. Please give me some space. I promise I won't do anything. I won't tell anyone.'

'Sorry, Gem,' he looked at her. 'I'm not fuckin' well going anywhere, you might as well get used to it.'

She sighed. 'OK. But I'm going to have a shower. You'll have to stay out here.'

'Wait,' he went into the bathroom, checking the window.

'Don't worry. I'll never get through that little gap,' she said.

'Alright,' he replied. 'I'll be here waiting for you.'

'Make yourself at home,' she knew that she sounded sarcastic. 'Have a coffee, anything you want.'

He ignored her sarcasm. 'Thanks, I will. Do you want one?'

'Alright. I won't be long.'

She went in and locked the door, listened as she heard him filling the kettle in the kitchen, then she flushed the toilet and opened the small window at the top of the window frame. She could just about see out into the back alley behind the flats. There was a car park at the end which serviced the shops below. She wished she could climb out of the window. Now she was in her flat she was not sure what she could do, and cursed herself for not having done something before they'd reached the flat. It was too late now and she would just have to play along with him - hopefully there'd be an opportunity later. He couldn't stay with her for every hour of the day and night, surely? Soon enough he'd need a fix of something, either smack or at least some tranqs or alcohol.

It was almost as if he was reading her mind, or maybe she just knew him too well. When she emerged from the bathroom, he was pacing about and sweating.

'Are you alright?' she asked, sitting down on edge of the sofa. 'What's up, need a fix?'

'No!' he snapped back at her. 'I don't feel too good, that's all.'

'Well, I haven't got anything to make you feel better. If you need anything, you'll have to go and get it.'

'I just need to make a phone call,' he answered. 'Where's your phone?'

'You're not bringing any of your dealer friends in here.' Gem bristled.

'Don't worry, I wasn't planning to. I just need to make a call. Where's the bloody phone?'

'It's in the kitchen, on the fridge. Where it's always been.' She sat and waited while he moved into the kitchen. She could hear him talking on the phone. He was agreeing to meet his contact in the precinct in half an hour. Good, that'll be my chance to be alone and to get away from him. But then she heard him change his mind. He was telling his dealer to come to the flat. She was furious and stood in the doorway, glaring at him. 'I said not here!' she shouted. He waved his hand at her to be quiet.

As soon as he was off the phone, she started on him again. 'I said I didn't want any dealers in here, and I meant it.

You really don't care what you do to other people, do you? He's not coming in. Do you understand?'

'Don't worry, I won't let him in. But I can't trust you yet. When he gets here, I'll go downstairs and get the stuff. You won't even have to see him. There's no way we're going out to the precinct or anywhere else yet.'

Gem's hopes sank as she grasped about for another way out of this. 'I don't want you using drugs in my flat,' she said. 'You promised me that you'd stop, and here you are only a few days later, bringing stuff in here. You've already injected me once and nearly messed up my treatment. I don't like it, Billy. I know you've been through a bad time but using more drugs isn't going to help.'

Even as she spoke the words she knew that he wouldn't have been able to stop using with all of this going on. It was hard enough to do it when things were settled in your life. The only way out was to ask for help, to get on a treatment plan, or go to a rehab where you couldn't get hold of anything, where you were completely cut off from everything - drugs, people, chaotic lifestyle, even your family for a while. Even after getting through all that it was hard. It was so easy to slip back into using once you'd had a taste for it. Life could be a bastard sometimes.

'I will stop,' he said. 'I just need to get through this and I'll be fine. I will do it, but not today. Just stick with me. I friggin' need you, can't you see that?'

'How can you pay for it, anyway?' she asked. 'You've got no money coming in at the moment. Are you dealing yourself?'

'No. Of course not.' He paused. 'I had some money at the house.'

'You mean you took it from your Aunty?'

'No. I didn't take any money. I sold some stuff. Some old crap that wasn't needed any more.'

'Your Aunty Joan's things? You took them from her room?'

228

'Stop it! Stop it!' He grabbed her shoulders, his grip painful as he shook her. 'That's what he said! I'm not a thief!'

'I didn't say you were. Christ, Billy, calm down. I only said ....'

'He said I was a thief. And the other one said that I was a murderer. I can't bleedin' stand it. They went away for a while but now you've made them come back, so shut up about Aunty Joan, will you!'

Just then there was a knock at the door.

'That was quick,' she said, almost relieved to have something to distract Billy from his tormenting voices. She went to look out of the window to see who was there. 'It must be him. I don't recognise him.'

Billy moved to her side and looked out, then started down the stairs. 'Stay here,' he looked up at her. 'And just keep quiet.'

She could hear him talking to the guy at the door who seemed keen to come into the hallway. Billy let him in but kept him downstairs and soon he was back with her, after sending the dealer on his way again.

He started to lay out his paraphenalia on the dining table.

Gem turned away. 'I don't want to see this,' she said and went into the bedroom, slamming the door behind her. She sat on the bed, her head was thumping, her hands were shaking, she felt sick and she realised she was actually craving for a fix herself. I don't need it, she told herself, over and over, I don't need it and I don't want it. If Billy wants to keep ruining his life then that's up to him. I'm not going to let it get to me. But even as she was saying the words to herself she knew it was getting to her and it was only a matter of time before she would fall into the trap herself.

She started pacing the floor, looking out of the window at the sky, even the clouds seemed to be laughing at her, telling her she would never be free of this prison that addiction to heroin was. Once in your blood, always in your blood.

Chapter Forty Eight

Kevin

I really wish I hadn't gone to the house after all. It was worrying me to think that Gem might be involved in whatever had happened to Joan. She didn't look very happy as they came out of the house but she was with him, with that young man who was there when I was in the cellar. How could she have been with him? She must have already known him before. Before all this happened. Of course, that's it. When we went there the first time she acted very strangely after she looked in the window and saw who was in there. She knew him all the time!

I don't know what to do now. I've been thinking about it all night. I tried to talk to Mother about it but she was watching Countdown and wouldn't listen to me. I'm getting very confused about it all. I should go to the Police. I really ought to but I'm scared to. The last time I spoke to a Policeman he wasn't nice to me. I will do it, though. Today. But first I have to look after the shop. It's Catherine's afternoon off and it's supposed to be me and Gem here today but it's already half past one and she's not here yet. She's obviously still with that man. Oh, dear, I do hope she's alright. What should I do? Stop thinking about it and get on with my work. Yes, that's what I'll do. There's so much to do in the shop this afternoon. Being on my own isn't right but I will cope. I will.

Chapter Forty Nine

Billy

Having the fix made me feel a bit better. The voices seemed to go quiet for a while but everything's still in a mess. The trouble was I couldn't just relax because I was thinking about Gem wanting to get away from me. So I only had a small amount and as soon as I felt more chilled I went into her bedroom with the needle all ready for her. She didn't make much of a fuss about it - it seemed as though she wanted it. She's been having this battle with herself but I knew that the drug would win in the end. As soon as she saw how cool I was, she held out her arm and let me give her the stuff. Alright, I do feel a bit guilty about getting her back on it. I know how effin' hard it is when you're trying to stop but I didn't have any choice. She might have gone to the cops and then I'd be in deep shit. I was feeling that it would all be OK now. I could beat anything if Gem was with me.

I woke up much later. I wasn't sure where I was at first, or even what day it was. Then as I came round I remembered - Gem's flat, the fix, and my worries about her grassing me up. I was wishing that I'd not shown her Aunty Joan in the freezer. It all felt wrong now. I looked at the clock - it was ten o'clock. I'd been out of it all night. Then I noticed that she wasn't in the bed with me so I jumped up and ran out of the bedroom. The flat was empty. She wasn't in the bathroom or anywhere in the flat. The bitch had run out on me. How could she do that after all I'd done for her. I'd shared the smack with her, hadn't I? I really thought she was with me and now she'd gone.

The voices started talking to me again. First it was just 'Murderer. You murdered Aunty.' Then it was 'Thief. You're a thief.' But there was something else. Another one telling me that I was a dirty junkie.

I started answering them back. 'Just fuck off, will you? I'm not a junkie, nor a murderer. I'm not.' I couldn't stand it and started to think that maybe they were in the flat with me. I looked everywhere. I pulled open all the cupboards and threw all the stuff onto the floor so that no-one could be hiding anywhere. But they were too good at hiding. I pulled out the drawers in the bedroom and in the kitchen too. I couldn't find anyone anywhere. I sat down at the kitchen table and cried but they kept on at me. I knew I had to get out of there. But it was dangerous everywhere so I grabbed the carving knife from the draining board, and hiding the knife under my jacket, I left the flat.

I made my way back to Station Road, sure that Gem must have gone back there. I didn't really believe that she'd been a grass. It's just not in her nature but I hadn't got very far along the main street before I bumped into Dan.

'Hey mate,' he said. 'Where've you been?'

'Just sorting things out with Gem,' I answered, reluctant to let him know exactly what was going on, even though I was sort of relieved he was still about. 'What's happening about the van?' I asked.

'That's why I was looking for you. I've sorted it. We get the van tonight. The sooner we get it done the better. I'm getting sick of having this little problem hanging over us.'

'Yeah, me too,' I said. 'I was just going back to the house now. You coming?'

'I've got a couple of things to do first. Have you got rid of that bitch then?'

'Not exactly,' I said. 'Don't call her a bitch. We're together - at least I'm hoping that we are. You'll just have to accept that, won't you?'

'You idiot! We don't need a woman around to mess things up.'

He was really starting to get on my nerves, but I held my tongue. It'll all soon be over, I thought.

Just at that moment, she came out of the Co-op carrying a bag of groceries. She almost collided with me and her face lit up. Then she saw Dan, gave me a filthy look of disgust and walked away, back in the direction of her flat.

'Gem,' I called after her but she just kept on walking, faster this time.

'What's up with her?' Dan asked.

I turned to him, told him I'd see him later and then I ran after Gem. I caught up with her just outside her place and grabbed hold of her arm. She spun round to face me.

'I'm sorry, Billy, but I just can't like that man. There's something about him that gives me the creeps. I wish you'd keep away from him.'

'I just bumped into him. I was looking for you,' I tried to explain. 'I thought you'd ran out on me.'

She held up the shopping. 'I was getting some food in. Look - let's get inside shall we. We need to talk.'

As soon as we got in the flat she saw the mess I'd made when I was looking for where the voices were coming from. It looked at though someone had come in and turned her place over, which was in fact what had happened. Only I knew it was me. She was shocked. I realised then that the knife was still there, under my jacket so I went into the kitchen to get rid of it before she noticed. Suddenly I couldn't think why I'd picked it up in the first place.

'Someone's been here! The bastards!' she was saying as she ran from room to room. Then she looked at me funny like. 'It was you, Billy, wasn't it? You did this after I went out.'

I couldn't deny it, could I? 'I was upset. I thought you'd friggin' grassed me up. Then I started to get those voices again. I thought they were hiding in your cupboards. That's what it sounded like. They're not there all the time. They just come and go and I can't stand them. If you'd been here with me it would have been alright.'

So she came over and held me, just like she used to in the early days. She started stroking my hair and telling me it was OK but of course I knew it wasn't really. 'We need to sort this out,' she said.

'It's better when you're with me. I just want you to stay with me and the voices won't be so bad. Will you stay?'

She didn't say anything for a long time. In the end, she just looked at me. 'Let's tidy up this mess. I can't do anything with all this mess.' And she started moving about the flat, picking up stuff and putting things back in the cupboards and drawers. 'Don't just stand there watching me, you did it so you can help clear it up,' she said. Eventually, it was looking more like it did before I went beserk. She put away the shopping and we sat down in the kitchen. That was when she started talking seriously to me.

'Right, Billy. I've been thinking about us, the drugs, everything. I didn't want to ever get back with you and I certainly never wanted to get back on the smack. Now it seems I've done both the things I said I didn't want. At first I was just doing it because I could see you were in trouble and wanted to find out what you were up to.' She paused, looking at me. 'Don't look at me like that,' she said. 'I was worried. And when your Aunty Joan went missing and people at work were snooping about at the house, I realised you were in it up to your neck. You can't blame me for worrying. When I saw you at the house I thought I'd ask you what was going on, to give you a chance to make whatever it was you'd done right. Before anyone went to report her missing to the Police, I mean.'

'What about now - I've told you what happened to Aunty.' I suddenly felt afraid. 'Who else have you spoken to? Who else knows?'

'No-one. I haven't told anyone what you told me. To be honest, I didn't believe you at first, but when you showed me the body - well, that scared me and now I don't honestly know what to do about it. I want to help you and I don't want to see you in prison.'

'You can help me by just being with me.' I was pleading now.

'Maybe I can,' she said. 'But there's more going on with you now. I'm worried about these voices you keep on about. It's obvious there's more wrong with you than you realise. You need help, Billy. Going to prison won't help you, will it?'

'You can, though.' I was scared to death she was going to leave me.

'I can't, Billy. I'm out of my depth with all this going on. I can't do anything about the fact you've killed your Aunty, can I?'

'I didn't bloody well murder her!'

'I'm not saying that. It was an accident, wasn't it? Only, you're going to be in trouble when they find her body. You should have owned up straight away and it would have been alright. I think it's messing up your mind, I really do. If you can sort it out, maybe the voices will stop.'

'It will be alright once we've moved her out of the house. It's going to happen soon. Dan's got the van sorted. We're moving her tonight.'

'Where to? You can't just dump her somewhere. I don't like this, Billy.'

'You don't have to be involved. We're going to bury her somewhere nice. Somewhere a long way from where anyone goes. It's for the best.'

'Even so, it's wrong, Billy. It makes me feel sick to think you're going to do this.'

'Don't fuckin' say that! You've got to be on my side, Gem.'

She was up on her feet now and pacing about the room. I hated it when she was like this. I shouldn't have told her anything. Maybe Dan was right. Then the voices started up again, this time telling me she was a bitch and I shouldn't listen to her. I shook my head to try and get rid of them but they kept on at me.

'Shut up! Just shut the fuck up!' I shouted. She looked at me in a bad kind of way. 'I didn't mean you,' I said. She ran from the room and I follow her. She was at the top of the stairs when she turned to me.

'I'm going for a walk,' she said. 'On my own.'

'Don't leave me!' I shouted at her and grabbed hold of her arm. She lost her balance then and the next thing I knew, she was falling backwards. I tried to keep a hold of her but I lost my grip and she was tumbling down the stairs. Suddenly everything went quiet. I don't like the quiet. I scrambled down to where she was lying in a heap and tried to get her to talk to me but she was out cold.

That's when I panicked and ran from the flat.

Chapter Fifty

Karen

She stood outside number fifty nine, just about to ring the doorbell wondering why she was hesitating. She supposed it was thinking about Kevin's account of being in the cellar. She had a bad feeling about this. Maybe she should have just phoned the Police or at least gone back to the office to talk to her supervisor about it all before she did anything. She shrugged her shoulders, thinking to herself she'd never been one to do things by the rule-book, and rang the bell. There was no sound coming from inside so she waited a moment and then knocked. Still nothing. Looking about, the street being empty, she went to the window and tried to peer in through the net curtains. She couldn't see anyone moving about and wondered if she should try the back of the house. The only way round was to go along to the end of the street so she made her way along the footpath and soon found herself in the alley.

She was just approaching what she thought must be the back gate to number fifty nine when there was someone coming out of the garden. He didn't notice her though but quickly walked off down the alley in the opposite direction.

So there must have been someone in there when I knocked, she thought. I wonder why he didn't answer the door. He's tall so it's possible that he's the man that Kevin described although he could be anyone. She wished he'd given her a more detailed description now.

Karen waited for the man to disappear round the corner before she made her way into the garden. She passed the shed where Kevin had said he'd hidden and walked on down the path to the house. There was a cellar window, low down on the wall. It was barred and there were wooden slats leaning against it which were loose and easy to remove. She tried to see into the cellar. It was pretty dark down there but she could just make out the shape of what looked like a chest freezer.

Suddenly she felt the prescence of someone behind her.

'What the fuck do you want?' She jumped.

She stood up and turned. It was Billy.

'What do you think you're doing?' he demanded. 'Who are you?'

'I'm sorry,' she started to explain. 'I was looking for Mrs. Clarke. This is her house, isn't it?'

'She's away,' he said sharply. 'Who are you? What do you want her for?'

Karen hadn't thought that far ahead. She wanted to ask about Gem but something was telling her not to let on she knew her.

'Well?' he said.

'My name's Karen. I was told she might have some clothes to sell. They gave me her address at the charity shop where she works. When will she be back?'

'She didn't say, but I'll tell her you called.'

'Alright, thank you.' Karen just wanted to get out of there and started to walk away up the path.

'Hang on,' he called after her. 'Did you say your name was Karen?'

She stopped and turned. 'That's right. Why?'

'You're Gem's Karen. Her key worker. She told me about you.' He walked towards her. 'What are you really doing here? You snooping about looking for Gem?'

'No. I told you, I came here to see Mrs. Clarke. I do know Gem, though,' she admitted. 'Is she here?'

'No, she's not. I haven't seen her. We finished months ago.' He looked away from her and then back again.

'You're Billy, aren't you?' Karen held his gaze.

'So she's told you all about me, has she?'

'Only that you were together for a while and you'd split up. I knew that. Look, I have to go now. I'm sorry missed Mrs. Clarke. Just tell her I was looking for her, will you?'

'When I see her, I will.'

'Thank you,' Karen quickly walked to the gate and hurried away before she turned back to see if he'd followed her. The lane was empty. She breathed a sigh of relief and made her way back towards the High Street, determined to try Gem's flat again before she went back to the office. Then I really must take this to my supervisor, she decided, feeling completely out of her depth.

Chapter Fifty One

Gem

When she opened her eyes the first thing she saw was the bottom of the front door. She was lying in an awkward position, her head against the wall and her legs splayed up the stairs. Slowly she started to remember. Billy had been shouting at her and the next thing she was flying through the air. Then nothing.

The thought of what was going on with Billy was making her feel sick, or was it the way she was lying crammed in the small hallway? She tried to sit up. Her legs and back were sore but she managed to get herself onto the bottom step while she tried to get her breath back. She was aware things had got completely out of control, not just with what was going on with Billy, but with herself. Only a few days ago she had felt her life was starting to get back on track. The methadone programme was hard but she'd been able to manage it. If only Billy hadn't come back into her life she could be looking forward to a good future. Now she'd slipped right back into that bad place that had been so hard to get out of before.

Stop blaming Billy, she told herself. Take responsibility for yourself and do something. She got herself up from the stairs. Luckily she didn't appear to have any broken bones. Slowly making her way back up to the sitting room she gathered her bag and keys and left the flat. As she walked away, she was still not sure what to do for the best but found herself making her way to the Drug Clinic. Then, as she reached the precinct she saw Karen walking towards her.

'I was just going to your flat,' Karen said as they stopped to greet each other. 'Where have you been? You weren't in when I called earlier and you haven't been to the shop either.'

'I've just come from my flat,' Gem said, still unsure of how much she should tell. 'I was coming to see you, actually.'

'You didn't turn up for your appointment. I was worried.'

'I know, and I'm sorry I didn't let you know. Something's happened.' Gem told her. 'Can we go to the clinic and talk?'

'Of course.'

Gem had to sit in the waiting room while Karen went to get a room. Sitting on a plastic chair that was bolted to the floor, she could feel the clamminess of the plastic through her jeans and started wishing she wasn't there. Karen seemed to be away a long time and Gem was starting to get paranoid - was Karen talking about her to her supervisor? The last thing Gem wanted was to lose her script. She got up from the chair and started to walk about the room, wondering whether to leave while she still could. But Karen was soon back.

'Come through, Gem,' she said.

Pausing for only a moment, she followed Karen through into the interview room. She'd been in this room so many times before. It was filled with memories of bad times as well as times of hope for her. She didn't know if today would be one or the other. She felt pretty scared because whatever she said she knew it would be bad for her in some way or another. And she was still feeling rotten about grassing Billy up, whatever he'd done. They sat down in the low chairs, set to make you feel ready to reveal your innermost secrets. This made her feel even worse - she's trying to make me feel at ease, to lower my guard, so that I'll tell her stuff I don't want to.

'Well, Gem,' Karen finally said. 'Do you want to tell me what's going on?'

'It's hard,' Gem replied, hesitating. 'I don't know how much to tell you.'

'Let's start with your charity shop job,' Karen said. 'How are you getting on there?'

Gem knew Karen was already aware she hadn't been in. She's just trying to catch me out, she guessed, so she told Karen the truth.

'I was getting on well. But I haven't been in today. I missed a shift yesterday too. Something came up and I couldn't get in.'

'Do you want to tell me what happened?' Karen asked again.

'I do. That's why I wanted to come here today.' As Gem moved in the chair she could feel her back twinge. She groaned and made a face as she tried to settle into a more comfortable position.

'Are you alright?' Karen frowned. 'You look like you're in pain.'

'I fell down the stairs earlier today. I'm alright though,' Gem added hurriedly. Karen was looking at her. She was probably going to insist she get to see a doctor or something and Gem didn't want to do that.

'OK, so what's been going on?' Karen asked.

Gem was still reluctant to tell her everything. It was so hard knowing Karen would be pissed off with her and she could lose her script.

'Come on, Gem,' Karen said. 'You need to be truthful about this. I need to know what, if anything, is going wrong so I can help you get back on track. Never mind about losing your script if that's what you are worrying about. You won't lose it but we need to know how to help you. Please.'

She wanted to but when it came down to it Gem couldn't bring herself to tell Karen about old Mrs. Clarke in the freezer. So she found herself talking about getting back with Billy and that she'd had some heroin. She'd find out about that anyway soon enough. Karen asked about Kevin and what he'd said about being tied up. Gem made out she thought he had a good imagination and was always making up things. When it came down to it she couldn't grass on Billy although she did tell Karen about Billy's voices, hoping that she might have some good advice. She just said that he should come in and ask for help himself.

In the end Gem was let off with just having to come in twice a week for urine tests. She could still pick up the methadone as long as she was clean in the future. Leaving there feeling a mixture of relief and uncertainty, she still had the problem of Billy and his aunty's body in the cellar to deal with.

Chapter Fifty One

Karen
Karen was still worrying about Gem when she left work to go and pick up Lucy from the school. She had the feeling Gem hadn't been completely truthful and wondered how she could get to the bottom of whatever was going on. She drove into the school car park and waited whilst various children were leaving the building and walking down the drive, or getting into waiting cars. She was so engrossed with her work that the minutes passed without her really noticing. It was when she saw Lucy's teacher walking across the car park towards her car she realised she'd been there for nearly half an hour and Lucy hadn't come out. Karen wound down the window.

'Is Lucy still inside?' she called. 'She's usually one of the first out.'

'Lucy didn't come to the after-school club today. She went home on the school bus at three thirty.'

'Oh, that's alright then,' Karen said. But she was feeling uneasy all the same as she drove home, immediately thinking of Peter and that somehow he had got to Lucy. All her old fears flooded back. Fears of being trapped, caught up in something she could never get out of. Fears of losing Lucy which had never gone away completely. By the time she arrived at her house she was visibly shaking and when she saw Lucy sitting on the doorstep she burst into tears and swept the young girl up into her arms.

'Where the hell have you been?' she yelled. 'I've been to the school to collect you. What were you thinking?'

'Sorry Mum,' Lucy sobbed. 'I forgot and got on the bus. I came straight home. Please don't be angry.'

Karen could feel the relief sweeping over her. She smiled at Lucy. 'It's alright. I didn't mean to shout at you. I was very worried when you weren't at school, that's all. Come on, let's go in and get something to eat, eh? We'll have tea on our laps in front of the tv.'

'Can I have spaghetti?'

'With fish fingers and chips?'

'Thanks Mum.'

They went indoors and Lucy went up to her room to change. Karen stood in the kitchen leaning against the sink, staring out of the window, still trying to calm the fears that wouldn't seem to go away. I'm starting to imagine the worst, she thought. Peter threatened me - said I'd regret it if I reported him and I know he can be dangerous. He believes I'm to blame for him going to prison and I wouldn't put it past him to do something stupid. Still, he wouldn't come here, would he? And he doesn't know where Lucy goes to school. Then on the other hand it wouldn't take much for him to find out. Lucy goes on the school bus every day, and that bus only goes to one school. If Peter wanted to, there was no way I could stop him from following either myself or Lucy. I've got to stop thinking like this. I'm just getting paranoid.

She was about to turn away from the window when she saw him. The back gate was slightly ajar and he was standing there, looking straight at her. Fear held her for a second then she ran into the hall and out of the back door but he was gone. She walked briskly to the gate and swung it open. There was no sign of him anywhere.

'Where are you, you bastard?' she whispered to herself. She walked to the end of the short road behind the houses and looked both ways into the main street. It all looked as normal as it ever did, no stranger's car parked anywhere. She shook her head and ran back to her house suddenly frightened as she remembered she'd left Lucy on her own. She ran up the stairs to Lucy's room. She was still there, sitting on her bed, perfectly safe.

'Is dinner ready yet, Mum? I'm starving.' Lucy looked up at her Mum, smiling.

'Nearly. I just came up to talk to you,' Karen sat on the bed. 'I wanted to ask you whether anything happened at school today. What made you come straight home instead of staying at the after-school club? You didn't forget did you?'

'No.' Lucy looked sheepish. 'I didn't want to go to the club. I don't like it. Why do I have to go to it?'

'It's because I have to work later some days, you know that. Tell me what it is you don't like. You used to enjoy it.'

'There's some new kids who go and I don't like them.'

'I see. What is it that you don't like about them? Are they being unkind to you?'

'A bit. They laugh at me because I always talk about horses and do my drawings. I don't want to play with them. I just want to be by myself and do my drawings.'

'Well, sometimes it's nice to be on your own, but playing with other children is fun too. Perhaps you could try and play sometimes.'

'I don't want to. I don't have to, do I?' Lucy pouted.

'No, of course not. But you will have to go to the after school club again. It's only once a week and I can't get anyone to look after you at that time. I'm sorry, Lucy, but you'll have to get through this somehow. I could talk to the teacher.'

'No. Don't do that. It'll make it worse.' Lucy said.

'Alright. Let's just see how it goes,' Karen sighed and hugged Lucy. 'Is there anything else?'

'Well, you know I said I came straight home from the bus? I did speak to someone. I'm sorry Mum, I know I shouldn't talk to people I don't know, but this man spoke to me. What do you do if a stranger speaks to you? I didn't talk back to him at first. He said he knew you and he was going to come and visit you. He wanted me to bring him home with me. He said we could go in his car but I told him to go away and ran away.'

Karen felt cold inside. 'What did he look like?' she asked although she already knew the answer.

'He was tall with short curly hair. He seemed quite nice at first. He was smiling but I was scared. I was scared to come home in case he followed me so I ran the other way and hid from him. I don't think he followed me so after a long time I came home. I'm sorry Mum.'

Karen could feel the anger mixing with the fear that she already had inside. 'You did the right thing,' she said. 'Don't worry. I think it might be a good idea if I take you to school next week. No more school bus for you for a while.' And she went downstairs to phone the Police.

Chapter Fifty Two

Peter

Peter was sitting in his car, parked in the square, just around the corner from Karen's house. He felt so good. His mood was high, because he knew things were going to start going his way soon. He had been so close to getting Lucy in his car. He hadn't been planning to hurt her, he'd just wanted to scare Karen, to get his own back on her for all she'd put him through. She needed to know she couldn't hide from him - couldn't treat him like she had and get away with it. It was a pity her kid, Lucy, hadn't been taken in when he'd said she should go with him. Now it would be more difficult to get her to trust him. He'd have to think of something else. Still, he was happy he'd scared the life out of Karen. He'd felt a thrill when she'd seen him from the window and he had just slipped away in time before she'd come running down her garden path. He laughed to himself, started the car and drove away.

His Mum was in the kitchen when he arrived back home in Gosport. He still thought of his Mum's house as home even though it had been some years since he'd lived there and he was only staying for a while until he could sell the house in Salisbury. He didn't want to go back there after what had happened with Carol. It just made him so angry to think she'd just gone the way she had. Being in his childhood home helped. Not that there was anything wrong with him. It was just he needed time to get his life back on track. And he knew he wouldn't do that until he'd finished what he had started with Karen. What was it, they called it? Unfinished business. That was it.

The welcome smell of cooking wrapped around his senses as he entered the house, his Mum smiled at him, wiping her hands on the towel.

'Dinner's nearly ready,' she reached to kiss him on the cheek. 'Are you alright? You look upset.'

'I'm fine. Don't fuss,' he said. 'I'm going up for a bath.' The look of concern on his Mum's face was so irritating. He wished not for the first time she'd just leave him alone. Why was it she was always watching him, picking up on his every mood. He pushed her away and went up the stairs two at a time, to run his bath.

The bath was soothing - he could feel the tension dropping away and the elation building up again. It was like he was floating in a pleasant dream. He thought about what he could do next to make Karen's life miserable. He loved the thought of creating a little hell for her to live in and the fact that she had Lucy made it even better, an easy way in to hurt her, he thought.

He was still relaxing when he heard the knock. He listened as his Mum opened the door - heard the sound of a male voice. He felt uneasy - then his Mum was knocking on the bathroom door.

'Peter. You have to come down - there's a Policeman here to speak to you.'

He felt a chill in the air as he pulled himself out of the now tepid bath, dried himself and got dressed. The bitch! She's called the Police. He hadn't really thought she'd do that - being such a stupid weak woman - he couldn't have imagined she would do that. Why hadn't he thought of it?

Now the Police officer was asking him questions.

'Where were you this afternoon between three thirty and four?'

'I was at work.'

'And where is your place of work, Sir?'

He's calling me Sir, Peter thought, wondering if that was a good sign. 'I work in Salisbury at Jenkins and Jones Accountants. But I was with a client in Romsey for most of the afternoon. I can give you the address. I've got it written down in my brief case.'

'That would be helpful, thank you.' The officer smiled.

'Can you tell me what this is about?' Peter asked.

'We have had a complaint, Sir. Did you approach a young girl in Wickham Square this afternoon? She says you tried to get her to go with you in your car.'

'Oh, you must mean Lucy. She's my ex-wife's daughter. Karen, that's my ex, she asked me to pick her up from the school bus.' He looked at his Mum, giving her a warning look and a little smile.

'Are you sure, Sir?' the Police officer looked surprised. 'Only she says Lucy was approached by you and neither of them knew anything about you picking her up. Your ex-wife has made the complaint - she also says you have been following her, watching her, intimidating her. The child Lucy was very shaken up about this.'

'I'm not surprised she's shaken up. Her mother never was good at communicating. I never would have gone to the school bus if I'd known she was going to do this. She's not well in the head, never was, and now it seems like she's gone back to her old ways.' He paused. 'Of course, you will believe her over me, won't you?'

'She was very sure that you had been intimidating her.' He looked at Peter. 'So you're telling me that none of this happened?'

'That's right, Officer.'

'Perhaps you could tell me exactly what happened at the bus stop, then.'

'Karen asked me to collect Lucy when she got off the school bus. She said she couldn't get time off work and asked me to do it for a favour. When I got to the bus stop, I told Lucy and she just ran off. That's all.'

'So, did you contact her Mother to tell her what had happened? Weren't you worried about where the child had gone? Didn't you try to find her?'

'No. I just left. OK, maybe I should have gone after her but I was annoyed at having wasted my time. I was only doing Karen a favour and I didn't want to upset the child.'

The Officer was writing down on a pad. He looked up at Peter and gave him a long hard look. 'The address of your client, Sir?' he asked.

'Yes, of course.' Peter went into the sitting room and took a card from his brief-case. He handed it to the policeman.

'Thank you, Sir,' said the officer. 'I will be speaking with Mrs. Edwards again about this matter. In the meantime I think it would be best if you kept away from your ex-wife and her daughter.' He stood up. 'I will be keeping in touch.'

As soon as he'd left, Peter's Mother closed the door and turned to face her son. 'What the hell are you playing at, Peter?' she demanded. She was shaking.

'It's nothing,' he smiled. 'Don't worry, I had no intention of doing anything wrong.'

'But you just lied to the Police. Karen would never have asked you to pick up Lucy.'

'So what? They'll never prove it. I'm just teaching her a little lesson, that's all.' He took a step closer to his Mother. 'Just keep quiet about it - you keep quiet. Do you understand? No-one's going to be hurt.'

Margaret looked at him in disgust. 'I thought you'd changed,' she said as she turned away and went back into the kitchen.

Chapter Fifty Two

Billy

Things seemed to be going from bad to friggin' worse. I couldn't believe I'd pushed Gem down the stairs. No, I didn't push her, I was trying to stop her from leaving and she slipped. I'm not a murderer, I'm not. I just wish I hadn't ran away like that. I've been worrying about things ever since, wondering if she's alright. I should have gone back to her flat to check but after that bloody woman, Karen, came round snooping, I couldn't go back there. They would know it was me, wouldn't they? I have got to calm down and stop panicking. Think. Right - tonight we're getting the van and then we can move Aunty's body out of the cellar. I know once she's gone I'll be able to think straight again. But what about if I have killed Gem? Perhaps I should go round to her flat to make sure. If she's dead, we'll have to get rid of another body. I can't bear to think of Gem as being dead - lying there at the foot of the stairs, all twisted and looking weird. No - I can't go there. Maybe I should send Dan around to see? But I don't have a key to get in. Just as well, then. I can't do anything about it now can I?

I was still thinking all these thoughts when there was a knock at the back door. I was so relieved when I saw that it was Gem so I opened the door quickly and let her come in.

'Thank God,' I said as she came through the door. I wanted to hold her but something stopped me. She didn't look too happy to be honest. 'Are you OK?' I asked.

'No thanks to you, Billy,' she snapped. 'You left me unconscious. I could have been dead.'

'Don't say that, Gem. I wouldn't have hurt you. It was an accident.'

'Then why did you leave me there?' She asked, giving me a look.

'I was bloody scared. The voices were at me,' I tried to explain but she didn't let me.

'Never mind. I'm alright, luckily for you. I think it's time we tried to sort out this mess that you're in.'

I breathed a sigh of relief. Now Gem was back everything would be alright again. She would help me sort out everything.

'We're getting rid of the body this evening,' I started to tell her. 'Then it'll all be sorted.'

'Billy, you can't bury her in the woods,' she said. 'We have to do the right thing and tell the Police what happened. They will see that it was an accident.'

'No!' I couldn't let her do this. 'They'll blame me, I know it.'

'There'll be a post mortem,' she said. 'They'll be able to tell how she died. It was an accident. It'll be obvious. You may have to go to prison for a while - hiding the body was a stupid thing to do, but you're not guilty of anything else, are you?'

'No. But you can't tell the fuckin' Police. I can't let you do that.' I was feeling uneasy now. I had to convince her not to go to the law. 'Promise me you won't do anything. You have to let me sort this out.'

She seemed to back off a bit then. 'Alright,' she said. 'I won't do anything today. But please think about it. It's not right to bury a person in the woods. She deserves a proper burial, with a service and that. Surely you can't be happy with letting your Aunty be stuffed in a grave in the woods?'

'I can't think about it now,' I said, shivering. 'I don't want to talk about it any more.'

She smiled at me but it wasn't a real smile, it was strained. Then I remembered that woman, Karen coming round. So I asked her about that.

'This woman, your key worker, Karen. Did you tell her about me?'

She blushed so I knew she had. 'Why do you think that?' she asked.

'She's been round here looking for Aunty Joan. Why would she do that unless you told her about her? What's going on, Gem?'

'I only told her about seeing you again. I don't know how she knows about your aunty.' She looked at me with those eyes. 'Maybe she went to the shop and they might have told her about it - I don't know.'

I couldn't really believe her any more. I couldn't trust her like I wanted to. I knew I had to make sure she wouldn't tell the the Police but how could I stop her? 'Promise me that you won't do anything, Gem. Promise me.'

She looked at me and sighed. I thought maybe I had her now. On my side, I mean. 'What are we going to do, then?' she asked. 'It's not too late to sort it out. You can't keep running away from the truth, Billy. Whatever you do with the body someone will find out sooner or later. And it's wrong not to let your Aunty have a proper burial. You can't put her in the woods somewhere. I know I keep saying the same thing but just think about it, please.'

She reached out and took my hand. It felt so good. Then I heard the voice in my head again. 'Don't trust her, she's a lying bitch!'

'Stop it! Stop it!' I tried to make it go away but it just got louder. And there was another one arguing with it. 'Gem's the only one can save you, murderer!' 'Don't trust her, she's a lying bitch,' said the first voice. Soon they were a jumble in my mind - it was like they were leaking out of my ears and into the air around us. Gem looked alarmed. She must have heard them too. She was still holding my hand but gripping it tight now.

'Stop it!' I shouted again, first at the voices, then to her not to leave me. She put her arms around me and held me there, gently rocking me, making soothing noises. Gradually, the voices started to fade away. I knew I would be safe now. Gem was not a lying bitch. She was there for me.

'You've got to stay with me, Gem. Only you can keep me safe.'

I could hardly hear her answer but it sounded like she said OK.

Chapter Fifty Three

Gem

She couldn't understand herself sometimes. How did it come to this? Always making the wrong choices. But what could she do now? Run off and leave him in this state - call for help and get him sent to prison, or hospital? Deep inside she knew going for help would be the best thing to do. She just couldn't seem to make herself do that. So she convinced herself to stay with him and that to see him through this mess was the best way. She sat on the edge of the sofa where they'd ended up after his meltdown in the hallway earlier. He was beside her, more relaxed now the voices seemed to have faded away, for a while at least. She groped in her bag for a cigarette and lit up two, handed him one and watched him as he smoked it. She didn't really want one herself but took a long drag on hers, started to cough and stubbed it out in the ashtray.

'I thought you'd given up,' Billy said.

'So had I. I don't know why I did that. Something to do, I suppose.' The smoke was getting to her. She stood up and moved towards the door.

'Where are you going?' Billy was on his feet.

'Nowhere. I'm not a prisoner am I?'

'No. I just don't want you to leave me on my own.' He reached for her hand. She took it.

'I won't,' she said. 'I just wanted some air, that's all.'

'I'll put the fag out,' he said and screwed it out into the ashtray next to her discarded one. 'See. No more smoke.'

Just then she heard a key in the front door. Shit, she thought as Dan slammed the door behind him and came into the front room. He looked at her with a smirk.

'Well, well,' he said. 'The lovely Gem is back.'

'Shut up, Dan,' Billy snapped. 'Gem's staying.' He looked at her then. 'Listen Gem, we need Dan to sort this out. I can't do it on my own. He's got to stay.'

'What's going on, Billy?' Dan grabbed a hold of Billy's arm and tried to drag him out into the hall. 'What have you told her?'

'She knows about Aunty, and she's cool about it,' Billy said. Gem recoiled to hear that. Was she cool about it?

'You bloody idiot!' Dan shouted at Billy. 'How can you trust her?'

'I can trust her - she's helping me. I don't care what you say Dan, she stays.'

'Well more fool you. What about moving the body tonight? Are you still up for that?'

'Yes, of course I am. We've got to get her out of here.'

'And you think that she will go along with it and say nothing?' He flicked his head in the direction of Gem.

'She promised,' Billy said.

There was a long silence whilst Dan seemed to be weighing it all up. Finally he just shook his head and went upstairs. Billy turned back to Gem.

'Well?' she asked. 'What now?'

'It'll be alright,' Billy said. 'We'll get the body out of here and then we can wash our hands of Dan. We won't need him any more. I promise - just be patient, Gem, please.'

Gem could feel the fear swimming about in her belly. She couldn't think straight any more. It all seemed like a weird nightmare - she felt out of control and didn't know how to get out of it.

'I can't do this, Billy,' she said finally. 'I'm sorry but I have to go.'

She didn't hear Dan coming back down the stairs. The first she knew about it was as she moved towards the door and there he was, standing at the foot of the stairs, pointing a gun straight at her.

'You're not going anywhere,' he said with a smile.

Chapter Fifty Four

Peter

He felt calmer now - he could see an end in sight as a plan started to form in his mind. Fooling those Police had been easy, easier than he'd expected and hearing the polite way they'd spoken to him made him want to punch his fist into the air and shout 'Yes!' Maybe life could be good again. He just needed to punish Karen for what she'd done to him and all would be perfect again.

He sat in his car. It was starting to rain, the sky darkening by the minute. Soon there were rivulets running down the outside of the windscreen. He remembered watching the rain on his bedroom window way back when he was a child, alone in the house, his mother at work. She'd always seemed to have been at work. He hated the rain. He used to have races with the raindrops, chosing one and watching how fast it could reach to bottom of the window.

He brought his thoughts back to the present. His feet were cold and the windows were misting up. He wasn't sure how long he could sit there, watching her house. There were other cars in the street but she would easily recognise his now, which was a pity, but then she couldn't do anything about him parking there, could she? He was only waiting by the shops. If anyone asked, he'd say he was only going shopping. But no one would ask. Look at the way the Police had reacted after all - they'd believed him, not her. He laughed quietly to himself, took a cloth from the glove compartment, and wiped the steamy window. He looked out. Her house was silent. He wasn't even sure whether she was in or not. There was no sign of her car. Maybe he should take a closer look.

Peter carefully folded the damp cloth and placed it back in the glove compartment. He took one more look about the street and got out of his car. Soon he was standing at the back of the house. The wall enclosing Karen's garden was just the right height for him to see over the top. He stood watching. From here he could see straight into the window

The light was on and he could see Karen moving about in the kitchen. He almost hoped that she would look up and see him. Then he'd just walk away again, like he had done before. He'd enjoyed seeing the look of horror on her face and would love to see it again. But she didn't look up and soon the light went out as she left the room.

He wondered whether he should get nearer to the house, maybe try the back door. He doubted whether she'd think to lock it. Soon he was standing there, right by the door. He peered through the small window into the hall. It was in darkness. She must have gone upstairs, or maybe she was in a room at the front of the house. He tried the door, carefully turning the door-knob. It was locked. Damn. She wasn't as stupid as he'd thought.

He was still standing there when the door into the front room opened and Lucy appeared as a silhouette in the hall. She stopped when she saw him looking in at her and let out a scream. Before he could think any more about what he was doing, he dashed back down the path and out of the gate. He guessed that Karen would see him if he went back into the street so instead he disappeared down the lane behind the houses and soon was in the woods and out of sight. He cursed Karen as the rain was falling much heavier now. It ran down his neck, cold and unforgiving. Bitch, he thought. I will get her. Just when the time is right.

He waited for what seemed like an age, then eventually made his way out of the woods and took a long way round back into the street. Soaking wet now, he got into his car, wiped his hands on the cloth he'd used earlier, and drove off back to Gosport.

Chapter Fifty Five

Karen
She'd known all along that Peter would never leave her and
Lucy alone. Even after the Police had been to see him, and
coming back to re-assure her that he had been warned not to
go anywhere near them, she couldn't feel at ease in her home
any more. And now this. She made up her mind then that she
would have to get Lucy out of here and take her to somewhere
safe. Somewhere Peter knew nothing about. But where? She
immediately thought about Evelyn, now living in her little
bungalow in Fareham. She would be delighted to have Lucy
stay with her for a while. She'd often stayed there in the past
and Lucy had always loved being there. Lucy was like a
Grandchild to Evelyn who had never known her own
daughter. She had given birth when only a child herself and
her baby had been taken away from her before she was sent to
the local Mental Hospital.

Evelyn smiled and welcomed them in. Karen still was
amazed every time she saw her - how much she had changed
from the mute woman she'd first met only a dozen or so years
ago. Now in her mid-fifties, she was independent and
confident, her past merely an unpleasant distant memory.
     Her bungalow was small and neat. It was filled with
the old furniture she'd inherited from her Mother's terraced
cottage in Trinity Street. The old mahogany table covered in
red chenille, the brass vases which had held pride of place on
the mantle piece, now on the side-board. Two or three old
sepia portraits looked down from the walls, the faces of early
twentieth century soldiers and women in black dresses gazing
with stern faces into the distance. There were a couple of
comfortable arm chairs placed either side of the modern gas
fire and although the room was cluttered, it had a kind of
cosiness too.
     Evelyn, like her Mother before her, was tiny, her eyes
twinkled with amusement as she opened the door and let

Karen and Lucy in. She was wearing a comfortable pair of black trousers, topped with a red blouse and cardigan with voluminous pockets wherin could often be found a bag of boiled sweets or a packet of mints.

Karen watched as Evelyn took Lucy into her arms and hugged her. Lucy's blonde hair bouncing in its pony tail, Evelyn's short grey hair, smoothly cut into a modern style. She was smiling at Karen over the top of Lucy's head.

'Thank you so much for letting Lucy stay,' Karen said. 'I hope you really don't mind.'

Evelyn smiled. 'Of course not. Now, if you'll just let go of me for a minute, I'll get you a drink of juice.' She looked down at Lucy. 'I might have some of those chocolate biscuits you like. What do you say?'

'Yes please, Nanny Evie!' And they both went into the kitchen.

Soon Karen was on her way, feeling relieved that Lucy would be safe. At least that was one place that Peter knew nothing about. Now she could go to work and not worry about her. But it would only be a matter of time before he tried something else. She knew he wouldn't give up easily.

Chapter Fifty Six

Gem

Seeing the gun put a chill of fear in Gem's heart. He was waving the thing in her face, making her back off into the front room again. She looked at Billy. His face was white but he said nothing. Just shook his head briefly before looking away.

'Right, you'd better sit back down,' Dan was saying. 'Go on, move it!' The gun was still aimed at her. She sat down heavily onto the sofa.

Gem looked back at him, then at Billy. 'Are you going to let him do this?' she asked. Billy still said nothing. Dan laughed.

'He does what I say.' He looked at Gem, a smirk on his face. 'Billy knows who the boss is around here, ain't that right, Billy?'

'OK Dan, that's enough.' At last Billy spoke up. 'Put the gun away. Gem's with us on this. She's gonna help, aren't you, Gem?' His eyes were wide as he looked at her, willing her to agree with him.

'I want to help,' she replied cautiously.

'Oh, yeah, as if I would believe that. You were about to leave before I came down. Where do you think you were going?'

'I wasn't going anywhere,' Gem said. 'I just wanted to get some air, that's all.'

'Well I don't trust you.' He turned to Billy, still pointing the gun at Gem. 'We should get rid of her, like the old lady. One more won't make any difference.'

'No!' Billy shouted. 'Aunty was an accident. Gem's my girlfriend - we can't hurt her. I'll make sure she stays with us. She won't say anything - will you Gem? You promised you wouldn't grass me up. You did, didn't you Gem?'

'Yes. I promised,' Gem agreed reluctantly.

Dan stood there looking at her, a sneer on his lips. He seemed to be thinking it through. Finally he smiled. 'OK. You want some fresh air - you can come with us in the van. If you help us then I'll be sure you don't tell anyone.' He stuck the gun right into her face, close enough for her to smell the metal. 'Come on,' he said. 'Get up and let's get the body out of the cellar and into the van. We need to get going.'

Billy looked at her and shrugged his shoulders. 'Come on, Gem. It'll be alright.'

'Course it'll be alright!' snapped Dan. 'Because you'll do exactly what I tell you. Now, let's go!'

Moving poor Mrs. Clarke out of the freezer and up the cellar stairs wasn't easy. It took two of them to carry her. Gem felt sick as she helped to lift the carpet-wrapped body and between herself and Billy, eventually half-dragged her up the stairs. The body was cold and her hands were numb. Dan didn't help. Too worried about her running off, she supposed, he held the gun aimed at her throughout the whole operation. Eventually they got the gruesome package into the back of the van. Dan told Gem to get into the front seat in between himself and Billy and they were off.

She watched through the window of the van as the rain began to fall. The windscreen washers scraped and squeaked across the screen as though they were calling out for help. Gem was silent, frantically trying to think of a way out of this. It had all gone too far now and she could see no way she could get herself, never mind, Billy, out of this mess.

They drove past the hospital on the hill and carried on up to the top. She could see the whole of Portsmouth stretched out below, the lights twinkling across the city, reflecting like jewels in the raindrops on the windows of the van. They carried on into the darkness of the countryside. Gem could feel every bump they hit in the road and winced, thinking about the body in the back. She looked at Billy but he was staring straight ahead at the road, seemingly concentrating on his driving. She reached across to touch his hand but immediately felt the gun in her ribs.

'Don't you even think about it!' Dan snapped. 'Keep your hands to yourself.'

Gem gave Billy a long hard look. He glanced at her and shook his head. She held his gaze for a moment and then sighed as she placed her hand back on her lap.

Soon enough they were pulling into a side road and driving along a winding lane under some trees. A car park spread out before them at the end of the lane.

'We can't do it here,' Dan was saying. 'It's far too open. Drive through there.' He indicated a gate leading into the woods. 'Go and open it, Billy,' he ordered.

Billy jumped out and walked over to open the gate.

Once alone with Dan, Gem tried to reason with him. 'You don't have to keep prodding me with that gun,' she said. 'I'm not going anywhere. I only want to help Billy, so why would I grass you both up? Can't you just back off a bit - it's scaring me.'

'Good,' Dan said. 'I don't like you and I don't trust you. I'm not stupid and I know what you think of me, so just shut up and do what I say.'

Billy climbed back into the van and they drove through the gates. The lane meandered deeper into the wood, out of sight of the car park. They pulled to a stop in a small clearing where the different lanes met at a crossroad.

'Put the van under the trees,' ordered Dan. 'Out of sight, you idiot.'

Billy managed to drive the van closer to the edge of the lane and stopped the engine. 'This'll have to do,' he said. 'I'm not driving any further in - the ground's quite muddy here and we'll end up getting stuck in if we go any closer.'

Dan opened the door and climbed down, still holding the gun at Gem. 'Come on you, get out,' he said. 'We need you to help dig a grave.'

Gem shuddered as she got out of the van and stood shivering. The rain had stopped but the ground was wet and a night chill had settled. Rain dripped from the trees onto their heads and ran down her back.

'What's up? You cold?' Dan sneered. 'You'll soon get warm when you start digging.' He laughed and shoved a spade into her hands. 'Go on, over there.'

Billy looked at her and mouthed a 'sorry' before moving off ahead to a spot under some trees. It was hard work digging - even though it had been raining and the grass was wet, there had been a long, dry spell of weather and the ground was hard. This, combined with the roots of the tree they were digging under, made it almost impossible.

'This is stupid,' said Gem. 'We'll never do this. A grave needs to be deep otherwise wild animals will get at the body.'

'Shut up, Gem!' Billy snapped. 'Don't think about it, just keep digging.'

'Yeah, shut up!' Dan echoed. 'We don't want your opinion.'

'You could at least help,' Gem said. 'Just standing there, waving that gun about isn't doing any good.'

'Yeah, you'd like that, wouldn't you. Anything to distract me so you can get away.' Dan sneered.

'Forget it then,' Gem turned back to the digging. 'We'll be here all night at this rate though.'

'Just get on with it!' Dan said. He turned away at that moment, distracted by a flash of light through the trees. 'What the fuck is that?'

'Someone's coming,' Billy whispered. 'We've got to get out of here.' The light seemed to be coming closer.

'Who knows about us coming here?' Dan was waving the gun about again. 'You told someone didn't you?' he spat at Gem.

'How could I have? I've been with you both all the time and I didn't know what you were planning before then. Don't be stupid.'

'Don't call me stupid, you Bitch!' Dan retorted.

Just then, Gem saw another light, further away, like a torch sweeping in the darkness. Her heart soared with hope.

'There's someone else!' Billy shouted. 'What's going on? We're gonna have to go.'

For just a moment, Dan took his eyes off Gem. She hesitated for a second then took her chance and ran into the darkness of the woods, trying to get as far away from Dan and the gun as possible. Her summer shoes weren't the best things to be running in and the ground was uneven and soggy with dead leaves. Brambles were all around her - she could feel them scratching her arms and tearing at her clothes. Pure panic kept her going, a fleeting hope in her mind she could run towards the lights and safety. But first she had to get away from Dan. She glanced over her shoulder and was dismayed to see he was only a few yards away from her. She ran on, aware that at any minute now she would feel a sudden pain if he chose to shoot her in the back. She wouldn't have put anything past him at this moment. Don't think about that, she told herself as she stumbled on through the brambles. Suddenly she felt a sharp pain across her waist. He's got me! She thought. Then she realised she was caught in a barbed wire fence. She was trapped. Spinning round to face him, her shirt tore away from the wire. She could feel the blood trickle from the cuts on her belly as she took a deep breath and looked straight at him.

'What are you going to do now?' she asked, with more bravado than she felt.

'Teach you a bloody lesson, that's what,' Dan was panting, trying to catch his breath, but still holding the gun. 'Thought you could get away? I knew we couldn't trust you.'

Gem looked about her into the distance, hoping that whoever was out there may have come closer. There was a light coming towards them. 'Help! Over here,' she called.

'Shut up!' Dan spat. 'Just keep quiet.' He grabbed her arm and dragged her down on to the wet forest floor. She could feel the cold of the gun barrel against her neck. 'One more noise from you and I'll finish it,' he said. 'Don't think I won't. I've already killed one annoying female so don't think I can't do it again.'

'What do you mean?' Gem's throat tightened with fear.

'What do you think?' he was sneering now, almost bragging. 'Billy thinks he finished off his aunty, doesn't he? He couldn't kill anyone if he had to.' He laughed. 'No, I finished her off after he left her unconscious.' He was breathing close to her ear now. 'She was just a nuisance to him. I could see that the best thing would be to get rid of her so I did.'

'You let Billy think that he killed his own Aunty? How could you do that?' Gem was horrified. 'You know it's completely messed him up?'

'He's always been flaky. You can't blame me for that.'

'You're a murderer.'

'Don't call me that!' he tightened his grip on her arm.

'That's what you are,' Gem said more quietly now. She looked past Dan and saw the light was much closer now and she could hear someone running through the undergrowth. Her hopes were momentarily raised but soon came crashing down when she recognised the silhouette of Billy against the moonlight. Still, a flicker of hope remained now she knew that Billy hadn't killed his Aunty. 'Billy, over here,' she called. 'I need to tell you something - you didn't kill your aunty.'

'Shut up you stupid tart!' Dan prodded her under the chin with the gun. 'I'll use this on you and then on Billy if you say anything. Get up, bitch.'

'What's going on?' Billy reached her side and looked from one to the other. 'Say what?'

'It wasn't you, Billy.' Gem said.

'What wasn't me?' Billy looked confused and then looked away. 'Stop it!' he said to the air. 'I can't hear properly when you go on like that.'

'She's off her head, Billy. You can't trust her - I told you she'd run if we brought her with us. You should have got rid of her when you had the chance.'

'Never mind that,' Billy grabbed Dan's arm. 'We have to get out of here, now! At least Aunty's still in the van. Just get back to the van and we'll go. Come on.'

'What about the lights we saw? Have they gone now?'

'I think so. We should get going before they come back.' He gave Gem a sorrowful look and started back to the side of the lane. Dan pushed her along in front of him as he followed Billy. She stumbled several times before they reached the van again.

Billy picked up the spades and threw them into the back of the van, glanced at Gem and told her to get back in the front seat. She walked round to the side of the van and opened the door. Dan was still behind her with the gun, pushing her forward to get in quickly. Her feet slipped in the mud which was deeper on this side and as she stepped up to climb into the van one of her shoes slipped off and was stuck in the mud.

'My shoe,' she wailed, but Dan shoved her from behind and followed her in before she could protest any further. Billy was already starting the engine. She could hear the wheels spinning in the mire. For a moment she wondered if they would be stuck but soon they were moving out of the shelter of the trees and back up the lane towards the gate again. Gem looked about, hopefully wondering where the lights had come from, maybe a forester who'd found the gate open, investigating lights seen in the woods. But there was no sign of anyone, the gate was still open and before long they were back on a darkened and quiet road heading to God only knew where.

Chapter Fifty Seven

Billy

After we left the woods we drove around in the countryside. I didn't know where the hell we were going only it seemed we were driving around for ages. I just kept turning right at one junction and then left at the next until we were lost in the middle of nowhere. I remember driving through a few villages but couldn't tell you the names of any of them. At one point we passed a church which seemed to be set nowhere near any village, just a lonely church in a dark country road. I slowed the van down as we were on a sharp bend and looked out at the graveyard. That was when I came up with the idea so I pulled up outside the gates to the church and got out of the van.

'Where the hell are you going now?' Dan asked.

'Just having a look around,' I said and shut the van door on him.

The church yard was quiet and to be honest, fuckin' spooky. I have to admit I felt pretty scared being in there on my own. The moonlight was shining on the faces of stone angels who looked down at me with that look on their faces like I was something dirty. I glared back at them. Most of the graves though were marked with old stone slabs, the dates of the dead going back over a hundred years. Weeds grew over the graves which seemed neglected, some decorated with rusty flower containers, long forgotten by the looks of things. I glanced about and soon found what I had in mind. At the rear of the church was a section with those huge concrete slab tomb-like graves, with rusty gates and steps leading down into family crypts. One of these would be perfect for what I wanted. Surely it would be better for Aunty to be buried in a church yard? Gem had said as much, hadn't she? OK, it wouldn't be her own grave and I couldn't put a gravestone on it for her, but it was better than leaving her to rot in the woods, surely?

I tried a few of the gates before I found one loose enough to break open. Once inside though, I admit that I hesitated. Too creepy to do this on my own, I made my way back to the van and told Dan what I planned to do. It would have been so easy if Gem hadn't started her effing whining again, saying stuff like, 'You can't do that, it's not right.' Of course it's not right, but it's the best idea yet and between her and the voices telling me I'm a murderer and a thief and that she's a bitch, I was getting bloody well stressed with it all again. So I told her to shut up and help me move the body which she did do, but with Dan waving that gun about again. I wish he hadn't brought the gun along with him. It was making me even more nervous.

We managed to get Aunty out of the van and carried her round the back of the church to the place where the broken gate was. As we stumbled along I could hear those voices telling me I shouldn't trust Gem and I should get the gun off Dan. I kept telling them to fuck off and eventually we got to the crypt. At the bottom of the steps was a door which I hadn't tried before, being a bit keen to get back to the others and not wanting to be on my own in a place with dead bodies in it. Luckily it opened with a bit of a shove and we half dragged, half carried the parcel containing Aunty into the middle. The crypt was cold and damp. I looked around in the darkness to see if there was a decent place to put her.

'You got a lighter, Dan? I can't see a friggin' thing.'

'Just leave her there and let's get out of here,' he replied. I guess he was spooked too.

'I can't just leave her on the ground,' I protested. 'There's probably rats in here.'

'She's fuckin' dead. The worms'll eat her anyway.'

'Don't say that!' I shouted. Then the noises in my head started again.

'The worms'll eat her. The rats will. It's your fault. You should have got rid of Gem,' and stuff like that.

I tried not to listen to them all coming at me from every direction. 'Leave me alone,' I cried.

'We will if you get rid of Gem,' they answered. 'She's trouble. You can't trust her. She told that Karen about you. Don't trust her. Get rid of her and it will be alright.' They kept on, first one voice, then another. Gem was staring at me. I knew then what I had to do but still couldn't let Dan hurt her. I moved to the door. 'Wait here,' I said.

'Where are you going?' Dan asked.

'Going to get a torch,' I said as I ran up the steps and back to the van.

I came back with the torch and some rope. I shone the torch into the darkness and could see several slabs, some with stone coffins laid on. I hesitated to look into any of them - I didn't want to know what may have been in there. The light shone on a nearby slab which was empty. 'We'll put Aunty on that one,' I said. 'Gem, get hold of that end and help me lift her.'

I felt a bit better seeing her there on the slab, even though she was still rolled up and wrapped in a carpet and polythene. 'Sorry Aunty,' I whispered to her.

I turned to Gem. 'Now you. Sorry Gem, but we can't trust you any more. Give me your hands.'

'Billy, no. Please don't...' Gem started to plead with me but I wouldn't listen any more. I'd had enough of her whining and lies. My voices were looking out for me now and I had to do what they said to get through all of this. I tied her up really tight and even though Dan said that we should finish her off I couldn't go that far. I know I killed Aunty but that was an accident and I don't care whatever anyone says, I'm not a cold blooded murderer. A murderer maybe, but never cold blooded.

I tied her wrists together really tight. I couldn't look her in the eye - I still had feelings for her didn't I? She kept saying my name over and over, 'Billy, Billy, please, don't do this.' I couldn't stand hearing it any more so I tied a rag I'd brought from the van around her mouth, stopping her from saying anything else. 'Sorry, Gem,' I said. Dan still had the gun on her. I made her lie down on one of the other empty slabs and tied up her legs so she couldn't run for help. I don't know what I was thinking. I just needed to get out of there. I thought maybe Gem would see sense if she was left in there for a few hours. I'd go back for her and everything would be alright again. We could make a fresh start.

'Come on hurry up,' Dan was saying. I touched Gem on the cheek and turned towards the door of the crypt. Soon we were out in the night air once again. I pulled the door to until it caught on the latch and made my way up the steps with a feeling of relief.

'You can put that gun away now,' I said. Dan looked at me kind of strange, he seemed to be thinking about it. Then he smiled and put the gun in his jacket pocket. 'Now you owe me, Billy,' he said. 'Big time,' as we walked back towards the van.

I didn't want it to happen like this. If Gem had only been nicer to Dan, we could have made a good team together, at least until we'd got rid of Aunty. I want her to be there for me but she had to see there are some things you need a mate to help with. Like burying a body I guess. Now we're in an even bigger mess. Gem was helping me sort out those voices in my head but she wasn't really telling me the truth when she said she would stay with me and not tell anyone. The voices tell the truth. They said that she was a liar and she was - is. Don't think about her in the past tense - she's still alive and I'm sure that everything will get sorted out soon. I just don't know how now she's not around to talk to me. I will go back and get her as soon as this settles down and the voices go away. They muddle my thoughts so much that I can't think straight.

Chapter Fifty Eight

Kevin

Another day had passed and still nothing had been resolved. He had thought when that woman, Karen had spoken to him, she would be able to get everything sorted out but there he was, back in the shop and still there was no sign of Gem or Mrs. Clarke. He really should have gone to the Police in the first place. Why, oh why had he listened to Gem? It could have all been resolved by now. But then, the Police were often stupid and wouldn't have believed him. He made a decision. He would go back to the house one more time and if Mrs. Clarke wasn't there, he would go straight to the Police Station.

His working day had seemed to drag but now at last he was free to go back to Station Road. He wondered whether maybe he should have gone home first to tell his Mother he was going to be in late for tea but he knew she would be fussing and questioning him about what he was getting involved in so he decided he wouldn't bother. She would just have to worry wouldn't she? This was far more important and could be a matter of life or death. Oh, dear, he wasn't sure what to do. He walked to the end of the road, hesitated, then decided to go straight home after all. He would have tea with his Mother and then go out later. If she asked questions he would tell her it was important business to do with work and she mustn't worry. And anyway, he needed to have a shower and change out of his work clothes. It didn't do to go about with dirty clothes on and smelling of the charity shop.

Mother smiled when he got in and they sat together for a while before tea. She cooked him his favourite, macaroni cheese, so he was glad he'd gone home first. There was nothing worse than stodgy dried up macaroni cheese. His mother was always fussing about something and today it was the next door neighbour's dog. It had been barking all day apparently and really getting on Mother's nerves. Kevin listened patiently and made all the right sympathetic noises.

He even suggested that Mother should go round and speak to the neighbour but she said she shouldn't have to and it was the last thing she wanted to do, to have a confrontation with someone.

As soon as he'd finished eating his tea, he made his excuses and said that he had to have a shower and then sort out some things in his room. In his bedroom, everything was in its place as usual and there on his bedside table was the jade rabbit. Feeling guilty that he still hadn't taken it back to the shop, he slipped it in his pocket. I will take it back first thing in the morning, he thought. This time I won't forget. When he slipped out of the front door some time later, he still hadn't told his Mother he was going out. He had meant to but she was in the middle of watching The Bill on the television and didn't like it if he disturbed her.

By the time he got to Station Road it was nearly dark. There was a white van parked outside the house and he wondered whether Mrs. Clarke could be back after all. But she wouldn't be in a white van, would she? Anyway, the van looked rather dirty and scratched, hardly the kind of transport old Mrs. Clarke would have used. Kevin waited at the end of the road, wondering what to do. If he was honest with himself, he was rather scared of meeting up with those men again. He couldn't see enough from this far away but it would be useful if he could just get a little closer to the house so he could watch what might be going on. He started to walk in the direction of the house, wondering if he could get away with sitting on that seat again. It was a bit too close for comfort though, he thought, and as he was hesitating a blue car drove past and pulled up a few yards ahead. It was that woman who knew Gem, Karen. The one who said she would sort everything out. What was she doing here? The driver's door opened and Karen called him to get in. At first he wasn't sure whether he should - he didn't really know her, did he? Still, after a bit of hesitation he decided things couldn't get any worse than they already were, so he got into the passenger seat.

'What are you doing here?' he asked. 'Have you come to sort everything out like you said you would?'

'I'm not sure,' Karen said. 'I'm looking for Gemma. She's not at her flat and she said she would keep in touch and she hasn't. I was worried, I had a bad feeling, that's all. Anyway, I could ask you the same - what are you doing? Not planning to go to the house on your own, I hope.'

'I came to see what was happening. I thought I would check to see if Mrs. Clarke has come home yet and then I was going to go to the Police. I know you said to leave it and you would sort it out, but she's been gone a long time now and we've heard nothing from her and I am very worried. I don't think we should leave it any longer. If she is only on holiday then the Police will find out, won't they. Better to be safe than sorry, I always say.'

'Yes, I know. I suppose that's what I was thinking too. Shall we both go to the door?' Karen asked.

'I don't know. Perhaps if one of us stays in the car it would be safer. Then if anything goes wrong they could go for help.'

'That sounds a bit drastic,' Karen laughed. 'Still, better to be safe than sorry, as you say. OK. We'll do that then.'

'I'll go to the door. You wait here.' Kevin felt he should take charge.

'Alright, but be careful,' Karen said. 'Whatever you do, don't go into the house. Just stay on the doorstep where I can see you.'

He was just about to get out of the car when the door to the house opened and the short man with ginger hair came out and opened the back doors of the van.

'That's him. He's the other one. Not the one that hit me but the one who came in just before I passed out.' He could feel his heart beating very loudly at the thought of being in the cellar again. 'What's he doing?'

'That's Billy. I met him a few days ago. He knows Gem. Just watch,' Karen said.

They watched as the man went back into the house. A few moments later he was back, this time struggling to carry one end of a rolled up carpet. The other end of the package emerged from the house carried by a woman. It was Gem!

'It's her!' Kevin said. 'Gem. She's in with them. I knew it! What are they doing?'

'I don't know, but I don't like the look of this,' Karen said. 'Wait. There's the other one coming out now.'

Another figure came out of the door. He was wearing a jacket and had his hands in his pockets. 'He doesn't seem to be doing much,' Karen said.

'He's the one who hit me. He's probably got a gun in his pocket,' said Kevin. He shuddered.

'You've got a good imagination, Kevin. Don't be daft. Things like that don't happen in everyday life.'

'Don't you be too sure of that,' Kevin snorted.

They watched as the rolled up carpet was hefted into the van and the doors were banged shut. Billy got into the driver's seat and Gem and the other man got into the other side. It seemed as though Gem was being cajolled into going along with them but you couldn't be sure. Kevin wondered what was going on. Where would they be going with an old carpet at this time of night?

'Come on. We'll have to follow them and see what they're up to. Do your seat belt up, Kevin.'

Chapter Fifty Nine

Peter

After getting home, he'd first of all breathed a sigh of relief he'd got away with it again. He knew he must have put the fear of God into that brat and Karen would be lying awake worrying about her all night. That made him feel good. Then he started to seethe - he felt like she'd stopped him yet again from getting what he wanted - what he deserved. What she deserved was to be punished and he wasn't going to let her go on living in peace whilst he was suffering. She thought she had the perfect life, didn't she? The perfect house, good career and even her own little family. And what did he have? Nothing, thanks to her and her meddling in his life. If she hadn't got pregnant with that brat in the first place, they could have had a family of their own by now and would have been living happily together, just as things should have been. It was all Karen's fault for being such a slut. Well, she would soon see that he wasn't going to sit back and do nothing about it.

He waited until his Mother was settled in front of the tv then slipped out of the house, driving quickly to Wickham. He saw that Karen's car was still there, parked outside her house. He drove past and down the street far enough away not to be seen by her and waited. It wasn't long before she came out, slammed the door shut and got into her car. No brat with her then? She must have someone in to look after her. Still, it wouldn't make any difference to him - it was Karen he wanted, not that kid. He still couldn't understand why Karen had chosen her over him.

He started the engine and moved off, following Karen at a distance. There weren't many cars about on the roads and the last thing he wanted at this moment was for her to get wind of him behind her. As he drove he mentally made a plan - what would be the best way to teach her a lesson? He'd already tried to frighten her and she had still bounced back. He wasn't sure how far he would go before, but now he could see there was only one outcome which would make him completely free of her. She'd told all those lies about him trying to kill her before, hadn't she? So, she'd wanted her dreams to come true, that's what all women wanted, wasn't it? He could think of a few ways to do that for her, and maybe have a bit of fun with her first.

He looked at his watch - it was already nearly eight o'clock. He felt excited, the adrenaline rushing through his body making him feel good again and ready for anything.

His senses were so heightened that he nearly forgot to make sure that she didn't see him and he felt a mild panic when he got too close at a road junction. His heart beat slowed as he realised that she hadn't noticed him. He pulled out and followed, again at a distance, more careful this time, wondering where she was going. Maybe she was going to meet a man. He decided that he'd soon put a stop to that. Alright, she wasn't technically married to him any more, but she was still his woman and she needed to be taught a lesson. And if she was seeing someone else, then he'd have to sort them out too. If he couldn't have her, then no-one would.

His thoughts raced on so fast that he nearly missed it when she began to slow down at the corner of Station Road. He drove on past and watched in the mirror. She'd stopped and was talking to a young man. So - he was right! She was seeing someone. He drove on a little further and watched as she disappeared around the corner. Damn, he thought, and quickly turned into the next road, driving slowly back to the end of Station Road from the other end. He could see Karen's car, parked half way down the street. What was she up to now? It was so frustrating, being so near yet so far from his goal. He stopped the car and turned off the engine, wondering whether he should leave it for another time, when she was alone. He didn't want to have to deal with another man as well. Then he noticed the white van which had been parked further down from where she was parked. The van pulled out, moving away and Karen's car moved off to follow it. At least, it seemed as though she was following. He couldn't really tell from this distance. All of this was getting more and more complicated but they wouldn't stop him, he told himself. He started his car and followed the little convoy, wondering where it would all end.

Chapter Sixty

Catherine

Sitting in her garden, trying to enjoy the peace of the evening after the summer rain, Catherine couldn't put out of her mind the developments of the week. She'd never had such a lot of problems with staff - Gem had seemed to be reliable at first but had let her down this week. She had known there must have been something about that girl from the first day, she'd wanted to give her the benefit of the doubt and now it seemed like she was going to be proven wrong. And Kevin had been acting so strangely too. She was having serious doubts about his sanity to be truthful. He'd always been annoyingly particular about how everything was done - in the past she'd coped with his ways and let him get on with things. The work was always done, so why should she worry. But this week - he'd certainly pushed her to the limits of patience. His obsession with Joan and whether she was in danger was really getting on Catherine's nerves. Then again, what if he was right? The stories he'd told her about going to the house and getting into a fight and then being locked in a cellar - she couldn't believe anything like that could happen in the real world. Kevin was just out of touch with reality, surely? But then, maybe she should at least have walked round to Joan's house and checked it out for herself. Oh this is all getting on my nerves, she thought. I can't stand it any more. Trying not to think about it she went inside to make her supper.

Two hours later and Catherine couldn't settle to anything. She had thoughts of Joan, Gem and Kevin running around in her brain. Something wasn't right. What if Kevin wasn't making it up? She'd never forgive herself if something was really happening and she'd done nothing about it. She poured herself a glass of wine and went outside again to sit in the garden. It was dark now and although it was warm earlier after the rain, the air was cooler and there was a cold lump in her stomach which she couldn't ignore any longer.

She finished her wine and went back into the house to pick up the telephone. I can't lose anything by telling the Police, she decided. They can go to Joan's house and check it out. Feeling better at having made a decision, she dialled the number and waited.

Chapter Sixty One

Gem

She was hurting. Every part of her was hurting, and she couldn't move. The rag in her mouth was making her feel sick, she was gagging and her eyes were streaming. She tried to control the reflex in her throat, tried to calm her breathing, tried not to think about where she was and what was going to happen next. Lying in a crypt with coffins filled with skeletons, Billy's Aunty Joan trussed up in a carpet, and heaven knew what else. She tried to still her breathing so she could listen to the sounds around her. Once the door had banged shut silence had descended on the tomb but now she could hear a faint scuffling sound. She tried to look about but it was pitch black. Don't think about what that might be, she told herself, as images of giant rats came to mind, together with snake pits like the ones in those films where the hero is trying to find the treasure in the temple.

She focussed on the pain around her ankles and wrists where the ropes were rubbing against her skin. Her thoughts kept wandering to all that had happened over the last few days. She was shocked at how things had got to this point. Only a week or so ago and life was starting to get better. She could have kicked herself at getting involved with Billy again just when things were going so well. But then, she couldn't have ignored it when she'd realised that he'd got himself into a mess with his Aunty. And he'd thought he'd killed her, but it was Dan after all. She felt better knowing that Billy hadn't done it, but him believing he had was probably what had tipped him over the edge with his voices. Gem had seen this happen before when people used too many drugs. It wasn't necessarily the heroin, that was a clean drug, apart from what it might have been mixed with - no, the weed was worse - it made you paranoid, and she'd seen a lot of people who'd been completely messed up with it mentally - hearing voices, sometimes even seeing things that weren't there. And it could make you quite aggressive too. So much for the myth that

weed just chilled you. And Billy had always liked his wee
too - thought it was a soft drug, no worse than smoking a fa
or having a beer. She'd seen he was quite fragile in the pa
although he hadn't been smoking much lately. No, it was ju
heroin at the moment as far as she could tell. She guessed
was the same with most drugs - alright in moderation but ev
if you had too much or you couldn't hack it.

She wished that Billy had listened to her when she wa
trying to tell him that Dan had actually finished off Joan an
she had still been alive when Billy had left her. She didn
think it would make him feel any better though, but it migl
have made a difference to Gem being left in here wondering
she'd seen the last light of day. She twisted her wrists, hopir
that the rope might have loosened but all she felt was mo
pain.

Chapter Sixty Two

Karen

She slowed the car as the van ahead turned off the main road and disappeared through the car park of the forest. She recognised the area - it was a place where she'd often come for walks with Lucy. So peaceful during the day, at night it seemed sinister, moody and dark. What the hell is going on? Why would they be going into the woods at this time of night? She stopped the engine and turned to Kevin.

'I don't know about this,' she said. 'I don't think we should drive into the woods - they'll see our lights following.'

'I've got a torch,' Kevin reached into his pocket. 'We can follow them on foot from here.'

'That's not a good idea, Kevin. If they see us, we could be in trouble.'

'What do you suggest, then?' he glared at her.

'We should find a phone box and call the Police. We don't know how dangerous this could be.'

'Are you scared?' Kevin asked. 'Because I am - of course I am, but we can't waste any time going off looking for a phone box. Gem may be in danger.' He opened the door of the car and got out before Karen could protest any further. She hesitated for a second more and then followed him, locking the doors behind her.

The van had stopped at the end of the car park. They watched the driver get out of the vehicle and open the gate, then get back into the van and drive on through, leaving the gates open behind them. They watched as they followed, the van driving slowly deeper into the woods, along the down-hill winding path until it finally stopped out of sight of the car park.

'Keep the torch low,' Karen said. 'We don't want them to see us.'

The night was dark, cloud covered the moon, the recent rain made the ground surface wet, the mud sticking to their feet as they stumbled along. Rain dripped from the trees

Karen shivered, wishing that she was anywhere else but there. It seemed that the lane went on for miles although it was probably only a few hundred yards from the car park to the place where the van had parked. She was trying to think about what they could do when they got to the point where they were face to face with Gem and the two men. The nearer they got, the more convinced she was that this was a very bad idea.

'We should go back,' she whispered. 'This is a stupid thing to do. We won't be able to do anything.'

'Sshh!' Kevin stopped and crouched down. 'We'll just watch from here.' He pulled Karen down beside him, behind a fallen tree trunk. That was when she noticed that one of the three had broken away from the others and was thrashing through the trees. Karen wanted to follow but Kevin gripped her arm, holding her back. 'Don't be silly, the other one may have a gun.'

She doubted that but something made her stay crouched, watching to see what would develop. She thought for a moment she heard someone calling out for help, but it may have been an owl in the trees. 'Did you hear that?' she looked at Kevin.

'No. It's just the wind I think. Look, they're back.'

Sure enough, the three figures were back at the van and driving away again. Karen and Kevin waited until the van had gone back up the lane and they quickly made their way to the point where the van had been parked. The ground was muddy and Kevin slipped, stumbling over something in the mud. He reached down and picked it up.

'It's a shoe. Looks like one of Gem's,' he said.

'Why would she leave her shoe behind?' Karen wondered.

'She must have been brought here by force. We've got to help her. What shall we do? We need to get back to the car quickly before we lose them.'

'I know a short way back,' Karen said and led the way through a smaller path, back to their car. They jumped in and waited, hoping that they wouldn't be spotted by the others when they came out of the car park. Karen looked at Kevin. He looked awful. 'Don't worry,' she said. 'We must be mad doing this, but it will be alright.' She wasn't convinved herself, but couldn't think of anything else to say at that moment. She breathed a sigh of relief when the van appeared and turned the opposite way, driving into the darkness of the countryside once more.

'Now where are they going?' she wondered and started the engine. As soon as the van was out of sight she followed, keeping a good distance behind, trying not to think about what may happen next.

Chapter Sixty Three

Peter

Well, well, well, this is getting very interesting, Peter thought as he sat in his car on the edge of the woods. He'd followed Karen and watched her and that young man walking into the woods with a torch. At first he thought they were looking for somewhere to have a bit of the other in the outdoors and he was thinking it was a bit wet on the ground for all that. However it seemed as though they were actually following those others in the van. Peter couldn't work out what they were up to but he didn't really care. This could be the opportunity he was waiting for although with two of them to deal with, it could make things a bit tricky. And then there were the others in the van. He wanted to follow them but there was no way he was going tramping through the forest on foot. He waited until their torch-light was a good distance away and drove slowly into the car park. He only went as far as the gate though - he didn't want them to see him following. Anyway there was plenty of time - they would have to come back this way - so he moved the car to the other side of the car park and stopped under some trees. He turned off the headlights and waited.

Soon enough, the van was driving back up the sloping lane, but where was Karen and that man? Then he spotted a flash of a torch making its way back to the road where her car was parked. She was going and if he didn't hurry he'd miss her. Damn!

Frustrated, he had to wait until the van passed through the car park before he could follow. The last thing he wanted was to be caught up in whatever they were up to. Eventually, the van turned into the road again and Peter started his engine and began cautiously to follow. He stopped just before the exit out of the woods and waited. He was just about to give up, thinking he'd missed his chance when he heard the sound of another motor. Karen's car, passing slowly, obviously still following the van! He moved off, keeping his distance, his heart in his throat, without a thought of where this would end.

Chapter Sixty Four

Kevin

We followed the van all around the winding country roads. I was impressed with how well Karen could drive but was a bit scared we would get too close to the others and they would see us and turn round to confront us. But they didn't, thank heavens, and eventually the van slowed down by a church yard in the middle of nowhere. I said we should call the Police at this point and we could have done as we had passed a phone box a short while back but Karen said it was a bad idea and we needed to keep them in sight and the Police wouldn't even know where to start looking as we didn't really know exactly where we were. I was thinking about that and was about to tell her the location would be in the telephone box when she suddenly stopped driving. She reversed the car a bit so we were just out of sight on the other side of the church which was where the van had parked.

If there's one thing I hate it's churchyards at night. I don't know what it is, maybe I watched something on television when I was little, but I have a fear of gravestones. You never know what's in the graves, do you? Well, you do, I suppose - there has to be a dead body underneath and that is what I don't like - the thought of all those dead bodies, skeletons probably, or the rotting flesh of those more recently buried with worms eating away at the bodies. Not a nice thought.

So when Karen told me to wait in the car whilst she went to investigate, I was more than happy to do that. She said I had to keep watch and if anything happened to remember the phone box which was only a few hundred yards up the road. So I sat and waited.

I hadn't been there for very long before I saw another pair of headlights in the rear view mirror. I don't know why but something made me duck down. I didn't want to be seen sitting there in case whoever it was in the car stopped and wanted to talk to me. The car drove on past and I was feeling quite relieved for a while until I realised that whoever it was had pulled up about a hundred yards along the road and was getting out of the car. I could feel my heart thudding as I wondered whether it was a friend of the bad men who were living in Joan's house. I didn't know what to do but I know I was scared. What if he'd seen Karen walking through the church yard? What would happen to her and to Gem now? I didn't want anything bad to happen to Gem. I had become quite fond of Gem. I know she was not the sort of young woman that Mother would approve of for me, but there was something about her that I liked. Perhaps it was because she was different, like me.

As the man neared the gate to the church, I ducked down again, then waited a moment before I decided that I should do something. What I couldn't decide was whether to follow him - maybe I could do something to help Karen save Gem - or to go back to the phone box and telephone the police. In the end, I thought that the best thing would be to telephone for help first and then go and see if I could help - then at least I'd know that whatever happened I'd have all events covered, as they said in those police programmes on the television. I opened the car door and stepped out, then, closing the door behind me as quietly as I could I made my way to the telephone box which was just around the bend of the road, out of sight of the church gate.

All sorts of things were going through my mind as I walked along that dark road. What if Gem was part of the gang? It seemed like she was one of them, going off with them in their van like that. But what if she'd been forced to go along with them? I don't think she would have left her shoe behind in the mud, would she? But I couldn't be sure. I thought she was a good person, and I wanted to think the best of her. Oh dear, it was all so difficult. Then, what had really happened to Joan? I was still hoping she was just away on holiday or visiting someone but there was something wrong with all of this. I really didn't believe she would go away without letting us know at the shop and I'd a bad feeling about her disappearing from the start. And now Karen had got involved in it all. I hoped she would be the one to help me sort it all out and thought maybe she still would, as long as she didn't get hurt, creeping about after them in the graveyard so late at night. And now there was this other person - the one who'd just turned up. I wondered what his connection was to the others and why he wasn't around before? It was too much, it really was.

It seemed like ages before I reached the phone box but it was probably only a few minutes and soon I was telling the operator all about what was going on. It took some time for her to understand how important it was they send a police car as soon as possible but eventually I seemed to get the message across. The operator said I should wait at the telephone box so I did for a while but things kept rushing into my mind about what might be happening and I couldn't just wait there. I looked out into the night. The wind was picking up and the trees looked pretty spooky. I didn't like being in there - I felt, well, vulnerable. I looked at my watch but it had stopped. How long had I been in there? What was going on out there in the churchyard? I was scared to stay in the phone box but I was scared to move out into the night too. I counted to one hundred, then another, then another. It seemed like I was there for hours and I couldn't wait any longer, so I held my breath and started to make my way back along the road to the church.

Chapter Sixty Five

Billy

As soon as we got to the top of the steps to the crypt, the feeling of relief slipped away. I had this thing like a fuckin' lead weight in my stomach, thinking about Gem lying down there in the dark. I knew I couldn't go back now though, not with Dan watching me. I don't like people watching me and although he was supposed to be my mate, I didn't trust him any more. My mind was a complete friggin' mess of what was right and what was wrong. I kept thinking about what Gem said about me not killing Aunty Joan. If she was right, then all of this needn't have happened. I couldn't believe it. Surely Dan wouldn't have done that, what she said he did. I didn't know who to believe any more. It was all so bloody mind blowing.

I looked about. It was still dark in the graveyard and I was glad I had the torch. Still I kept hearing those voices talking to me, telling me I was a murderer. And now there was another voice added to all the others. I couldn't make out at first what it was saying and I was trying not to take any notice, just wanting to get back to the van and away from there. I don't know what I was thinking. I didn't really want to leave Gem alone in there, I wanted to go back and get her out but I couldn't.

Dan was watching me all the time. That's when the penny dropped - Dan was going to kill me - he knew that I was a murderer and he would get rid of me before I did him in too. I could tell by the way he was walking, looking over his shoulder at me and I could have sworn he had a kind of sneer on his face as if to say, I know. I don't know how he could have known but he must have. He could look into my mind and read my thoughts. Walking along behind him in the dark was horrible and when he turned around again and asked me what's the fuck up, that just confirmed it to me so I decided I had to protect myself from him.

I still had the torch in my hand luckily so I had something heavy I could hit him with. Before I could do anything though, I saw another shadow moving amongst the graves towards us. Dan must have seen whoever it was as well as he ducked down behind a grave-stone and waved his hand at me to do the same. We both crouched there, waiting to see what would happen next.

The voices were getting on my sodding nerves. I tried not to listen to them. I tried to concentrate on what was happening, on who else was creeping about in the grave-yard, but they were too loud. Murderer. Don't trust him. Do him in and you'll be safe. Gem was your only friend and now you've killed her too. They just kept on and on until they were all shouting at once and I couldn't really hear what they were saying to me any more. I wanted to scream out to shut them up but I was too scared. I was doing my best to work out how to stop it all and decided if I got rid of Dan this would be the answer. Then I realised the person wandering about was a woman and as she drew nearer I recognised her as that nurse Karen. My fear lifted a little as I thought maybe she would save us from all of this. Then I remembered she'd been snooping around the house, looking for Gem and she was probably on to me for doing in my aunty so I kept quiet and waited, hoping she would go away so we could get out of this fuckin' place. I wanted to get rid of Dan as well so I could go back and rescue Gem and then everything could go back to normal.

It seemed as though Dan had different ideas as he had taken out the gun again and looked like he was ready to use it. I was frozen at that moment, really bloody scared, so much so I couldn't think any more. It seemed like time went on in a void. All I could hear was the drip, drip, drip of the raindrops from the trees and the soft footsteps of that woman as she moved nearer to where we were hiding. I remember thinking if she came any closer then Dan would finish her off once and for all but it wasn't to be, not yet anyway, because I heard the sound of a car door closing and the next thing I saw was a flash of light on the far side of the church. It was making it's way towards us. Bloody Hell, I thought, This place is like Albert Road on a Saturday night!

Chapter Sixty Six

Karen
Karen was terrified. She didn't want to think about what was going to happen in this awful place. If she had stopped to think, she probably would have given up and gone home long ago. Something kept her going, probably the feeling that she wouldn't be beaten. She knew it had got her into trouble in the past and briefly wondered when she would ever learn her lesson. Still, she couldn't go back now when she believed Gem was most likely in danger. Wondering fleetingly whether she should have waited for the police to turn up, she hesitated at the gate to the churchyard and was about to turn back to the car when she heard the clanging of a metal gate coming from across the other side of the dark shadowy place.

She began to make her way towards the noise. Her feet crunched on the gravel path, sounding so loud to her ears so she made her way on the grass between the graves. Still, it seemed as though she was making enough noise to wake the dead. She laughed to herself at the thought of what had popped into her head - waking the dead? Stupid thought and not at all appropriate bearing in mind where she was.

She realised she was blundering along without a plan of what to do if she actually came face to face with anyone. It was just at that point she decided perhaps it would be better to go back and wait by the gate after all. As she turned to go, she saw the light of a torch making its way through the gravestones towards her. She stopped, crouched down and waited. The grass was over-long here and wet, the ground slippery under her feet. She felt herself sliding and gripped hold of the gravestone she was hiding behind. The sudden movement alerted the torch carrier. The light flashed over the graves and shone in her eyes for a brief second. She ducked her head and tried to be still, hoping she hadn't been seen but knowing in her heart that she probably had.

So many things went through her mind. Wondering if maybe it was Kevin coming after her, or perhaps the Police, she felt a little better - then she realised that the Police would have made more noise, perhaps shouted out or something. That's what they did wasn't it? But it could still be Kevin. Then Kevin would have called out if he'd seen her hiding there. She was still thinking all these thoughts when she saw the person was getting closer and it was too late to run without being seen. She looked up and felt a chill of fear rush through her as she recognised the shadow as the one person she never wanted to be face to face with again in such a lonely place - Peter.

Chapter Sixty Seven

Peter

He wasn't very happy. Chasing after Karen all over the countryside in the dark was not his idea of a fun night out. Still, he could see the end to all his troubles - if he could just catch up with her, he'd sort things out at last. It wasn't long before she'd stopped near a church which was out in the middle of nowhere. He drove on past until he was out of sight and stopped the car. He was anxious not to lose track of what she was up to so he got out of the car and made his way back to the bend, hid under some trees and waited.

Soon she had got out of the car and was walking towards the church-yard gate. Peter watched until she had passed through the gate and was making her way through the graves. She seemed to be looking for something, or someone maybe. He was just about to follow her when he saw that man getting out of her car. He waited as the man turned away and started walking back along the road the way they had come. He wondered what the man was up to but he couldn't follow both of them and anyway, it was Karen he wanted, not the man. The further away he was, the better.

Taking out his torch he crept through the gate after Karen. The ground was wet under foot and the trees were still dripping from the recent rain. The wind gusted, causing a shower of rain to splatter down his neck. He shivered, even though it wasn't that cold. Shrugging his shoulders he turned his coat collar up against the dampness. The next time he looked around, Karen seemed to have disappeared. Damn it, he thought, Where's the bitch hiding now? He guessed that she must have seen his torch flashing about and cursed himself for having a light and giving himself away. Still, she couldn't have gone far, could she?

Peter shone the torch across the graves, looking for any movement. He knew she couldn't have gone far and sure enough, there, just ahead of him less than ten feet away, he shone the torch right into her eyes. Yes, she had ducked away quickly enough, but not fast enough for him not to be able to recognise those eyes with the look of disdain in them she always had when she looked at him. Or maybe it was fear. He hoped it was fear - she deserved to be afraid after all she'd done to him. He was going to make her pay and he'd enjoy every minute.

Peter almost felt himself wanting to laugh now he knew all of this would soon be over and then he'd be able to start a new life completely free of her and what she'd put him through. He could move on at last - have closure as they said in America. He was excited at the thought of finally sorting it all out.

No longer feeling the need to creep about, Peter stood tall and strode over to where he knew she was hiding. He stood over her.

'Well, well, Karen, there you are at last.' He shone the torch into her eyes. 'What were you thinking of? Coming out here to get some time on your own with your new boyfriend, eh? Did you think you could fool me? You must think I'm stupid, driving all over the countryside to lose me - well it didn't work, did it? And what have you done with that brat of yours? Don't think she's safe either. I'm going to sort you both out, don't you worry. But first of all, you.'

It was such a good feeling, knowing he was in control of her at last. The look in her eyes confirmed he was doing the right thing. He could swear she was laughing at him - not out loud of course, she wouldn't dare do that - but laughing inside, as though she knew something that he didn't. He wasn't going to let that get to him though. He'd come prepared, not really sure anything would happen tonight, but just in case. He drew out the knife from his inside pocket. It had been uncomfortable carrying it there. All the way here he had been aware of it, digging into his side as he drove along. Now he didn't have to carry it any more. He'd use it and then get rid of it, after carefully wiping his prints from it, of course.

He loved the feeling he had when she looked at the knife in his hand. She must have realised she was looking at the end of her tormenting him at last. He felt good about the way the light in her eyes changed from laughter to fear. He wanted this moment to last forever - it was better than the best sex he'd ever had. In fact, he felt himself getting a hard-on and wondered fleetingly whether he could have her one last time. It was only a fleeting thought - he knew he couldn't do it while she still had a bit of fight in her. Maybe if he made her unconscious first? Not kill her right away - he couldn't make love to a dead woman, could he?

But she was speaking to him, drawing his thoughts back to the present.

'Peter, I don't know what you're talking about,' she wheedled. 'I'm here looking for someone. She's gone missing and I think she's here somewhere. I don't understand what's the matter with you - you've been following me around, I know, but what I do with my life now is nothing to do with you. It's not your business any more. I've already been to the Police once - you've got to move on.'

'How can I move on when you're still alive, enjoying your life. You ruined mine and now you're going to pay.' He shook his head, determined she wouldn't get the better of him again. It was time. He grabbed her by the wrist and dragged her along the path.

'Where are you taking me?' she hissed, her feet scuffing the path.

He wasn't exactly sure but thought they should go somewhere drier, maybe inside the church if it was open. I would be more comfortable in there for what he wanted to do with her. Before he could take a few more steps, however another figure appeared ahead of them - it was a man - the man in the car, he thought and he was shouting at them. Well this was the last thing Peter needed. He'd suffered enough. He felt a great anger well up like a volcano about to erupt as he launched across the grass. Too late, he realised that the man was waving a gun in the air. Too late, he only noticed after the shots were fired.

Chapter Sixty Eight

Kevin

I'd only got as far as the church gate when I heard the shots. At first I thought they were coming from the woods on the other side of the road and my first impression was there must have been someone shooting pheasants or deer or something. I knew they did quite a bit of hunting around here. But I soon realised the noise was closer. And I could see there was a bit of a commotion going on across the other side of the church yard. My first instinct was to run away again. I thought that perhaps I should wait for the Police. It would certainly have been the safer option. However, I knew that Gem was probably in there somewhere and Karen, of course. I couldn't just hang around and wait, could I? That would have been the easiest thing to do but not the right thing, would it?

So I gritted my teeth and moved across the graves as quickly as I could, towards where I could see a light shining on the grass. As I drew nearer, I saw that there was someone bending over what looked like a dead body on one of the graves. I recognised the figure bending over as that one called Billy who had been with Gem. I thought he had hurt her. He seemed to be doing something to the body. I was thinking that it might be Gem and ran to try and stop him. That was when the other one who must have been hiding a little way off appeared. He was waving a gun about and shouting at Billy - or maybe he was shouting at me - I couldn't be sure. It was all a bit confusing to tell the truth and not something that I like to recall. I hesitated when I saw he had a gun. The other one, Billy, was shouting back at him. Something about being stupid and not hurting the nurse. Then I understood that the figure on the ground must have been Karen, not Gem. I wasn't sure at that moment whether I was relieved or not. At least Gem was still alive. Or hopefully, anyway. I wondered where she was.

I stumbled backwards and nearly fell over something else lying behind one of the gravestones. I looked down and shuddered. It was a man's body and he looked very dead. I wasn't sure at first but when I reached down to check I felt the hot stickiness of what I thought was probably blood as his life seeped away onto the wet grass. I felt sick.

Suddenly not wanting to be there any more, I thought about Mother, sitting at home and wondered if she was missing me. I didn't even know what the time was but imagined she would be watching one of her programmes and maybe looking at the clock and fretting as to where I was. She wasn't used to me being out in the evenings. I thought for a moment maybe I wouldn't be going home again.

I was just mulling all this over in my mind when I noticed the man with the gun had moved and was standing over Karen. He was arguing with the one called Billy, telling him to get out of the way so he could finish her off too. He didn't seem to notice that I was there so I looked around frantically for something heavy that I could use as a weapon. There was nothing near that would have been any use. Then I felt the weight in my pocket and fumbling in there I took out the jade rabbit. I gripped it in my hand and crept towards the man, who still had his back to me, thank goodness. I swung back my arm and cracked the rabbit on his head with one swoop. The sound of the stone against his skull was sickening but at least he fell to the ground and lay there without moving. I looked at the rabbit in my hand and wiped the blood off on the grass. I remember thinking I would have to take it home to wash it now.

I turned to Billy next, hoping he wasn't going to have a go at me after that. He seemed to accept it was over though and sank down onto the grass with his head in his hands. I picked up a stick from the ground and carefully took the gun from the man's hand without touching it, and was going to put it into my pocket. I didn't feel that happy with having a gun in my pocket though so I hid it behind a nearby gravestone. Better to be safe than sorry.

Karen seemed to be alright. She got up and gave me an odd sort of look. 'Wow, Kevin,' she said. 'I'm not sure what to say, but I think you may have saved my life.'

'Never mind that, we need to find Gem.' I turned to Billy. 'What have you done with Gem?'

Billy shook his head. 'I didn't want to hurt her,' he said. 'I had to do something but she is alright, really she is.'

'Where is she?' Karen was speaking now. 'Come on Billy, don't make this worse for yourself. Is she somewhere here? In the church?'

'I'll show you,' he said, and led us to the top of the steps of what looked like a family crypt. I had read about crypts in one of the books I got from the library a while back and I wasn't very keen to explore any further. Only the thought of Gem being locked up in there made me quite angry and determined to venture where I would never normally go. After all, I thought, I've been locked in a cellar already once this week - it can't be much worse than that, can it? So I followed Billy down the steps and waited whilst he pushed open the door at the bottom.

There was a funny smell in the crypt - a kind of sweet smell, like bad meat. It wasn't very nice and was too dark to see much. Billy had a torch though and flashed the light around the damp, cold space. There was something on the nearest stone platform - a carpet rolled up. That seemed to be where the smell was coming from as it got stronger when I walked over to have a closer look. I had a sudden memory of what I'd seen in the freezer and shuddered at the thought of what was in there.

'Over here,' Billy said. His voice was shaky. 'I'm sorry, Gem. We've come back to get you out. I didn't mean anything.' And there she was, tied up and laid out on the top of another of the platforms which were really meant for the coffins to lie on. It was all a bit of a muddle but between us Karen and I managed to untie the ropes around her feet and hands and helped her down from the slab. Billy seemed to have been taken over by something a bit overwhelming and was talking to himself in the corner of the crypt - something about Aunty Joan and being a murderer and a thief.

'Let's get out of here,' Karen said and we helped Gem up the steps and out into the fresh night air again.

Gem sat down on a nearby grave and leaned on the headstone. 'Thank God,' she said. 'I thought I was going to die in there.' I handed her my handkerchief to wipe the tears that had started to run down her cheeks.

'You'll be alright now,' I said but I was shaking inside.

Billy was still in the crypt when the Police arrived a few minutes later. I told them about how I'd knocked out the man who was attacking everyone and about the gun behind the gravestone. I assured them that I hadn't touched it with my hands. I think they were pleased even though they didn't say much. I remember Gem calling out that Billy hadn't known what he was doing and they shouldn't be too hard on him. That made me a little bit cross because I kept thinking about all he had done to us over the past few days. She is too soft, I think.

I didn't get home until well past midnight. Mother was already in bed when I crept up the stairs and I don't think she even noticed. The first thing I did was to wash the jade rabbit which was still in my pocket. I decided I wouldn't tell the Police about the rabbit - it felt wrong somehow, knowing it could be classed as a weapon. I would take it straight back to the shop as soon as possible and say nothing.

The Police said I had to come to the station in the morning to be interviewed. I wasn't really looking forward to that but I supposed it had to be done. I just hoped Catherine could manage in the shop without me as I was supposed to be working there in the morning. I couldn't sleep all night, I kept thinking about everything that had happened. That poor man who got shot - I did wonder who he was and what he had to do with everything. I supposed I would find out when I went to the Police Station.

Chapter Sixty Nine

Billy

I don't know what the time is. It seems as though I've been in this fuckin' cell for ever. It must have been quite late by the time they put me in here last night. They took me first to the interview room and tried to get me to confess. It should have been easy - I was ready to tell them everything. Only I couldn't think straight as things kept popping into my head, like I was having four or five conversations at once. I'm trying to remember what happened after Dan and me left the crypt. There were lights in the churchyard - I remember that and thinking there were a lot of people about. That nurse, Karen was there. I don't know how she found us but I know Dan was going to get rid of her and I had to stop him. He's been the problem all along I think. I can't trust him anymore.

I told the police about killing Aunty Joan and leaving Gem tied up in the crypt. At least I've got that off my chest. I'll go to prison now - I know, and I'm fuckin' dreading it but it feels a bit better now I don't have to keep secrets any more. The voices are still there but not as bad as before. The trouble now is I haven't had a fix for hours - I don't know how long it is but it must be a bloody long time. I'm starting to hang out and if I don't get something soon I'm going to be suffering. I tried to tell the copper who was interviewing me and he said that they were going to get me seen by a Police Surgeon. He seems to be taking his friggin' time though. I can't sleep. I wish it was the morning. I don't like the dark even though it's not a proper darkness in here. There's a light still on in the corridor and it's seeping through the gaps of the door. And it's bloody cold. I can feel myself starting to shiver. I wonder if they'll let me have another blanket.

I feel so bad about Gem but she seemed to be alright with me after they got her off the slab and untied her. I heard her shouting to the coppers and I'm sure she said I hadn't meant to hurt her which was the truth really. I always meant to go back and get her out again. I think.

Chapter Seventy

Karen
There was no denying it - she had been scared when Peter suddenly appeared before her in the dark and when he started to drag her away towards the church, Karen had panicked, wondering if she would ever get away from him again. It all happened so quickly after that - the man, Dan she thought, shouting at them from across the graves. She hadn't realised he was the one with the gun until she heard the shot. A split second before the shooting, Peter had been holding onto her - then he seemed to lose it as he dropped his grip on her and lunged towards the man. The sound of the gun appeared to be so close to Karen - it felt as though she'd been hit herself. She remembered falling to the ground and lying there, stunned for what seemed like ages. When she finally opened her eyes again, she saw Billy was standing over her, shouting something she couldn't make out. It turned out he was shouting at the other one, Dan, who still had the gun. Billy was saying something about him not hurting the nurse. It dawned on Karen then that he meant her.

Before she could get her wits together, Kevin appeared from nowhere, it seemed, and the next thing, Dan was on the ground. She felt a rush of relief when she saw Kevin was there - Billy seemed to collapse as soon as Dan was knocked out. She tried to get some sense out of him but he was rambling on about a crypt. Of course, that was where they'd hidden Gem. Karen hoped she was alright and got Billy to show her and Kevin where the crypt was. She was shocked to find Gem had been trussed up and left on one of the platforms where the coffins were kept. It was pretty gruesome and the smell was horrible. It soon became apparant there was a dead body rolled up in a carpet on the next platform. Only later it came to light the body was Joan Clarke's, who was Billy's aunty. Billy seemed to collapse once we untied Gem and sat in the corner of the crypt, responding to voices which were obviously tormenting him.

Once the Police had arrived Gem was taken to hospital just to make sure she was alright. Billy and Dan were led away to be questioned at the station, and Kevin and Karen were allowed to go home once they'd given the Police their details. They expected to have to make statements the next day.

As for Peter, Karen didn't want to think about what had happened to him. Just thinking about him made her feel like crying. Whatever he had done to her, she had loved him once and to end his life being shot was the last thing she'd wanted. It was difficult to understand how he'd turned into such a monster of a man and she kept wondering about how Margaret would take it. He was her son, after all, and Karen knew what it felt like to be a parent.

She got home well after midnight and was sitting in the dark, the curtains open. She could see the clouds changing shape in the night sky, the moon was rising, not quite full, and she wondered if she would ever be able to sleep again. So much was going through her mind - she thought about Kevin and how he'd probably saved her, then there was Dan shooting Peter - he had saved her too she supposed. And of course there was Gem and the mess she'd got herself into. Karen hoped she could still help Gem get back onto some kind of settled life.

But her first priority had to be Lucy. Turning her thoughts to more positive things, Karen started making plans for tomorrow, when she would spend some time with Evelyn and Lucy and then see about bringing her dauhter home. It was time to put the past behind her.

Chapter Seventy-one

Gem

When the metal door to the crypt had slammed shut, Gemma had felt like her life was at an end. She couldn't see any way out of there, unless Billy came to his senses and returned to get her out but she had little hope of that whilst Dan was with him. It seemed like a long time and she was on the point of losing hope when she heard the gunshot. Her first thought was that Dan had shot Billy. She struggled with the ropes at her wrists but it was useless and she felt the tears of frustration and fear pricking at her eyes. She didn't doubt Dan would come back and finish her off too but she couldn't hear anything else so she just lay there, waiting.

Eventually, the door opened and a beam of light flashed across the dank space. She couldn't see who it was at first but it was more than one person. Perhaps Dan hadn't shot Billy after all, she hoped, then she felt her hopes fall away as she realised they had probably both come back to kill her. After all, why would they leave her alive when they'd already killed one person? So who was shot then? She couldn't work it out.

'We've come to get you out,' Billy said as he took the rag out of her mouth. 'I'm sorry, Gem,' he sobbed.

There were two others there beside him. Karen and Kevin.

'How did you know?' she asked Karen, feeling so relieved that it was all over at last. Karen and Kevin untied the ropes around her feet and hands.

'We followed you,' Kevin said. 'The Police are on their way too.'

'Thank you. I was so scared. Thank you.'

As soon as she was freed she looked around in the dark for Billy and saw he was slumped in the corner mumbling to himself. She felt so sorry for him, sitting there She could tell he was being tormented. 'Are you alright

Billy?' she asked but he didn't answer. He seemed to be oblivious as to where he was or who was there.

The others helped her out of the crypt. The fresh night air was so good, she took a huge breath and thanked God she was alive and free. Feeling sick she sat down on a grave, and couldn't hold back the tears any longer. She remembered that Kevin had given her his hanky - a proper cotton one, not a paper tissue. She smiled to herself thinking about it.

The Police arrived as they started to move away from the crypt. She heard Karen speaking to one of the Officers and they started to make their way to get Billy out. Gem couldn't help calling out for them not to be too hard on him. He obviously wasn't well.

They took her to the hospital in an ambulance. Karen had spoken to the driver about the methadone script so she would be looked after properly and not have to suffer from any withdrawals. Gem felt ashamed of herself as she hadn't admitted she'd been using again before going out that night. Still she was grateful for the help and only stayed in for a few hours whilst they checked her over. Even so, her wrists and ankles were sore for days after, and her back ached from all the shoving about Billy and Dan had done.

Gem was shocked to hear Dan had shot that other man, Peter, who turned out to be Karen's ex. He'd been stalking her apparantly. It just goes to show that you should never make assumptions about people. Just because Karen was her nurse, and seemed to have her life all in order - she had a kiddie, Gem knew, it didn't mean she didn't have problems and struggles of her own to cope with. Gem found out later all about Peter's vendetta to get back at her. Anyway, he was out of the way for good now. As for Dan, he too would be put away for a long time. Kevin only just stopped him from hurting Karen - it looked as though he was about to shoot her when Kevin hit him over the head with a rock or something. Gem smiled, thinking about Kevin. She'd never known he had it in him. He's a bit of a hero.

The day after leaving the hospital, she was sitting at home during the evening with so many thoughts spinning in her head. She started thinking about how life could throw so much at you. She still had feelings for Billy and hoped he could be helped with his voices and all that paranoia stuff. She'd told the Police about how he'd been lately and told them about how Dan had bragged that he had killed Mrs.Clarke, not Billy. Her fall had been an accident and she could have probably been saved if they'd got an ambulance straight away. 'I know Billy will most likely have to be locked up for what he did,' she thought. 'But I'm hoping that they'll send him to one of those secure hospitals for treatment instead of just putting him in prison. He needs to get a detox from all the drugs and then specialist help to get back to normal, whatever that is. I will visit him, if I can, but I'm not sure about whether to give him any hope of us being together in the long term. It'll just have to be one step at a time, as they say, and then we'll see.

'Catherine came round to see me this afternoon. She told me she had called the Police that evening as well as Kevin. We had a good chat - we both had come to the same conclusion - that we should have got the law involved earlier, then maybe Peter wouldn't have been killed. Still, he's not much of a loss is he? At least Karen can get on with her life now without looking over her shoulder all the time.

'Catherine's a good person. I knew she was frustrated working in a charity shop after all her years in Woolworth's and I wasn't surprised when she told me she'd got another job - in a proper shop, she'd said. And she was putting forward Kevin to manage Charlie's Choice. He loved to be in charge and it would be great for him to have a job with a bit of a wage to take home.

'I know at the start Kevin and I had struggled a bit with our relationship, especially in the shop with his annoying ways, but I started to warm to him and I'll always be grateful for him being there at the end. I'm even looking forward to going back to work now.'

Chapter Seventy Two

Catherine

She was standing in the shop, looking around, feeling a mixture of pride and regret. She smiled to herself. Only a while back, she'd been feeling dissatisfied with this place, wanting nothing more than to be back in her old job, working with professional shop workers, not all these volunteers - this company of what may be termed inconvenient people. And now, she'd soon be leaving them all to move onto managing what she had once thought of as a proper shop. But she had to admit to herself the service provided in Charlie's Choice was just as, if not more, important than making profits for a big corporation.

Catherine felt sad that Joan wouldn't be coming back. She knew she couldn't have stopped her from coming to an end like she did, but wished she had done something about her being missing before, then maybe things could have been stopped from going as far as they did. She wondered when the funeral would be. 'I'll get some flowers for her. It's the least I can do.'

On the other hand, she supposed Peter getting killed, although unfortunate, had saved Karen from being hurt any more. Catherine was completely horrified when she'd heard the full story from Gemma. As for Billy and Dan, they would get what they deserved, she guessed.

Kevin would be good as the shop manager. Even though he could be extremely irritating, he knew how to run a store and he had a good way with the customers. She just hoped it wouldn't be too stressful for him and he would cope with the difficult side of running a shop - like the rota for instance. The first thing he'd have to do was recruit more staff. With herself going and Joan no longer there, they would be two people down. She wondered if Gemma would take on more hours. 'Not my probelm now,' she thought.

The shop-lifting was another problem and didn't seem to get any better. She still couldn't fathom out how people could steal from a charity shop. They must be either greedy or desperate. She knew that some of their customers were desperate, with no money to spare for clothes for the family but there were others, she was sure, who stole to sell on stuff in car boot sales. She'd seen them herself on a Sunday morning, doing just that and had recognized things that had been in the shop only days before. They had no shame.

Chapter Seventy Three

Kevin

He hadn't been surprised to hear Gemma had a drug problem. He knew all along there was something about the girl although you couldn't help liking her. She had nice ways and Kevin was positive she would steer clear of anything bad in the future. He hoped so, anyway.

Kevin walked across the shop floor, a duster in his hand. He'd noticed the bric-a-brac shelf needed a good bit of tidying up and since he'd had taken his eye off the ball so to speak, things weren't always as neat as they should be. He would be making lots of changes as soon as Catherine left and he was totally in charge. She had been very good though, showing him all the things he needed to know about running a charity shop. He thought he would probably miss her for a while but she had said he could phone her at any time if he got stuck with anything. He didn't think he would though. This was what he'd always wanted. And the thought of a wage packet at the end of the month made him feel very proud of himself. Mother was delighted too although he thought she made too much of a fuss about the whole thing, almost as if she didn't think he could do it. Well, he would certainly show her.

He picked up the jade rabbit and was dusting it, happy it was now back in its rightful place. He was thinking about all that had happened in the past few weeks since Gemma had started working there. He remembered the first day when she had come in. It was raining and she was looking at this very same jade rabbit. At the time he'd been very suspicious of her - he thought she was another one of those shop-lifters and he'd been a bit surprised when she'd spoken to Catherine and asked for a job. He was even more surprised when Catherine took her on. She had certainly shaken up things, but then, Joan would have died anyway. That wasn't anything to do with Gemma even though it was her friend who turned out to be Joan's nephew and if it hadn't been for him living with Joan she'd still be alive now. So many ifs.

Kevin snapped back to the now when he heard the shop door open. He straightened his back, carfeully replaced the rabbit on the shelf and turned to smile at the customer. 'Good morning, Madam,' he said. 'How can I help you?'

Chapter Seventy Four

Karen
It was hard seeing Margaret again after all that had happened.

They stood together in the church. Even though the sun was shining outside and the day was promising to be another hot one, there was a chill in the air inside. Karen felt numb and wondered if that was why she felt so cold. Remembering all that had happened in the last few weeks was hard. She was looking forward to it all being in the past, properly in the past. She just had to get through this day, that was all.

Many of her friends had thought she was crazy coming to the funeral but she said it was important to her to say a proper goodbye. She'd had some good times with Peter in the past and strangely, still had some feelings for him. She wasn't sure what those feelings were, but still she was going through a kind of grief process. She acknowledged those feelings were mixed with relief and guilt too, if she was honest. It had been important to her to be here today, that was all.

Chapter Seventy Five

Margaret
Margaret's face was grey, her mouth set in a firm line. She looked ahead, not wanting to catch the eye of any of the other mourners who'd turned up. She knew they were only there out of curiosity and she doubted any of them cared for Peter or what had happened to him. Even Karen - she shouldn't have been there, but had insisted on coming.

Margaret couldn't help wondering if only she'd done things differently when she was bringing him up, perhaps things wouldn't have ended up like this. She felt heavy, heavy with grief, heavy with remorse that she hadn't been a better mother to him. And also feelings of regret for Karen. She should have been more careful with Karen when she was fostering her. If only she hadn't encouraged Peter to marry Karen, he might have met someone else and had a happy marriage and Karen too, may have had a different, happier future. It was all too painful to think about. She turned and looked at Karen as they brought the coffin into the church and noticed that the girl had a tear in her eye.

Chapter Seventy Six

Gem and Billy
They stood together at the side of the grave, holding hands.
The wind ruffled Gem's hair but it was a warm wind and a
relief from the heat of the sun. She squeezed Billy's hand and
he smiled at her.

'It seems like only yesterday,' she said.

'Not to me,' was Billy's reply. 'It's been a long five
years for me, stuck in that place.'

'I know, but you're out of there now and can start a
new life.'

'Oh, don't get me wrong,' he said. 'I know I needed
to be in there. I couldn't cope any more the way things were
for me and I needed all the help I got. And there's been no
more voices for over a year. I just have to stay clean and I'll
be alright.'

'I know. I'll help you, you know that.' Gem said.

'I couldn't have done it without knowing you were
there for me, Gem.'

'Yes you would have, you know. You're stronger than
you think.'

'It wasn't hard staying away from drugs in that place.'
he explained. 'There was stuff about, you know, but the
thought of you waiting for me kept me going. The nurses
were good to me, too. They helped me through some bloody
dark days - and nights.'

'I'm glad you got through it, Billy,' Gem said. 'And
I'm glad it's all over now.'

Billy looked down at the gravestone. 'I can't believe
all that happened now. It seemed like a fuckin' bad dream to
me while I was away. It's only now, seeing her name on the
headstone that's made it real. Poor Aunty Joan. I did love
her, you know. She was good to me. And she loved me too. I
feel so bloody guilty - if I hadn't been living with her, if I
hadn't pushed her, she would still be here now.'

'You have to put it in the past, and move on.' Gem said. 'You're home now and can make a fresh start.'

'Home?' Billy asked. 'Can we really be together?'

'I've told you already, Billy. You've been watched over for five years and even when they let you out for short trips, it was like you were being watched. You were always under some kind of "Big Brother" black cloud. Now you're more or less on your own, apart from me, that is. It's going to be difficult for me too. I don't know how it will work, to be honest. I've got used to being on my own and I kind of like it.'

'It sounds like you've made up your mind.' Billy said and laughed nervously.

'Not really,' she replied. 'I'm just being realistic. I still feel fragile sometimes. No - I feel fragile a lot of the time, about whether I would ever be tempted to use smack again. I'm doing well at my job in Tescos, I have a good laugh with my mates there. It's hard work and sometimes I get stressed with things and that's when I get scared I might go off the rails again. The last thing I need is to get out of control and I couldn't cope with being on Methadone again. It took me months to get clear of it last time and I still get night sweats sometimes if I can't sleep. I know they say it's not possible to have withdrawals after so many years, but I do. The doctors say it's psychological but it's still bloody awful. It feels like it's in your bones. So you must understand I'd be taking a big chance on having you living with me again.'

'So, what do I do now?'

'You've got the hostel and they'll give you a lot of help to keep straight. It can't be all down to me.'

'But I thought....'

'I know, and I'm sorry, but it's gotta be down to you alone. I've got too much to lose.'

They stood for a while, each in their own thoughts. Finally, Gem broke the silence.

'Are you going to put those flowers on the grave, then?' she asked as she crouched down and gathered the

349

dried, dead flowers from the pot and stood up. 'There's a bin over there, and I'll get some fresh water,' she said and walked away.

Billy was alone with his aunty. He knelt down beside the grave and carefully placed the flowers in the pot. Now he was on his own, he felt the tears well in his eyes. The sadness was almost too much to bear, knowing what he had done to her. 'I'm so sorry, Aunty,' he whispered. 'I wish I'd been a better nephew to you.' Then he made a promise. Whether it was to his Aunty or to himself, he wasn't sure, but he said it out loud to make it more real.

'I promise I will be a better person, and do my best to be good to Gem in future,' he said.

'And to yourself,' Gem was standing behind him with the watering can full of fresh water.

'And be good to yourself,' she repeated, and smiled.

***

Lightning Source UK Ltd.
Milton Keynes UK
UKHW011826240219
337913UK00005B/58/P